Murder at the Mystery Castle

A Marcie Rayner Mystery

J.C. Eaton

CAMEL
PRESS
Kenmore, WA

Epicenter Press
6524 NE 181st St.
Suite 2
Kenmore, WA 98028

www.epicenterpress.com
www.camelpress.com
www.coffeetownpress.com

For more information go to: jceatonmysteries.com

Cover design by Dawn Anderson
Author photo by Florine Duffield

Murder at the Mystery Castle
Copyright © 2018 by J.C. Eaton

ISBN: 9781941890691 (Trade Paper)
ISBN: 0978194180875 (eBook)

Printed in the United States of America

CHAPTER ONE

New Ulm, Minnesota

I don't know what happened first – Byron's "me yowl" or the thud on my chest as he used it for a launching pad. In any event, it woke me seconds before the phone rang on a rainy Monday morning in late April. The kind of morning that makes me want to reach for the covers and go back for another hour of sleep. Sometimes I can pull that off, but today wasn't one of them. I had an early appointment with a new client who referred to her situation as "delicate." "Delicate" in our investigative business usually meant one of two things. The client either thought his or her partner was cheating or they were worried someone in their past was about to disclose not-so-nice stuff on social media.

It was still hard to wrap myself around the fact that I was now a licensed private detective in the state of Minnesota. I'd reached the six-thousand-hour requirement while working as an investigative assistant for Blake Investigations, and my boss, Max Blake, paid the thousand-dollar fee because "the last thing I need is to break in someone else." Of course, he said that with a huge smile and a pizza party in the office.

Now, at some ungodly hour in the morning, Byron was meowing his head off for food and the phone was still ringing. At least I could manage two things at once. I picked up the phone, slid the arrow and took the call as I walked into the kitchen and poured some kibble into the cat's dish.

My mother's voice bellowed into my ear. "Oh good, Marcie. You haven't left for work yet."

"I just got up. Florida's an hour ahead of Minnesota time."

"Fine. Fine. We can discuss setting clocks back and forth some other time. I wanted you to know Alice Davenport called me a few minutes ago."

At the mere mention of that woman's name, I froze. *Not again.* Alice Davenport was my mother's neighbor in Delray Beach, Florida. They were both retirees from Minnesota. Alice was a schoolteacher who hired my boss, Max Blake, and me to solve a murder at the Crooked Eye Brewery in Biscay last year. Not just solve it, mind you, but provide her with chronological and detailed reports every step of the way. She all but graded them.

The only good news to come out of working with Alice Davenport was meeting my boyfriend, brewery owner and one-time suspect, Hogan Austin. Oh, and solving the murder, of course. Now, with a phone in one hand and a box of kibble in the other, I prayed Alice wasn't about to hire us again.

"Uh-huh." I literally couldn't get beyond mumbling. My mother, Iris Krum, had no problem picking up the conversation.

"Are you aware of Helena Heatherbrae's sudden death at that Mystery Castle in Mendota Heights?"

"The owner of that creepy mansion you took Jonathan and me to when we were kids? That Helena Heatherbrae? She was like a hundred years old when we were in elementary school. And the way she sat on the couch staring, Jonathan thought she was already dead."

"Yes. *That* Helena Heatherbrae. And for your information, she was only in her seventies when we visited."

"Okay. But what does any of this have to do with Alice Davenport?"

"Alice's cousin, Minerva Watson, was the cook at the Mystery Castle. I say was, because with Helena dead, she'll pretty much have to retire."

Byron had finished his kibble and was rubbing against my legs for milk. A bad habit I'd gotten him into. I had to get going. "I'm not following any of this, Mom."

"Minerva called Alice last night. And that's why I called you. Minerva believes Helena was murdered."

Oh no. Here it comes. Here it comes.

"Marcie, are you listening? Minerva wants you to investigate Helena's death. She's going to call your office sometime today to set up an appointment. You do have weaponry, don't you?"

"Weaponry? It's not the Middle Ages. And yes, I'm licensed to carry a gun. And why on earth would I need a weapon in order to meet with a client? Don't tell me Minerva is scarier than your neighbor Alice."

"Not the meeting with Minerva. The investigation. That mystery castle made Transylvania look like Disneyworld. You remember the place, don't you? It gave your brother nightmares for weeks. Poor Jonathan."

"Don't remind me. Look, I've got to get to work. If Minerva Watson does call us, I'll let you know."

"Oh, she'll call all right. I can practically guarantee it."

"How?"

"Because Alice threatened to fly to Minneapolis and drag her into your office if she didn't."

"Whoa. Guess I'll let Max and Angie know to expect the call."

"Good. And be careful."

"I will. Love you, too."

I quickly poured a bit of milk in a bowl for the cat and raced into the shower. Thank goodness I didn't have to fuss with my hair or make-up. A tad of eyeliner to accentuate the arctic blue tones in my not-quite almond eyes and a dash of blush so that my fair skin wouldn't look as if I needed a month in the sun. I was positive I'd inherited my facial features from my father, along with my height. Those extra two or three inches made my angular body look fit even if I didn't work out every day. My once layered bob had morphed into a shoulder style that somehow made the natural blond color appear to have ashen tones. I figured I'd give it another week or so and then decide whether or not to go back to my original style. Meanwhile, a quick brush-out still worked. With form-fitting pants and a tailored top, I looked every bit like the consummate professional.

Thirty minutes later I was out the door and headed to the office. My apartment was only a fifteen- minute drive, something that was likely to change if Hogan and I took our relationship to the next level. Even though we lived forty miles away from each other, we still managed to spend more than a few nights together each week. His place or mine. His felines or Byron sharing our sleeping space.

Angie, our office secretary, was just unlocking the door when I arrived. In spite of the rain, her frosted black hair looked perfect as did the stylish outfit she wore.

"Good morning, Marcie. I'll get the coffee going. Don't know about you, but I could always use a second cup. Looks like it's going to be a busy day. Your schedule and Mr. Blake's are both full.

"Speaking of the devil," I said, "here he comes now."

"Hold that door! Don't need to get any wetter."

Max charged inside the office, turned on the lights and tossed his jacket on one of the chairs in our waiting area. "I'm not going to be here long enough to bother hanging it up. I've got a meeting at Equis Financial on that Cresci trust. Should be back in an hour or so."

I took a step toward him and cleared my throat. "Um, before you head into your office, we may have another murder investigation."

"Here in New Ulm? Haven't heard of anything in this area.

Unless it's a cold case."

Angie looked up from the coffeemaker. "There was nothing on the news about a murder. Some robberies, a stabbing, and an Amber Alert near Mankato but that was about it."

"Okay, okay everyone. The murder, well, I don't know if it was actually a murder, but the person who's going to hire us thinks it was. Anyway, the possible murder took place in Mendota Heights, outside of Minneapolis to the east."

"Mendota Heights. Why does that ring a bell?" Max asked.

Angie answered before I could take a breath. "Because that's where that crazy Mystery Castle is. You know, the Heatherbrae estate. All forty acres and a building that rivals most European palaces. Except, the Mystery Castle is—"

"An architect's nightmare," I blurted out. "Part creepy castle, part Moroccan Casbah, part underground grotto…"

"You mean you haven't heard of it, Max?" she asked.

"Now that you mention it, yeah. Doris helped chaperon a school field trip there years ago. Said they were afraid they'd lose some kids in that place. It was impossible to keep track of anyone. So, tell me Marcie, where'd this so-called murder in Mendota Heights take place?"

I opened my mouth and paused. Long enough for Max and Angie to figure it out. They both spoke at once but Max was louder. "The Mystery Castle? Who the hell died in the Mystery Castle?"

"The owner," I said. "Helena Heatherbrae. Her cook thinks someone killed her."

Angie all but dropped the cup of coffee she was pouring. "Oh my gosh. I remember reading something about that not too long ago. If my memory serves me right, they said she died of natural causes. Wasn't she quite up there in age?"

"In her nineties according to my mother, who just so happened to call me this morning to tell me we're going to have another murder on our hands."

"Alleged murder," Max said.

Just then the phone rang and Angie took the call. It

was so quick Max didn't have time to reach his desk before she announced, "It's a Minerva Watson. Said her boss was murdered. Asked for Marcie."

Max smiled at me. "This is your mother's doing, isn't it? I suppose we should be thankful Iris is keeping us busy all the way down in Delray Beach."

"I'll get the info, Max, and have Angie set up an appointment so both of us can meet her."

"We don't need both of us."

"She's Alice Davenport's cousin."

Max turned to Angie. "You've got my schedule."

"Thanks," I said. "I'll take the call in my office. I've still got five minutes before my first appointment shows up."

Minerva Watson sounded older than death. Maybe it was the connection. Maybe it was the subject. In any case, she was willing to make the drive from Mendota Heights to New Ulm, a good hour and a half's drive west. *If* the highway traffic was moving.

"I don't care what that idiotic medical examiner said, Helena didn't die of natural causes. Someone in that house killed her. I need to hire you and your firm to find out exactly which member of our staff committed such a heinous act."

I reached across my desk for a pen to jot down what she was saying. "Your staff? You mean the household staff at the Mystery Castle?"

"Yes. Who else could it have been? Helena once mentioned a third cousin in Rochester but I thought he died. Or was it a she? Anyway, no relatives ever came to visit her. I know for a fact the only Christmas cards she got were from her employees or the companies that did business with the castle. You know, the plumbing company, the electricians.... Her murderer had to be someone on our staff. Anyway, we need to get moving on the case. I have no problem driving to New Ulm."

If Minerva was anything at all like her cousin Alice, I'd bet money patience wasn't her strong suit. While she was willing to make the drive, I knew Max and I would have to see that

Mystery Castle up front and personal, not second hand from Minerva's point of view.

"Miss Watson, if you're willing, I think I can save us some time. My secretary can email or fax you a contract. Once it's signed, we'll be able to secure information from the local authorities and begin our investigation. Does that sound acceptable to you? If so, we can set up a meeting nearby the Mystery Castle once we receive the paperwork."

"Send it over right away. My email is—"

"Wait. I'll connect you to Angie. That's the office secretary and she'll take it from there."

"Fine. I'll give her my schedule. Please don't dilly-dally."

My God, this was Alice Davenport's cousin if ever there was a relation.

"No problem. I'm sure we'll be conversing with you this week. Have a nice day. Please hold."

I transferred the call and tiptoed to Angie's desk. Whispering, I said, "Make sure Max is free to drive with me. I'm not doing this alone."

Angie picked up the receiver, held her hand over it and mouthed the word "chicken" to me before greeting Miss Minerva Watson.

CHAPTER TWO

I was right. My "delicate" Monday morning case fit in the infidelity category after all. My client, Loreen Larsen, was fairly certain her fiancé was cheating on her. Although she didn't have anything substantive to back up her allegations, she had a gut feeling he was screwing around. I couldn't imagine any guy in his right mind cheating on someone who looked like a super model. But what did I know? She pulled a strand of her long, light-red hair and wrapped it around her finger as she spoke.

"I don't want to say, 'I do' and then find myself married to someone who can't keep it in his pants. It's not like I'm anywhere near thirty and have to worry about being single the rest of my life."

No. Let that be my problem. And since when is it too late for someone turning thirty?

I forced myself to ignore her last comment. "What brought this on? I mean, it's not as if you found the proverbial lipstick on his collar or anything like that."

"No, but for the past few weeks Scott hasn't been in the mood. Claims work is tiring him out. Work. How much energy does it take to be a financial planner? He's not digging ditches or working on machinery. He's in wealth management. And he usually spends the weekends at my place. Now all of a sudden, he can't seem to get away. One thing after another according to him. I'm betting one woman after another. So, will you take my case?" I nodded and we had the paperwork drawn up.

SCOTT BYRD LIVED AND WORKED in the New Ulm area so surveillance wouldn't mean long hours driving. Loreen gave me the pertinent details and I assured her I'd have some information for her by the end of the week. That was two days ago and so far, I had managed to track the guy going into a Starbucks, his office and his house. Also, a fancy Italian restaurant but Loreen was at his side for that one. I planned on checking Scott's fitness center and golf club tomorrow, but today Max and I were on our way to Mendota Heights to meet with Minerva.

"There's a Cracker Barrel on Route 35 by Crystal Lake," Max said once we got on the highway. "I need a big plate of bacon, sausage and eggs. Doris is killing me with her damn healthy diet obsession. This morning I ate horse food."

"What?"

"Oh, you heard me. It was a dry breakfast bar thinner than paper. When I bit into it, it was like eating dust. Then I looked at the ingredients. Rolled oats, chia seeds and fennel. We're stopping at Cracker Barrel."

"That's fine with me. I've never turned down good pancakes."

"Whatever you do, don't get caught up with the scenery and miss the exit. My stomach's grumbling already."

Max's point was well taken. Even though it was barely spring and the trees were just starting to bud, it was hard not to take in the rolling hills and greenery that made this Twin City suburb so inviting. With the Mississippi River to the west and Pike Island, now a part of Fort Snelling State Park, smack dab in the middle, I couldn't help it if my eyes did wander a bit.

If he was worried about food, there was no need. I knew we'd have plenty of time to eat because our appointment wasn't until eleven and we left the office at eight fifteen. We agreed to meet Minerva at Fischerville Coffee House in Mendota Heights. It was fairly close to the Mystery Castle and unlike a restaurant, we could linger over a cup of coffee for hours. I prayed it wouldn't take that long.

Max devoured his meal at Cracker Barrel as if he was afraid someone was about to pull the plate away from him. Maybe that was something Doris did for fear he'd gain weight. True, he was in his early sixties but I didn't think his metabolism was going to slow down so drastically that he'd been relegated to eating nothing but health foods for the rest of his life. So far, I considered myself one of the lucky ones. I could eat like a racehorse and not put on so much as an ounce. Unfortunately, my mother's warning of the impending menopause weight gain scared me to death. Of course, she was talking thirty or so years from now, but it still made me shudder. According to her, "You just have to look at a cookie and boom! Next thing you know you'll wind up like Great Aunt Chessie."

My great-great-aunt Chessie was rumored to have sat on her husband, Nickolas, and broken his ribs. It was a story my mother told whenever the holiday desserts were placed on the table. I wondered if Max's wife had heard that same story...

It was ten thirty when we left Cracker Barrel and headed to the Fischerville Coffee House. I had offered to drive, mainly because Max was on the road so much with his cases, but mostly because I tended to be a control freak about driving. Somehow, I only felt safe if I was the one behind the wheel. Hogan was trying to change that. I think Max gave up.

The Fisherville Coffee House was a colorful stand-alone building off of Market and Linden Streets in the center of Mendota Heights. Along with the other establishments, it was part of a small triangle surrounded by residential property complete with large lots, an abundance of trees, and lawns that appeared to be well-cared for. The coffee house resembled one of those Hansel and Gretel cottages complete with white shutters and window gardens. Green and yellow booths framed the walls and small round tables filled the space that led to the large counter. A glass pastry display featured everything from scones and croissants to cookies and tarts. I imagined the place was packed during the early morning hours but there were only a handful of customers when we walked inside.

Max poked my elbow. "That must be Minerva Watson in the booth by the back window. She looks like Mrs. Doubtfire."

I studied the other customers, trying not to be too conspicuous. A young couple with a toddler. Two men reading newspapers, three or four "thirty somethings" glued to their laptops, and a heavy-set tattooed man who appeared to be in his forties or fifties.

"I think you're right. Let's walk over."

"Miss Watson?" I asked.

"That's right. You must be Marcie Rayner."

"I am. And this is my boss, Max Blake."

"Didn't expect the whole office to be here. I'm not paying double, you know. I already signed the contract."

Max reached over and offered his hand. "The fees are based on hours, not personnel. Nothing on that contract is going to change. Before we sit down, can I get you another coffee or anything?"

Minerva shook her head. "I still have a full cup but you might want to put your order in before the lunch rush hits this place."

"Good idea. Marcie, you get started and I'll bring us some coffees."

I watched as Max walked to the counter before I squeezed into the booth. For a man in his sixties, he looked more fiftyish with his dark hair and hints of gray. Face to face with Minerva, I strained to see if anything about her resembled Alice Davenport. Of course, I'd only seen one picture of Alice and that was taken eons ago when she stood over her fifth-grade class like a vulture hawk.

Nothing about Minerva's appearance was frightening. In fact, she looked like the stereotypical sweet old lady. Curly gray hair that framed her face, wire-rimmed glasses, a floral blouse and pearl necklace. But like her cousin, she was a formidable presence.

"Thank you for driving all this way to meet with me. Like I told you over the phone, I'm certain someone in Helena's household killed her."

Max had just returned with two coffees. He placed them on the table and slid next to me in the booth. Minerva kept talking.

"As I was saying, there was nothing whatsoever natural about her death."

I picked up my cup and took a quick sip. "Can you be more specific?"

"Helena was found lying flat on her bed with her head resting on a pillow."

"That's seems kind of natural to me," I said trying to eyeball Max.

Minerva shook her head. "I've cooked for that woman for over fifty years. Came to work as the assistant cook when I was twenty. For the past fifteen years she suffered from the worst kind of acid reflux disease. I should know. I had to prepare the special meals. No red sauce at dinner meals, no citrus drinks, no red wine, and absolutely no heavy spices."

"She should've met Doris," Max mumbled under his breath.

I gave him a poke in the knee and leaned toward Minerva. "What does that have to do with the way she was found in her bed?"

"Helena would never have gone to sleep lying on a single pillow. She had to sleep with one of those bed-wedge contour pillows or she'd risk having a GERD attack. And believe me, those aren't pleasant."

"So, you think someone killed her and staged the body? And what about her bed cushion? Where did that disappear to?"

"It didn't disappear," Minerva said. "It was one of those fold-up contour pillows. Whoever killed her didn't know about her condition. The wedge cushion was folded up at the foot of the bed. Helena was found dead by the maid before she had a chance to turn down the bed for the night."

Max tapped the rim of his cup. "Did you tell this to the police during their investigation?"

"There was no investigation. No inquiry. No nothing. Arletta, that's the maid, called nine-one-one after screaming her lungs out. I was downstairs in the main kitchen. I had put away the dinner dishes and was getting the ingredients organized for the morning breakfast when I heard her. We were the only two people in the house at the time. It was around five. Helena liked to eat early."

"What happened after that?" I asked.

"An ambulance came, Helena was declared dead and carted off to the hospital morgue or wherever they take you. A few days later we got the word she died of natural causes and they cremated her. No funeral. No nothing. The castle director said some sort of memorial would be planned for the summer. Anyway, Helena's ashes are going to be buried in the family plot somewhere. But there's nothing natural about her death if you ask me."

The tapping sound from Max's finger on his cup was getting louder. Finally, he spoke. "What specifically makes you think that?"

Minerva gave him one of those steely looks. "Helena was convinced someone was trying to kill her. She didn't say as much but she started taking precautions."

"Precautions?" he finally took a sip of his coffee as we both listened.

"Strangest thing. Like I told you, I've been her cook forever. Then, about a month ago, she insisted Arletta and I taste the food before she'd eat it. And that's not all. No matter the weather, she began to sleep with the windows partly opened. I think she was afraid of carbon monoxide poisoning or something. And she'd make Arletta shake out the blankets and re-adjust the sheets before putting down the contour pillow. Arletta thought maybe she was afraid of bed bugs but we've never had anything like that here."

I didn't know how to say this diplomatically so I took a chance. "Um, Miss Watson, is it possible Helena was, well, you know, slipping? Cognitively. I mean, she was in her nineties."

Minerva looked down but I could see the sheepish expression on her face. "She was getting a bit, well…impaired. Suspicious is a better word. She was getting suspicious. About personal things. Not the Mystery Castle enterprise. As far as that went, she was as sharp as a tack. Did her own banking and correspondence online. Only used the accountant for her taxes and that was because of the business."

"That's right," I said. "I forgot. The Mystery Castle was a tourist attraction and a source of income for her. It must have been hard separating out her private life from all of that."

"No different than Buckingham Palace, I suppose," Minerva said. "Only on a much smaller scale. Helena lived in an upper wing, closed off to the tourists. The tour guides never approached that part of the castle. Helena had her own kitchen where my assistant and I prepared most of the meals. The large kitchen on the ground floor was also used from time to time since it was better equipped. Not only for Helena's menu but for special events."

"I'm getting a refill," Max said. "But before I stand up, tell me, Minerva, what kind of staff are we talking about?"

"Well, Helena had her own people. Sydelle Alridge, my assistant, and Arletta Maycomber, her personal maid. Then there's Harry, her chauffeur. He's only been on staff for a few months. Replaced Townson O'Neil who retired. Townson was Helena's original chauffeur. Oh, and Greta Hansen, the housekeeper. Now the Mystery Castle itself is different. It's a business. Anna Gainson is the director and she has her own secretary. Then there are the tour guides as well as Ernie the gardener and Martin the handyman. When major projects take place, they're contracted out."

"What about the cleaning?" I asked. "I can't imagine one person cleaning a massive building like that."

"Good heavens, no. Anna's contracted out with a cleaning service. They arrive after hours a few days a week and clean the castle itself. Everything except Helena's wing. Greta takes care of that. When she needs additional help for deep cleaning and such, she lets Anna know and they make the arrangements."

"I need that coffee, now," Max said. "I'm getting tired thinking about running the place, let alone figuring out which person in that cast of thousands could have killed your boss."

"Ah-hah. You believe she was murdered, too. Is this right, Mr. Blake?"

Max took a breath. "Yeah, I do. The death scene does sound suspicious in light of her medical condition. And she was literally looking over her shoulder. So, all we need now is a damn good motive and some concrete evidence. We've already contacted the Mendota Heights Police Department and they've faxed preliminary reports to our office but we needed to meet with you first. Back in a second. "

He grabbed his coffee cup and went straight to the counter. Minerva motioned for me to come closer. "You must be discreet. No one in the Mystery Castle knows I've hired you."

I gave her hand a quick pat. A really quick pat. "You don't have to worry. As far as anyone is concerned, we're private investigators looking into Helena Heatherbrae's death. It's not unusual, especially in situations where large estates are concerned. Which reminds me, do you know if she had a will, and if so, who was named?"

"Everyone on staff received the same letter from Blair and Lowery Legal Services. Helena had left each of us ten thousand dollars. Hardly a motive for murder in my book. As for the rest of the estate, I honestly don't know."

"That's okay. Blair and Lowery you said?"

"That's right. But there's no one by those names working there anymore. Evanston Blair started the firm in the late 1800s and partnered up with Jamison Lowery. Then the firm got sold at the start of World War I. The only reason I'm aware of all this history is because the company had a founders' celebration not too long ago and it was in the papers. Their office is right by the college of St. Catherine in Minneapolis."

"That shouldn't be too hard to find. You wouldn't happen to remember the name of the attorney who sent you the letter, would you?"

"It wasn't signed by a lawyer. It was signed by their business manager, Warner VanWycke. I can mail you a copy if you'd like."

"Nah, that's all right. It doesn't matter. We'll have to meet with them anyway. And we'll need to meet with the director of the Mystery Castle as well. Max and I will need a tour of that building in order to put everything in perspective. Their staff will need to be interviewed, too. Before I forget, when's the best time for us to contact you?"

Minerva pushed her coffee cup to the side. "In the evenings. After seven. I'm still on staff to cook for special events at the castle but I'll no longer be doing the small grocery shopping I did for Helena. As far as the public version of the castle goes, everything is running as always with community fund-raising events and small private luncheons in the Garden Grotto. Now with Miss Heatherbrae gone, it wouldn't surprise me if they opened up her residence to the public. She was quite a collector, you know. Native American fetishes, ivory carvings, you name it. And weird things, too. She once showed me a piece of petrified dinosaur dung and some sort of a pin made from a dead beetle. "

"Wow."

Max arrived back at the booth just as Minerva stood up to leave. She clutched her bag with both hands. "I've got to get going. It was nice meeting the two of you."

Before she could take a step, I raised my voice. "Wait. Don't leave yet, there's one more thing."

"What's that?"

I blurted it out without thinking. "How do you want us to send you the investigative reports?"

"Investigative reports? Why on earth would I need those? That's your business. Just find out who killed Helena."

At that moment I could've given the woman a giant hug.

CHAPTER THREE

M ax plopped himself across from me in the booth and gulped his third cup of coffee.

"There're more people in that Mystery Castle than a Cecil B. DeMille production."

"A who?"

"Argh, I keep forgetting you're so much younger. He was a famous director. Literally invented crowd scenes. So, if I've got this straight, we're dealing with a small cadre of employees who worked for Helena plus the business end of the castle and everything in-between."

"Yep, sounds about right to me. Might as well start at the top with Anna Gainson like we planned. I suppose if she's too busy to spare a few minutes of her time, we can always set up a formal appointment for another time."

"My thoughts exactly. Which reminds me, how comfortable are you taking the lead on this one? I'm up to my elbows with court appearances and a surveillance case in Mankato."

"I'll be fine. Most of the stuff I'm dealing with right now is pretty routine. I'll be able to drive back here on Friday and the weekend. I'll need at least two or three days to scope out the place and interview the employees."

"Okay. Let's get a move on. We should be there in twenty minutes."

Max was right as usual. It was a quick jaunt from the coffee shop to the Mystery Castle. I thought I had a clear picture of the place in my mind since I'd been there as a kid but I was wrong. I didn't remember the long winding driveway that seemed more like a mountain road than a private entrance. And I certainly didn't recall the spectacular view of Minneapolis from the top of the hill.

"My God, Max," I said as we got out of the car, "would you look at the river and the city? This is breathtaking."

"Breathtaking. Good word to describe Helen's final dilemma. Come on, looks like the entrance is over there."

I parked in the front lot under one of two majestic Norway pines. There were at least ten cars in the lot. Undoubtedly tourists. A large artfully painted sign said, "Mystery Castle Tours" followed by an arrow that pointed to a small outbuilding adjacent to the castle.

"Must be where they sell the tickets," Max said staring straight ahead. "Maybe they know which entrance we need to use. Pretty damn imposing place, huh?"

Imposing wasn't the word. In fact, there was no singular word that could even come close to describing the architectural structure that the late Randolph Harvey Heatherbrae had built at the turn of the twentieth century as a wedding gift for his bride, Margaret Lee Wakefield. It was the legacy passed down to their only daughter, Helena. And, according to one unsettling Wikipedia comment, "The tomb that held Helena from the day she was born."

I squinted and eyeballed the place. "It's creepy if you ask me. The middle of it looks like a fortress with those turrets but the sides look more like a Persian palace. Look at the tile work on those arches!"

"I'm looking. I'm looking," Max said. "We could be here all day trying to find the door. Might as well follow the arrow."

The young man at the ticket window wasn't about to grant us access to the building without paying the fifteen dollar entrance fee and waiting for the next available tour guide, but at the mention of the words "murder investigation" and a swift move on Max's part where he reached for his business card while allowing the guy to see his holstered gun, we were directed to a side door framed by a huge stone arch.

"I'm phoning the office now," the man said. "Someone will be at that door to let you in."

We thanked him and headed to the entrance. Minutes later we were ushered inside by a petite brunette who appeared to be in her early forties.

"I'm Phoebe Leyton, Miss Gainson's secretary. Follow me, please."

Max and I didn't say a word as we were led down a long corridor whose maroon carpeting looked as if it was showing signs of age. Framed landscapes hung on the walls. Each one more depressing than the other. We passed two or three ornate wooden doors and I wondered what was behind them. Finally, we reached a cheery French door with glass panels that revealed a large business office inside.

"Please come inside and have a seat. I'll tell Miss Gainson you're here."

Phoebe knocked on an interior door, leaned in and then returned to the outer room where she took a seat at her desk. Other than file cabinets, plants, and a few computers, including the one on Phoebe's desk, the place looked pretty austere. I was about to say something to Max when a tall, well-rounded woman, probably in her late fifties, approached us. She ran her fingers through a long gold chain that hung down her silk ecru top.

"Hello. I'm Anna Gainson. I understand you're here about a murder investigation. Please, follow me to our conference room." Then, turning to Phoebe, she asked her secretary to bring us some water before we even had a chance to introduce ourselves.

The conference room looked every bit the part. Enormous oak table with matching captain's chairs, framed watercolors of the Mystery Castle on the walls and a huge window that overlooked the rear of the building.

Once Anna closed the door and took a seat, Max held out his hand and introduced himself, thanking her for taking the time to meet with us. I did the same.

"I spoke to the police the day after Helena was found. I'm not sure if there's anything I can add. And the police made no mention of foul play. Helena was in her nineties. I thought she died of natural causes."

Max cleared his throat, leaned his elbows on the table and clasped his hands, making a loud slapping noise. "It would appear that way, yes. However, there are certain incongruences that came to light and that's why my office was hired to probe further."

He handed her his business card and continued to speak. There was a certain directness to his voice that I think made Anna uncomfortable. A skill I'd have to pick up and learn fast if I was going to get the same results. And while my background as a crime statistician was helpful, it was no match for the street skills I needed to acquire. Anna Gainson didn't question us any further. In fact, she sat quietly waiting for Max to continue.

"Miss Rayner and I will need to interview all of the employees at the Mystery Castle this week. Those who work for the business enterprise and Helena's personal staff. Is that something you can arrange?"

"Only for those people who continue to work here."

Just then, Phoebe walked in and placed three bottled waters on the table before hurrying out. I reached for mine and caught Anna's eye. "It would be easier for us to conduct our investigation if you could provide us with a list of all the current employees as well as any who worked for Helena in the past year."

"That's not a problem. Hold on for a moment."

She stood up, opened the door and directed Phoebe to run

her an employee list.

"It should be available in a few minutes. I don't know what we'd do without technology and spreadsheets."

"Thanks," I said. "I haven't been here since I was a little girl but I remember being dazzled by this place. I still am. What's going to happen now? Now that Helena is gone."

I could detect a slight smile as Anna leaned back and spoke. I hoped Max noticed it as well.

"Helena treasured this place and wanted to share it with the world. It was deemed a state historic site years ago but only recently did Helena sign the paperwork to transfer it to the state national park system. The Mystery Castle is now officially a Minnesota state park, not unlike the Lindbergh house in Morrison County."

"So, um, you're state employees now," I said.

Anna nodded. "In a manner of speaking. There was a caveat to the transfer of property. All employees of her estate would continue working in their current capacity. The only exception being her personal staff. Not many state parks have private cooks or maids I'm afraid. Still, we were able to retain most of our employees. The Mystery Castle is quite unique. We host community events and rent the Garden Grotto to private parties for luncheons and the like."

I tried to act as if this was new information and opened my eyes a bit wider. "Sounds as if nothing will really change as far as the public is concerned."

Max made a groaning little "hmmm" sound, then asked, "What about her personal property? Furniture. Clothing. Jewelry. Family heirlooms. Seems I recall hearing that she had some relatives in Minnesota but I could be mistaken."

"Helena left a will. She was extremely well organized. You'd have to check with her attorney at Blair and Lowery Law Partners. They're handling the estate. In the meantime, her residence has been closed off until we get word from them about how to proceed. I had planned to hire an appraisal company to do a complete inventory of Miss Heatherbrae's personal art and jewelry. After that, a cleaning service would be hired to do a deep cleaning of the place. At this juncture in time, I'm not sure if the Mystery Castle will simply close off her residence for good or include it on the tour. Seems a shame to not open that area to the public as well. Of course, that would mean installing a security system. Only the first two floors and the basement of the castle are monitored. Not Helena's apartment."

So far, everything Anna Gainson said coincided with what Minerva had told us. I looked at Max out of the corner of my eye, unsure of where to go next. Thankfully he stepped in.

"According to the information from the police reports, it was her maid who found her and her cook who ran to the bedroom once she heard the maid scream."

"Yes, so I've been told," Anna said. "It was evening and I had already gone home for the day. Plus, I don't, I mean *didn't*, see Helena on a daily basis like her personal staff. We met a few times during the week to discuss business and that sort of thing. Last time I spoke with her was a few days before she died. We talked about the summer art show. A major outdoor event held on our lawn."

Phoebe knocked on the doorframe and walked in. "I have the information you wanted, Miss Gainson."

She handed Anna some papers and left the room, closing the door behind her. Anna immediately placed them on the table and slid them to Max.

"Here's the employee information you requested. Names and dates of employment. Contact information as well. I can set up times for you to meet with the tour guides, our handyman, and our gardener. I'm not sure what information they can provide since they didn't have any direct contact with Helena. It's her personal staff you'll need to see. The only exception is Greta Hansen, her housekeeper. Greta worked in the private and public part of the house. I can set up a time for you to talk with her."

Max rubbed his chin as he scanned the paper. "That'll be

fine. One or both of us will be back later this week. Preferably Friday. I'll have our secretary call your office for the appointment times. Make it later than nine. The rush hour traffic is a pain. Also, we'll need to take a look at Helena's residence and the rest of the castle. Can we wander around or do we need to hook up to one of those tours?"

"You're free to wander the castle. The exhibits are clearly marked and if you get lost, there are at least two tours going on so someone will be sure to help you. As for Helena's apartment, I'll see if Greta can show you the place. She's really the only one familiar with it. Well, her and Arletta Maycomber, Helena's personal maid. Arletta's no longer working for us as you've probably surmised. Anyway, why don't you check out the castle and come back here in an hour. Greta should be available by then."

"Sounds like a plan to me," Max said. "And one more thing. Were you aware Helena had some digestive issues?"

"Digestive issues? No. I would imagine that's something her cooks would have been made aware of. Why do you ask?"

"Just something in our notes. That's all. Anyway, thanks and we'll see you in an hour."

Anna led us out the door but instead of having us walk back down the long corridor to the side entrance, she opened another corridor door which took us into a small eastern looking reception area.

"This is the Casbah section of the house. On the table to your left are guidebooks to the house. I doubt you'll have any problems."

I opened my mouth to thank her but she had already headed back down the corridor.

"Wow. What did you think of that encounter, Max? And by the way, I've never seen you act so...so...intimidating. What am I missing?"

"Nothing. But she wasn't about to give us any information and would have put us on the defensive if I would've let her. Sometimes you've got to play the alpha dog."

"Well, woof to you, I guess. Where should we go first?"

CHAPTER FOUR

T he Casbah section was a series of small rooms separated by ornate alcoves. Each room resembled what I imagined the interior of a Moroccan Casbah would look like. The individual areas boasted highly decorative arched windows, some with stained glass, others with dangling beads but all of them with intricate window treatments. Martha Stewart would be in her glory. Max, not so much.

"How many of these sitting rooms did that family need? Yikes. This one's got a reflective pond in it. And more palm trees than Florida."

"Oh my gosh, Max. They're incredible. Some of these water features are mind-boggling. Look at the mosaic one on that wall. It's breathtaking. Funny, but I don't remember this part of the house when my mom took us here years ago. Of course, my brother was running all over the place like a wild man so we might have skipped this part."

"I'd like to skip this part. Let's move on."

We walked past the Casbah wing and entered what I could best describe as a royal tomb. Only it wasn't a tomb. Well, not exactly. It was a gilded gold room with a couch that resembled an ancient Egyptian sarcophagus. Max shook his head and kept walking.

Next, we entered a room that I did remember. It was framed in wood and filled with taxidermies of elk, deer, moose, and all sorts of animals that inhabited this part of the United States. Maroon and gold wooden chairs and a matching settee were smack dab in the center. I found myself edging away from the stuffed animals but for some reason Max was in no hurry to leave the room.

"Guess the old man must have been a hunter, huh?"

"Or he liked stuffed dead things," I said.

Then Max did something unexpected. He turned around and backtracked.

"Quick! I hear a tour coming down the hallway toward this room. I want to check on something."

We raced back to the tomb room and the Casbah section.

"Uh-huh," Max said, "Just as I thought. "Look carefully at the walls. What do you notice?"

"What do you mean? The decorations? What?"

"The spacing between the panels. It's not as obvious where there's wallpaper but it's really obvious where the builder used wood. That's when I first noticed it. When we walked into the taxidermy room. It was done intentionally. Those are doorways to another part of the house."

"You don't think—"

Before Max could answer, a second tour group entered the room from the corridor behind us. We were surrounded by at least fifteen or more people, most of whom weren't speaking English. They did, however, speak the universal language of smartphone and began taking photos and selfies.

"We're going to run into that other tour group," I said. "Should we just keep going?"

Max gave me a nudge and pointed. "There's a stairwell in the foyer right before we get to the tomb room. Hurry up, let's see what's upstairs."

By the time the second tour group had entered the tomb

room, we were almost to the top of the long winding staircase. It was one of those grand wooden stairwells that appear in all the old romantic movies. Like the floor below, the second story was also eclectic. There were bedrooms with canopy beds and frilly curtains, bedrooms with sleigh beds and small sitting rooms. There were also two large bathrooms both with claw tubs and pedestal sinks.

"I imagine their greatest achievement was indoor plumbing," I said as we moved down the hallway. There was only one more room to our left before we reached a formidable wooden door with a sign on it that read, "No Visitors Beyond This Point."

Max and I looked at each other and headed back to the first floor. It had been close to an hour and Greta Hansen would be waiting for us.

"What do you think Anna Gainson told Greta?" I asked as we got closer to the business office.

"Hard to say. Let's see what we can pry out of her when we take the grand tour."

Sure enough, Greta was waiting for us in the first reception area adjacent to the business office. She was wearing a white smock over a plain blue dress and looked as if we had interrupted her from some housework. Her short gray hair was tossed a bit and other than some quickly applied blush, she wore no other makeup. I guessed her age to be around sixty.

"You must be the private investigators Miss Gainson told me about. I'm Greta Hansen. I was Miss Heatherbrae's housekeeper until she passed. I'm lucky they kept me on. I need the work. Poor Arletta. Don't know what she's going to do. She wasn't planning on retiring right away. Oh my. I shouldn't be babbling on about this."

"That's okay," I said. "We need to know as much as possible about Helena and her staff."

Greta looked past me at Max. "I thought she died of natural causes. That's what I was told when I came to work the following morning. Arletta found her."

"That's our understanding as well," Max said. "But we need to be sure. Can you show us her residence? We can talk once we get upstairs."

Greta nodded. "Follow me. We're going down this long hallway that looks like someone threw up Persian seat cushions. Oops. Don't tell Miss Gainson I said that."

Max and I both laughed as we continued down the corridor. I expected us to take the same grand staircase we used before but when we entered the tomb room, Greta walked us past the sarcophagus to the closed curtains. She opened them to reveal a wooden door. Then, with a key, she unlocked the door, flipped a switch on the wall and lit up a straight stairwell with high steps.

"It's shorter this way. These stairs take us directly into Miss Heatherbrae's apartment. Please close the door behind you. It locks automatically."

"Um, how many people know about these stairs?" I asked staring at the back of Greta's neck.

"Why, I imagine everyone who worked for her," was the reply. Seconds later I swore I could hear Max mumble, "Oh crap."

The door opened into a small butler's pantry. I could see a dumbwaiter across from a prep sink and a glassed-in cabinet with all sorts of plates and cups. "Why is there a dumbwaiter here? The room below us isn't a kitchen."

"No," Greta said. "But the room below that one, is. Houses built in that era had the kitchens in the basement. Service kitchens. Not like today. The room below us is the day room. It used to be the main dining room."

I could've kicked myself for not remembering. Especially after watching all those episodes of *Downton Abbey* a few years back. Greta continued speaking without pausing for a breath.

"Miss Heatherbrae's kitchen is straight ahead. And by the way, she had another dumbwaiter installed from the opposite side of the pantry downstairs. That contraption is concealed behind those two cabinet doors."

I did a double take. "Wow. Could've fooled me. I thought they were regular kitchen cabinet doors."

"Nothing is regular here. Helena had it built when she took residence here a number of years ago. Other than that, she didn't want anything changed. Or very little changed, I should say. With the exception of the microwave, those are the original appliances and they still work. In fact, that's one of the best gas ovens around. Bakes perfect pies."

"I take it her cooks used this kitchen," Max said, "and not the one downstairs."

"They used both, but usually this one. The main one was and still is used for private parties or events. But Miss Heatherbrae hasn't held any of those in years, only the ones for the Mystery Castle and she wasn't doing the planning. Miss Gainson was."

The kitchen was vintage mid-century if ever I saw one. Vintage and spotless. Max and I both looked at the oven. It would be easy to leave it turned on and fill up the place with gas. According to Minerva, Helena was worried about carbon monoxide poisoning.

"This is Miss Heatherbrae's office." Greta said. "Everything's like it was when I last cleaned in here. She was at that computer at least two or three hours a day."

I glanced over at the monitor and could tell the system was an LG. "Was Helena left handed?"

Greta looked at me and shrugged. "I honestly don't know. Why?"

"The mouse is on the left-hand side of the monitor. Just curious, that's all."

The office opened up via large French doors into a stunning living area that resembled Old Russia. A large samovar sat in the middle of the room on a coffee table and Russian nesting dolls lined the built-in shelves. A few hand-painted lacquer boxes with fairy tale motifs were dotted here and there on the small end tables.

From the living room, we moved into her bedroom, passing

a small half bath in the hallway. Max headed toward the queen size English style bed and bent down to take a look under the dust ruffle.

"Did Helena eat a lot of sweets in her bedroom? Like taffy or caramel?"

Greta paused for a second before shaking her head. "I'm guessing not. Why do you ask? The woman had dentures. Sometimes I'd find them soaking in a glass in the bathroom."

Max held up a red Tootsie roll pop. "I found this under the bed. Kojak wasn't visiting, was he?"

I was about to ask who Kojak was but Greta spoke first.

"I'll be darned. Why on earth would she be chomping on something like that? Most likely Arletta dropped it. Maybe around the same time she found Miss Heatherbrae. I can tell you this much, it wasn't under the bed the last time I cleaned in here. And I happen to be a very conscientious cleaner."

My eyes darted from the Tootsie roll pop to Greta. "Has anything been moved since the um, discovery of—"

"The body? No. We left everything the way it was when Arletta found her. In case the police wanted to have a look-see. I was going to remove the bed linen and wash them but now I'm glad we waited."

"Who told you to wait?" I asked.

"Miss Gainson told us, us being Arletta of course and the cooks, to lock up her residence until further notice. Maybe she was waiting on one of the relatives or something. That is, if Miss Heatherbrae had relatives. I don't know."

Max took a step back from the bed and scanned the bedroom before stepping back into the living room. "So, nothing's been touched or moved since that night?"

"That's right," Greta said, "But you really should check with Arletta. She was Miss Heatherbrae's personal maid. She'd know if anything was disturbed. I clean the apartment but things get moved around in-between."

Max moved closer to Greta. "When was the last time you cleaned in here?"

"That morning. I clean every morning when Miss Heatherbrae goes downstairs to sit in the large day room."

"The day room." I looked at Max. "Were we in the day room?"

Greta jumped in before Max had a chance to respond. "The day room sits in the center of the house. It has an enormous couch that overlooks the front windows. Miss Heatherbrae liked sitting in there. She could look out and see all of Minneapolis from that spot. She also liked interacting with the visitors."

Interacting or scaring them half to death like she did to my brother?

"This is the first time I've been back in this room but it looks the same to me," Greta continued. "All of her knickknacks are still on the dressers and nothing's been moved. But then again, Arletta would know for sure."

"Have you been in contact with Arletta since Helena's death?" Max asked.

"No. Last time I saw her was that next morning after she found Helena. She showed up along with Minerva Watson, the head cook and Sydelle Alridge, Minerva's assistant. As soon as we got inside, Miss Gainson ushered us into her office and sent Arletta and the cooks home. Told me I could do some cleaning in the main part of the castle until it was determined who got to stay on. I learned later that they were keeping the cooks on a part-time basis but since Arletta was a personal maid, her services were no longer needed. Same with the chauffeur. At least Harry's on the young side so I don't imagine he'd have much trouble finding another job."

"I suppose not. You're certain everything looks the same in here?"

Greta walked around the room slowly, pausing every now and then. "It does to me."

"All right then," Max said. "We'll need to take a few pictures before everything gets cleaned out or rearranged."

Then, he looked at me and I got the hint. I immediately took out my phone and systematically went to work. Meanwhile, Max used that time to question Greta. I listened carefully.

"How long have you worked for Miss Heatherbrae?"

"I've been employed here for the past thirteen years. Had to find something when my husband passed away."

"Was Miss Heatherbrae having any problems with anyone that you knew of?"

"Problems? No. Nothing out of the ordinary. Except…"

"Except what?" Max's voice got a bit louder.

"She never used to sleep with the windows open but a month or so ago, she started doing that. Place was freezing when I'd come in to clean it."

"Anything else?"

"Not that I'm aware of, but like I said, I wasn't around her as much as Arletta. Is there anything else I can show you up here? Otherwise I need to get back to the downstairs dusting."

We thanked her and exited the apartment. Greta locked the door and gave the doorknob an extra turn to make sure it was secure. "I'll walk you back downstairs into the day room so you can see where Helena spent most of her time. There are a few more formal rooms beyond that, including an atrium."

We were halfway down the stairs when I had a thought. "Other than these stairs and the formal ones, is there another way to access Helena's residence?"

"Not unless someone wants to climb up the balcony. Well, here we are. The day room's on your left. It was nice meeting you."

Greta left us standing in an open foyer as she proceeded down the corridor. When she was out of earshot, Max spoke.

"I'm convinced more than ever someone knocked off our dear Miss Heatherbrae."

"Why? I mean, how?"

"Let's keep walking and I'll tell you when we get to that day room."

"You can also tell me who Kojak is."

CHAPTER FIVE

Max and I stood in front of the large picture window that was the focal point of the room. The Minneapolis skyline looked as if I could reach out and touch it. The tours hadn't arrived or perhaps they'd been through the room already. It didn't matter. We had the place to ourselves for a few minutes.

Suddenly Max laughed. "I can't believe you don't know who Kojak is. Think Monk only with Tootsie rolls instead of hand sanitizer. Telly Savalas played him in a 1970s TV series. Your mother would know. Sounds like something Iris would have watched."

At the thought of my mother, I grimaced. "I suppose. Anyway, are you going to tell me why you're so certain Helena was murdered?"

"Sometimes it's the little things that clue us in regarding someone's death. Greta told us nothing was moved or touched. It's April in Minnesota and two people confirmed Helena slept with the windows open. So why was the blanket folded up on chair on the other side of the room? Shouldn't it have been on the bed? Minerva said they had to shake it out before Helena would sleep with it. All I saw on the bed, other than the sheets, was that folded up cushion we were told about. Oh yeah, and that Tootsie roll pop under the bed. Strange thing for a woman with dentures to be eating. Hey, by the way, you were smart to question Greta about another entrance into the apartment but I already have the answer to that one."

"What?"

"Did you notice the large bookcase in that living room of hers? The one with those nesting dolls?"

"Uh-huh."

"I noticed the way in which one of the panels was rubbing against the other. Lots of temperature fluctuation and humidity in these parts. And, there was a slight gap that shouldn't have been there. I took a good look at the grain in the wood and noticed one of the knots. Right next to that green and gold doll, and not obvious to the untrained eye. I've seen that kind of thing before. It's a button. One push and I guarantee that panel would spring open. Great spot to hide something incriminating."

"My God, Max. The police really need to get a search warrant and find out. Someone probably used that door to sneak in and kill her."

"Slow down, kid. First of all, there were no signs of trauma or a struggle and the death was ruled natural. Our evidence isn't even at the circumstantial point yet. We'll need a whole lot more to go on before we can convince the police department to start their own inquiry. And by then, we might have it figured out for them. We've got a lineup of employees to question and we'll need to meet with her attorney."

"I'm planning on driving back here on Friday for the interviews Anna's going to set up. I can also see if I can get an appointment with Blair and Lowery regarding her will and the estate."

"Sounds like a plan to me. What do you say we head for home? This place is beginning to give me the willies. You know, I've lived in this area all my life but never came here. Doris and the kids did though, on more than one occasion. School field trips. I owe her."

"You can't head out right now. You haven't seen the creepiest part of this place. It's really the only thing I remember – the grotto."

"Yeah, didn't Anna mention something about the Garden Grotto?"

"That's a separate building behind the house. Looks like a merry-go-round surrounded by glass. I remember being forced to sit quietly with my brother while they served us cookies and lemonade. The grotto I'm referring to is in the basement. We'll have to check out the floor plan map to see how to get there."

No sooner did I say that when a tour group entered the room and the guide, a man in his early twenties, began to talk about Thomas Cole and Frederick Church whose landscapes hung on the walls.

I nudged Max. "When he catches a breath, I'm going to ask him how we can get downstairs to the grotto."

"We just came from there," a woman said. "I wasn't eavesdropping when I overheard you. You go out the door on the right and when you get to the small foyer with the big Grecian urns on the tables, you'll see a wooden door. It's a stairwell that takes you to the grotto. The guide told us you can also get there from outside but you have to climb down a slight embankment. I don't think many people would be doing that. Too muddy."

"Thanks," I whispered.

Max was already out the door of the day room and standing in the foyer. I hurried over.

"This must be it. No other doors in sight." he said.

He pulled it open and we were both relieved the staircase was well lit. Wall sconces shaped like lanterns were evenly spaced, making it easy enough for us to see where we were going. I was dying to give Max a heads-up about the room but decided to let him see for himself. Unfortunately, I kept laughing to myself the entire way down the stairs so he knew something was up.

"Holy Hell! Is this what you were giggling about? You could've warned me, you know. Again, Holy Hell! Are those real skeletons?"

"I think so. I think they were acquired back at a time when you could purchase such things."

"That's good to know. Wouldn't want to think they died that way. I've heard of marriages that went belly up but not the wedding itself."

Max was staring at the grotto's main attraction - an altar with a skeleton bride and groom surrounded by a wedding party. All of the guests were decked out in the finery of the day. It was laughable and eerie at the same time.

The grotto's other features included a small greenish pond, compliments of some decent lighting techniques, and assorted gargoyles and trolls that seemed to pop out of nowhere.

The room was illuminated by wall sconces and lanterns. I imagined at one time candles might have been used but had been replaced when the house was retrofitted for electric lighting.

"Aren't you glad you stayed for the best part?" I was still laughing as Max walked around the large room.

"Very funny. Hey, isn't there supposed to be a kitchen down here? The main one for the building."

"Um, now that I think of it, you're right. Everything's disjointed in this place."

Max let out a soft groan. "That's a good word for it. We're probably in a sub-basement. I'll wager the kitchen's a floor above us with access from another stairwell. We should check it out. Minerva and Arletta were supposedly the only ones in the building when Helena was found dead. They wouldn't have known if someone was downstairs in the kitchen. The main part of the building, yes. Those noises would carry. If Helena's cook and her personal maid didn't kill her, I'd like to know who else was in the Mystery Castle that night."

"It's already a little past four," I said. "I don't think Anna

Gainson would be all that thrilled showing us the kitchen, do you?"

"No, and she'll be less thrilled when I ask her to show us the blueprints of this house. When you come back on Friday to interview the employees, see if you can get one of them to show you that downstairs kitchen. That is, if Minerva isn't available. She'll have to play the part and be interviewed as well. Meanwhile, I've seen enough skeletons in this closet to last me a lifetime. Let's get on over to Anna's office before she decides to cut out early today."

Max was pretty intuitive with that last statement of his because the minute we returned to the director's office, Anna was on her way out. She had shouted for Phoebe to lock up and make sure the windows were bolted as well.

"I'm sorry, Miss Gainson," Max said blocking the doorway. "I hate to hold you up but Miss Rayner and I really need to take a good look at the original blueprints to this house. I'm sure you must have them filed or archived."

Anna had a pained look on her face that was hard to conceal. She was either in a hurry to get somewhere or she didn't want us to see the blueprints.

"Is that really necessary? Wasn't seeing Helena's apartment enough for your investigation? It wasn't as if anyone else was here during the time of her death."

"That's what we'd like to know. So, can we steal a bit more of your time and have a look? It shouldn't take us more than fifteen or twenty minutes."

"Follow me inside and have a seat."

Anna walked over to Phoebe who was still working at her desk. It was hard to hear the conversation except for Phoebe saying, "Yes, I'll be sure to do that." Seconds later, Anna returned to where we were seated and informed us Phoebe would be securing the blueprints for our review. We had a half hour to look at them before Phoebe went home for the night.

Max thanked Anna and walked with me to the conference room. It took Phoebe a few minutes to get the blueprints and she apologized when she placed them on the table.

"They were locked in a special file cabinet in one of the back rooms. There are two copies. Both the same. Can I get you anything else? Oh, and please be careful, these are very, very old. The paper's almost brittle."

"We'll be careful," I said. She closed the door and walked out.

"Um, I don't know about you, Max, but I can't read blueprints."

"Who said anything about reading them? Start snapping photos."

I don't know what we would have done before the iPhone and I didn't want to think about it. I snapped away. "So, who's going to figure this out for us?"

"My brother-in-law's a retired contractor. Not an architect but he thinks he is and who are we to argue? He can read these things. That's all that matters. Guess Doris and I will have to have him and his wife over for dinner sometime this week. Good. At least I'll get a good meal out of it. How's it going?"

"Um, fine I guess. Except...well, see for yourself."

I handed him the yellowing sheets of paper. "I think there're pages missing. We've got the basement floor plan, the first-floor plan, the second-floor plan and the attic but check out the lettering on the bottom of the sheets. It goes from A to C, D and E. Where's B? What floor is B?"

Max lined up the sheets and moved his head back and forth. "'A' must be that grotto because the other sheets are clearly marked with rooms. If I'm reading this right, and God knows, then the floor plan for the downstairs kitchen seems to be missing."

I leaned over to take a closer look when Phoebe knocked on the door and I all but jumped.

"Oh, I'm sorry. I didn't mean to startle you. I need to lock up in a few minutes."

Max pushed his chair back and stood up. "Is this the entire set of blueprints?"

Phoebe rubbed her hands together and shook her head. "This is what we have on file."

"It'll have to do. Thank your boss for us. We're better get a move on before it gets dark."

We were almost out the side door when Phoebe walked over to us. "Maybe Miss Heatherbrae's attorney might have what you're looking for. I wish I could help you but—"

"It's okay. The conversation we're having stays in this room."

"Thanks. And good luck. She was a lovely woman, you know. Strange, but sweet. I'd like to think her death was a natural one."

"Us, too," I said.

Phoebe closed the door behind us and we walked back to my car without saying a word. It was as if we needed a moment to process what had just happened. Then, Max turned to me and made a grumbling noise. "I'm running background checks on everyone, starting with Anna Gainson. She gives me that cold, creepy feeling I had as a kid watching a horror movie. Not her looks, mind you, she's fine in that department but there's something too cold about her and it has nothing to do with the Minnesota weather."

"I had the same reaction, too."

"Tough thing about this case is that we don't know for sure if the old lady was really murdered. But…if we could figure out a motive for killing her, it might offer up the evidence we need to be certain."

"And if we can't?"

"There's always a motive for murder. Like I said, we figure out what it is, attach it to the right person and boom! Case closed."

Of course, both of us knew it really wasn't going to be that simple but it made us feel better. We stopped for a quick hamburger in St. Peter, southwest of Minneapolis on the 169, before getting back to New Ulm. Max said he wanted to be sure he had "something substantial" in his stomach because "God knows what hellish gluten-free GMO-free vegan thing

Doris would have waiting for him."

Byron was on the counter yowling for food when I walked into my apartment. It was a little past his feeding time and he was letting me know. I put my phone on the counter and reached for his bag of kibble when I realized I had the thing set on mute all day. As Byron chomped away at his meal, I noticed a missed voice mail – Hogan's.

He called to let me know he had the weekend covered at the brewery so we'd have Saturday and Sunday to ourselves. I called back but that went to voice mail. Ugh. I told him Sunday was a "given" but I was up in the air as far as Saturday was concerned. If I couldn't squeeze in all those interviews on Friday, I'd have to drive back the next day. Tomorrow, being Thursday, was totally out of the question. I had to narrow down Scott's whereabouts so Loreen Larsen could either go ahead with her wedding plans or drop him like a sack of potatoes.

Smart woman, Loreen. I should have done the same thing with my ex-husband. Unfortunately, I married young only to find out he was a philandering son of a gun. We worked at the same college and when Max Blake, a friend of my late father's, offered me a way out as his investigative assistant, I took it.

I was so exhausted from a full day of driving and reliving a childhood excursion at the Mystery Castle that I didn't budge from the couch except to grab a can of soda from the fridge. Byron nestled himself at my feet while I channeled surfed until coming across an old movie that looked as if it would be interesting. I had gotten as far as the opening credits when I closed my eyes.

It was only when Hogan returned my call did I sit up and look around for the phone.

"Hey, you sound really groggy. Did I wake you up? It's only quarter to nine."

"Sorry. I must've dozed off. You won't believe the day I had."

I went on to tell him about the Mystery Castle and Max's reaction when he stepped into the grotto.

"I don't blame the guy," Hogan said. "I'd want to be warned, too. You know, I've never been to the Mystery Castle. Been to lots of other places in this state but never to that attraction. Look, if you have to return on Saturday, how about if I join you? You could interview those employees while I play tourist. After that we could go out somewhere for a nice dinner."

"I'm up for that. Angie's supposed to coordinate the interviews with Anna Gainson tomorrow. Anna's the director of the castle. All business if you ask me. Max had an interesting take on her as well."

"As in she might be a suspect?"

"As in she might know more than she'd ever be willing to share."

"Hmm. This new case of yours is sounding good. Good, as in interesting. Not good as in someone dying. Even if it was a ninety-something someone who literally had skeletons in her closet."

CHAPTER SIX

———

Thursday was a complete bust. Scott Byrd was tethered to his office most of the day and when he did go out to lunch it was with two other men from the same office. They ate at a sports bar not far from my apartment. I was able to sit inconspicuously and nibble on some wings while I tried to overhear what they were saying. Maybe Scott was into some dealings that kept him distracted and distanced from his fiancée.

The only bits of conversation I could glean had to do with sports - batting averages, trades and the odds of the Minnesota Twins beating out the Rangers. I did hear Scott say, "Next year at this time it'll be a different story," but that could've meant anything.

The guy's evening routine was even more boring. I followed him to his house near Flandrau State Park and thankfully the place had a carport and not a garage. That meant I could keep checking periodically without having to actually stake out the place for the next few hours. It looked to be a fairly new neighborhood with split-level homes like his and cookie-cutter yards. Nothing out of the ordinary.

At a little past eight, Loreen arrived at his house and I took that as my cue to get the hell out of there. I had parked diagonally from his place in front of an empty house with a For Sale sign in front. She didn't notice me and I doubted if anyone else did. So much for a wasted evening. I figured if the guy was cheating on her maybe he was doing it on the weekend. I had to be more productive with this investigation. When I got home I left a message for her to call me. I needed to know when she was going to be with him so I wouldn't waste my time.

As it turned out, I should've paid more attention in the first place. She did say he wasn't spending weekends at her place like he used to. If he was dallying around, it was a good guess Saturday night might be a starting point. I wasn't sure how Hogan would react if I asked him to join me on a quasi-stake-out when we got back from the Mystery Castle, but I figured I'd worry about it when the time came.

In between scoping out Scott's office and his house, I was able to get some paperwork done at my own office. Angie was as efficient as usual and had contacted Anna Gainson to set up those interviews.

"Here goes, Marcie," Angie said before I darted for another round of surveillance shortly before noon. "Miss Gainson was able to set up most of the interviews for tomorrow. She said you could use her conference room."

"Hmm. About that. I got to thinking maybe some of the employees aren't going to feel so comfortable talking to me in there. Can you give her a call back and tell her I'd rather chat with them on the wrap-around porch by the Garden Grotto? Even with an event on, we wouldn't be in the way. The porch is covered if it starts to rain and it's got plenty of room."

"No problem."

Angie handed me the interview schedule and I took a quick look.

"Aargh. Looks like Hogan will get to see the Mystery Castle after all. He said he'd keep me company on Saturday if I had to go back for more interviews. Actually, I think he's chomping at the bit to check out that place."

"Not that I'm being too nosey, but how are things going between the two of you?"

"I *really* like him," I said. "Really like him. And I don't have to try to impress him, I can be myself and it still works."

"He's probably thinking the same thing about you."

I smiled and took a closer look at the schedule. The gardener and the handyman were scheduled for the next morning starting at ten. Minerva was also scheduled but that was going to be a ruse. At least I'd be able to see what else she knew about the other employees. Greta had already given Max and me as much information as she was willing to share so that left Sydelle, the assistant cook, and Arletta, the personal maid.

Sydelle's appointment was for the early afternoon. I figured I could use the time in-between to have another look at the castle's interior. That left Saturday. Arletta Maycomber had agreed to meet with me but there was an asterisk next to her name and a note off to the side that read, "Made it clear she didn't have to do this but was only doing us a favor." Terrific. I made a note, too. A mental one. "Handle with kid gloves." It was an expression my mother used when my sister-in-law, Gale, was pregnant. "You don't want to upset her, no matter what," my mother would say. "Expectant mothers are more unpredictable than politicians. If she shows you some piece of clothing she's bought for the baby and it's hideous, just nod and say, "How nice.""

I muttered that phrase to myself forgetting that Angie was only a few feet away.

"What's nice?"

"Oh, nothing. I'm just thinking out-loud. All of the people I'm going to question worked for Helena Heatherbrae in one capacity or another. But only four of them would've been familiar with her apartment. The two cooks, her maid and her housecleaner. Unless…"

"Unless what?" she said.

"Unless Helena had visitors. Personal visitors. Acquaintances. That sort of thing. Anna Gainson wouldn't know about that because it had nothing to do with the Mystery Castle's business. The cooks wouldn't be privy to that sort of thing either unless they were asked to serve refreshments. That leaves Greta and Arletta. If Helena had company, one of those two ladies was bound to know about it."

"What are you getting at?"

"A wider list of suspects. Max would go nuts if I mentioned it. You know him by now. He likes to start with a small circle and widen it if necessary. I'll see how far I can get with the folks I'm meeting but I'll also find out what else they may know."

That's exactly what I did on Friday beginning with Ernie Diaz, the gardener, at ten thirty. We had the entire wrap-around porch to ourselves but I knew that could change at any minute. The tourists were everywhere. Fortunately, Ernie was easy to spot. He was well built, in his mid-forties, and his jeans were caked with dried dirt. I waved him over and we spoke for at least a half hour, mostly about the flower gardens. He told me he had worked for over a decade as the estate's gardener and had only seen "La Señora" on a handful of occasions.

"It would have been…what's the word? Oh yes. Improper. It would have been improper for me to speak with her," he said.

I immediately thought of my obsession with Downton Abbey and the rigid separation of social classes. Ernie still followed those antiquated rules and for the life of me, I couldn't imagine him having a motive to kill her. When I asked him if he knew of anyone who might have wanted to harm his boss, all he said was "I think they all would like her money." With nothing specific, I crossed his name off my list.

My conversation with Martin Vogel, the handyman, was more promising but not by much. He had been in and out of Helena's apartment on a number of occasions over the years, and, like Ernie, had been employed by the Mystery Castle for well over three decades. Talk about longevity. He was in his early sixties, having worked as an electrician prior to taking the position at the castle. He also had carpentry and plumbing skills.

He had taken Ernie's place at a small table overlooking one of the parking lots. It was a little past eleven and the tourists were trickling in and out of the castle.

"If half those people would keep their hands and feet to themselves, we wouldn't have to replace so much stuff," he said. "The kids are the worst and the parents don't discipline them. Last week I had to re-attach toilet paper holders in the men's room and replace a wall socket in one of the foyers. Someone stuffed gum in it. Can you believe it?"

"Yeah," I said. "I suppose I can. So, tell me, what kind of repairs did you make in Helena's residence?"

Martin ran his fingers through his thinning salt and pepper hair. I could see they were calloused and rough. "Let me think. Nothing too recent but about two months ago she had me change the locks to her doors. Wouldn't say why. Lots of time spent making up extra keys, too. And last month I had to change one of the wall sockets. It's an old house and some of mechanisms go way back. Of course, there's the light bulbs. Had to change a few of those, too. They're made in China now and they don't last no matter what the labels say. Other than that, we've had the HVAC guys work on the boilers because Miss Heatherbrae's apartment wasn't getting much output. Didn't want her to freeze to death during the night."

I thought about Helena sleeping with the windows open. "Do you know when that was?"

"Back in February. I had a week's vacation so I wasn't around. Miss Gainson took care of the arrangements."

Martin's recollection jived with what Minerva and Greta said. Whatever spooked Helena into thinking her life was in jeopardy had to be fairly recent. But what?

"At any time, did you ever notice anything unusual about Helena's behavior?"

Martin shook his head. "Not that I would know. I'd go into her place, make any necessary repairs and be on my way.

Sometimes she'd be there reading or working on her computer. Her head practically touched the screen. Other times, Greta would let me in the apartment because Miss Heatherbrae was downstairs in the day room."

I brushed some wisps of hair from my face and paused. "As you've probably been told by the director, there were some discrepancies regarding Helena's death and that's what we've been hired to look into. With that in mind, is there anyone on staff who would have benefited from her death?"

"You mean do I think someone here killed her?"

"Well, to put it bluntly…"

Martin rubbed his hands together and looked around. "You might want to have a good long talk with Arletta. If she'll let you. Never liked that woman. Always had the feeling she was up to no good."

"Can you be more specific?" I asked.

"Ever walk in on someone who had a look on their face like the cat who just ate the canary? That was Arletta. Whatever she was up too, Helena never found out."

"Like what?"

"That's the thing. I have no idea. Like I said, it's a feeling."

I thanked Martin, gave him my card and told him to call me if he thought of anything else. Then, I grabbed a granola bar from my bag and munched it while I waited for Minerva to show up. I still had twenty minutes so I took out my phone to see if there were any voice mail messages or texts having put the phone on mute when I first saw Ernie approaching.

No texts but two voice mails starting with the most recent – my brother Jonathan's.

"Hey, sorry about opening my mouth but she was relentless. Don't ask how, but she found out Ira Birnbaum's now working in my lab and wanted me to fix you up. Before I knew what I was saying, I told her you had a boyfriend. Geez, Marcie, I can't run interference on your social life. Gale says hi."

Oh hell no.

I bit my lower lip and listened to the next message.

"When were you going to tell me you had a boyfriend? At my future grandson's bris? Who is this boyfriend of yours? Does he have a job? You didn't meet him at some bar, did you? Call me."

No, I met him at a brewery when I thought he was a murder suspect.

I deleted both voice messages and put the phone in my bag when I heard Minerva's voice. "Good Morning. Hope I didn't keep you. I stopped in the office to pick up my pay stub."

"No, no, you're fine. Have a seat and I'll fill you in. Ernie and Martin spoke with me this morning and Max and I met Anna, Phoebe and Greta. Got the grand tour of Helena's residence from Greta. I get the feeling people know more than they're saying."

"Wouldn't surprise me."

"Minerva, how familiar are you with Helena's apartment? I mean, I know you and Sydelle cooked meals for her in there, but were you aware of any other means to get into her place other than the main stairwell and the back stairwell that opened into the butler's pantry?"

"Those were the only ways in as far as I know. Why? What did you see?"

"Not what we saw but what might be there. It's an old house. A mansion. And those places were notorious for hidden doors and passages. If your observation about Helena's body being 'staged' is right, then quite possibly someone found a way into her room to kill her. And to kill her in a way that made it look natural."

"I don't suppose Greta was any help, was she? And I wouldn't trust her anyway. She may have been employed by Helena but she took her orders from Anna."

The place was beginning to sound more *Dark Shadows* than Mystery Castle. I thought about what Martin told me regarding the boilers back in February. Something had to have happened between then and a few weeks later when Helena started acting strangely.

"Did anything ever look out of place to you in the kitchen when you came to prepare her meals?"

Minerva shook her head. "I didn't notice anything and Sydelle never said a word. Helena's kitchen seemed perfectly fine. Same could be said for the one downstairs."

"Oh my gosh. I haven't seen that kitchen. Is there any way you could take me there?"

Minerva looked at her watch. "Not today. I have a dentist appointment and I can't miss it. But you can ask Sydelle when you talk with her. Is she coming here this afternoon?"

"Yes."

"On second thought, don't ask Sydelle. Tell her. You haven't met Sydelle yet, have you?"

"No, is there anything I should know?"

"Yes, she's a liar."

I opened my mouth but it took a moment for the words to form. "Um…in general, like in exaggerating or more specific?"

"Let me give you an example. A few months ago, before Helena was insistent we taste her food, we made some vanilla biscotti. When the loaves came out of the oven, I told Sydelle to wait ten minutes, cut them and re-bake for another ten minutes. That's what gives them their texture and dryness. I had to leave early so she was in charge. So to speak. Anyway, I found out later when the biscotti was served to Helena, it was soft and mushy. I confronted Sydelle and she insisted she did a re-bake but those biscotti wouldn't have been moist. Sydelle lied about it. And that's not the only time. We had a lovely recipe for—"

"Did she lie about anything other than food?" I asked.

"Humph." The sound emanated from Minerva's mouth and lingered in the air. "A lie's a lie. That's all I'm saying."

"Would Sydelle have any reason to want Helena out of the picture?"

"Not likely. That girl had a cushy job and now she's lost it. True, we're still employed but the hours aren't the same and neither are the benefits."

"One last thing. This is important. Did Helena give any clue about what was spooking her? It had to be something that happened between the time the HVAC crew fixed the heating and when she first started asking you to taste her food and directing Arletta to keep the windows open."

"I'd check her personal calendar if I were you. Not that I'm telling you how to go about doing your job…"

"Her personal calendar? Would it have been on the computer? I know she did her banking online."

"It looked like a datebook. A floral datebook. She kept it in her desk and wrote down what we were serving in case she had a GERD attack. If so, she'd have us add that food to the list of meals to be avoided."

"Uh-oh. That's means going back into her apartment. We had a tough enough time getting Anna to let us in in the first place. And Greta wasn't too thrilled."

"No, I don't suppose she was. When will you be back here?"

"I'm meeting with Arletta tomorrow."

"Good. It's a Saturday. The office is closed. No Anna. No Phoebe and no Greta. The cleaning crew only works weekends except in emergencies."

"What are you thinking?" I asked.

Minerva reached in her bag but not before looking to her right and then to her left as if she was in a car about to make a turn. "I made a copy of the key to her residence. The locks should work fine. Martin replaced them not too long ago. Said the old locks were getting harder to work. Something about the tumblers. Actually, I made two copies just in case. Here, take this. Once you're done talking with Arletta, you can check that datebook yourself. Use either staircase. The key opens both doors. I'm sure of it. For all I know it may be a master key but that shouldn't matter. You'll be in the castle anyway. All you need to do is get into Helena's apartment."

"That's breaking and entering."

"No, honey. It's only entering and no one will notice. Haven't you done this sort of thing before?"

No, up until this year I've handled crime statistics for a small community college.

I tried not to sound whiny. "What about the tour guides?"

"Wait until you're sure they're in another area and if that doesn't work, act like you know what you're doing. Pretend you're a congressman."

CHAPTER SEVEN

M inerva told me she'd keep in touch and would let me know if she picked up any gossip relating to Helena's death. The key she had given me looked shiny and new in the palm of my hand and I put it in the small zippered compartment in my bag. Funny, but according to Martin, it was Helena's idea to change the locks. I wondered why he would lie about something like that.

I had an hour and a half before my meeting with Sydelle and I was starving. The granola bar didn't even put a dent in my hunger but I didn't want to waste time at a restaurant when I could be taking another look at the castle. I decided to opt for a Big Mac since I spotted a McDonalds not too far from the Mystery Castle. That left me approximately fifty-five minutes to wander back through.

The tour guides had been informed by Anna that Max and I were investigating Helena's death. No one questioned me when I showed them my Minnesota Board of Private Detective and Protective Agent Services license. But no one looked impressed, either.

Sauntering into the first foyer, I studied the wall hangings as if I was getting a Masters in Fine Arts. At least I made it look that way. I was actually trying to see where the wall gaps were that Max had pointed out. Two in the Casbah area and one in the day room. I didn't have time to scope out the rest of the building because I didn't want to keep Sydelle waiting.

I hurried back to the wrap-around porch and was immediately hit by the smell of fried onions and grease. It was Sydelle. A chubby brunette with a double chin. She was seated at one of the small tables, and the odor that had permeated her clothing was now polluting the air.

"You must be Marcie Rayner," she said reaching out her hand. I could see the faint lines of grease she hadn't yet wiped off. "You've got to excuse me. I'm working the Suburban Diner now so I didn't have time to run home and change."

Was I that obvious? "It's nice to meet you. I really appreciate you taking the time to talk with me, but I've got another request. Any chance we could have this conversation while you show me the downstairs kitchen in the castle? It's the one place I haven't been and I really need to see it."

Sydelle didn't budge. She pursed her lips and I knew I was in trouble. I should've just told her to do it like Minerva said.

"Seems Minerva should've given you the tour."

"She had an appointment. So, what do you say? It shouldn't take us that long."

I turned my back to Sydelle and took a step. *This better work or I'm SOL.*

"I only have forty-five minutes or so. I'm working the dinner shift at the diner," she said.

"That's fine. Which way is it? I mean, which entrance are we using?"

Sydelle had caught up to me and I found myself inhaling stale grease. "We're going in from the outside entrance. You can't see it from here because the bushes are blocking it. Keep walking."

Thankfully it hadn't rained since Monday so the ground wasn't soft and mushy. I was wearing light brown Beacon pumps and didn't want to ruin them. "Did you do a lot of cooking in the main kitchen?" I asked.

"Only when Miss Heatherbrae wanted special meals that needed lots of work space. Or for holidays like Thanksgiving and Christmas. Otherwise her kitchen was more than adequate. And there's nothing like cooking on a gas range. Or using a gas oven for that matter. So much easier to regulate the temperature."

"That's what I've heard. I've only ever used an electric stove."

Sydelle looked at me, half smiling. "You must not do a lot of cooking."

I shrugged. "Is that the entrance over there? Down that embankment?"

"Good God, no! That's the way into the grotto. Unless of course you go there from inside the house. It's a really steep embankment and that thick wooden door is tough to pull open. Whoever finishes the last tour has to bolt it from inside. The entrance to the kitchen is around the other side by the circular driveway. Keep walking."

If she says, "keep walking" one more time I'll scream.

"So, um, how do you like working with Minerva?"

"I don't work with Minerva. I work *for* Minerva. There's a difference. Everything has to be her way, even if my way is better. But she's okay. It could be worse. I could be working for Anna Gainson. I don't know how Phoebe gets through the day without charging after her with a letter opener and driving it into her chest. Oops. Sorry. Shouldn't have gone there. Anyway, here we are. The steps to the main kitchen. Watch it. They're steep."

Her description of Phoebe lingered in my mind as I took to the steps. "Geez, you're right. These are steep."

"Each one is a solid chunk of rock. Makes you wonder how the iceman ever carried those huge slabs on his back when this place was first built. Hold on. It'll take me a second to unlock the door."

"You've got a key to this place?"

"Minerva and I both do. Keys to the house and to Miss Heatherbrae's residence. When she was alive we'd have to be here at the crack of dawn. It's not that way anymore but no one asked for our keys back and we didn't offer."

"What about Greta and Arletta?"

"Arletta had to turn hers in but I'm sure Greta still has a set."

I expected Martin to have a key. That would go without say. After all, someone had to be on call for emergencies. But the cooks? And everyone else? Then again, they were long time staffers whom Helena trusted.

Sydelle flipped a light switch and I was standing in the brightest, whitest kitchen I'd ever seen. Two industrial size refrigerators took up most of the wall space directly across from where I was standing. An eight-burner gas stove and a smaller four burner one took up the other wall. A large double sink seemed to span the length of the third wall. Pots and pans hung overhead and a marble-topped island with assorted bowls and ladles on it stood in the middle of the room.

"It's been modernized," Sydelle said. "The cast iron stoves were removed before my time and of course the ice boxes met the same fate. The counter's new and so is the sink."

"Um, no dishwashers? Or is that done by hand?"

"Good grief, no. There are two dishwashers in the pantry behind the refrigerators. The only thing that remained from when the kitchen was first built was the dumbwaiter. It's in the pantry. Old ropes and all. I wouldn't trust that thing to carry a fly upstairs. A new system was installed on the opposite side of the pantry. It goes straight up to Miss Heatherbrae's residence."

"Huh? I wonder why they didn't just convert the old one. I mean, the shaft was already there."

"Don't ask me. Lots of things about this place are a mystery."

I walked around the kitchen unable to take my eyes off of the gleaming silver and white surfaces. Someone went to a lot of trouble to keep everything shining. I could see the opening to the pantry but there was also a smaller door adjacent to it.

"Where does that door go?" I asked.

Sydelle took a few steps and opened it. "To the root cellar. I think it's just used for storage now but when the house was first built, that's where they stored the potatoes, turnips and carrots."

"Wow. How do you know all of this?"

"From Minerva. She seems to know everything. Well, her and Anna Gainson."

"Have you ever been down there?"

"Nope. And I don't plan on starting now. There could be mice or spiders, not to mention—"

"I don't mind. And I'd really like to have a look. Is there a light?"

Sydelle sighed. "There's a wall switch but I can't be held responsible if something bites you."

"You won't be. I'll only be a second."

I had a hunch about this place and I had to see for myself. While I wasn't too thrilled about the mice, I was more concerned about the spiders. Didn't need to have an encounter with a brown recluse.

The root cellar was only five or six steps down and it was fairly well lit by the one hanging light bulb in the middle of the room. I could see wooden shelves with some old bottles and jars and the original stone masonry on the walls. Sydelle had mentioned storage but there wasn't anything much else that I could see other than a small half-door. Great if you're four-foot-tall but anyone my height would need to bend down in order to go through.

I knew I wouldn't have another chance to get back here so I grabbed the doorknob and gave it a pull. The door creaked but opened without a problem. Straight ahead dim greenish light flooded the place and I knew immediately where I was – the top of the grotto on a small landing.

Of course. It was all beginning to make sense. The basement and sub-basements had to be connected one way or the other.

If Max and I knew how to read those blueprints we would've figured it out.

"Find anything interesting down there?" Sydelle asked when I returned to the kitchen.

"No. I think I'll stick to the more populated rooms. Look, I really appreciate you showing me this part of the house. I don't imagine Helena came down here often."

"What? I don't think she came down here at all. She'd hang out in the day room giving visitors the willies when they walked by or sometimes she'd sit in one of those musky Casbah rooms. But she hadn't done that in a while. She pretty much stayed in her own apartment most of the time. Kind of reclusive if you ask me. Almost as if she was scared of leaving the place. What's that word for people like that? Not claustrophobia..."

"Agoraphobia?"

"Yeah, that's it."

"Uh, about that, are you aware of anything that might have unnerved her to the point where you and Minerva had to taste her food?"

Sydelle twisted the silver ring on her right hand and swallowed. "Like what?"

"Oh, I don't know. Maybe an argument with someone. Or something she witnessed. Something that made her question her own safety and security."

Sydelle's fingers moved faster as she twisted her ring. "No. I can't think of a thing."

"If you do, you have my card, right? Call me."

Sydelle started to exit the kitchen the same way as we had entered. From outside.

"Hold on a second," I said. "Can we use the interior exit? The one that goes into the house?"

"I suppose. If you don't mind going up a long staircase. Pain in the neck. At least the dumbwaiter carried the food for us when we'd have to cook in here."

"That's right. I remembered it from my tour of Helena's residence. But I don't understand. Dumbwaiters were built for the service staff to send food and dinnerware directly into the dining area. But that's not the case here, is it? I mean, the room below Helena's place is the day room."

"Uh-huh. It is now. But that wasn't always the case. It used to be the dining room. Helena had the rooms switched years ago and a new dumbwaiter built."

"Why?"

Sydelle shrugged. "When you have money, no one asks."

CHAPTER EIGHT

Hogan had gotten off work early at the brewery and had made himself comfortable on my couch. Byron, too, if wedged between Hogan's shoulder and the top of the couch could be considered comfortable.

"Hey, Marcie, mind coming over here and giving me a kiss? I don't want to disturb your cat."

"Oh brother."

I plopped myself down and shoved Byron onto the seat cushion so Hogan would have a free arm to wrap around me. "You're really spoiling him, you know."

"Yeah, well, he's a nice kitty. Wonder how he'll take to Foxy and Lady."

Those were Hogan's cats. Someone had dropped them off in front of the brewery a few years ago and he didn't have the heart to bring them to an animal shelter or make them brewery cats. At some point in time I figured the felines would finally meet and flush out that whole territorial top cat thing. Meanwhile, Hogan's neighbor had a fourteen-year-old girl who adored the cats and took care of them when he stayed at my place.

"Tell me, how'd it go with your investigation? Get any closer to figuring out who might have had it in for the old heiress?"

"Not really. I don't know what to believe. Or whom."

"Well, maybe you'll have better luck tomorrow. The personal maid, right?"

"Uh-huh. Arletta Maycomber. And while I'm trying to pry information out of her, you can knock yourself out wandering through the place. Anna Gainson, the director, gave me the green light and I'm unofficially giving it to you."

"Don't tell me you're going to have them think I'm an investigator, too."

"Course not. On Saturdays the office is closed. Only the tour guides are in the place. They already know me. I'm sure it won't be a problem. Until…"

"Until what?"

"Um, yeah. This is where it gets interesting. Minerva gave me a key to Helena's apartment. It's off limits to the public. And probably me, but that's beside the point. Sometime after February, Helena started to act strange. Suspicious, actually. Max and I think there might have been some sort of incident and I need to find out."

"By going into her apartment? Weren't you there already? With the housecleaner?"

"Yes, yes and yes. But it wasn't until I talked with Minerva today that I learned Helena kept a datebook where she wrote down daily musings and that sort of thing. Remember, she was an old lady. She wouldn't have been using a computer program. The only thing she used her computer for was to do her online banking. She had an email address but didn't email anyone. Her correspondence was done the old-fashioned way – snail mail."

"Go on."

"I need to sit down and read through that datebook of hers. Minerva said she kept it in her desk. A floral datebook."

"And I take it you need me to create some sort of distraction so you can sneak in there?"

"No. That only happens in the movies. We'll both sneak in there. After my meeting with Arletta. That shouldn't take more than forty minutes or so. I'll look for you in the Casbah section when I'm done. Then we'll go upstairs. There are two staircases. The main one opens into a large corridor, and Helena's apartment is down the hall. The door is locked and the place is off-limits to visitors. The back staircase is the one the staff uses. It opens into a butler's pantry. That door is locked, too, but I have the key. When no one is around we'll tiptoe up the staircase."

Hogan didn't say a word. He stood up and paced in front of the couch. I was beginning to get nervous.

"Please don't tell me you're uncomfortable with this. It's really common practice in my line of work," I said.

Then he laughed. And not a small laugh, a big, loud laugh. "Golly gee, Nancy Drew, we'll go into the bell tower when no one is looking."

I reached over and pulled on his belt giving him no choice but to return to the couch. Other than taking a break to eat the cold-cut subs he had stashed in my fridge, we pretty much stayed on the couch until we traded it for my bed.

"Where'd you say Arletta was meeting you?" Hogan asked the next day when we arrived at the Mystery Castle. Hazy morning sunlight had turned stronger by early afternoon and the place looked more welcoming than my first visit. "I'll park the truck at the closest spot but preferably in the shade."

"On a wrap-around porch. It's around back by the Garden Grotto. We're early. Let's go inside the castle first. The middle entrance is the one the visitors use once they buy their tickets from that booth over there." I pointed to the small out building on the side of the estate. "We shouldn't have any problem getting in."

I was right. The tour guide was the same one who was here yesterday and he recognized me immediately.

"Let me know if you need anything," he said adjusting

his wire rim glasses. I wasn't sure if they were prescription or costume ones used to make him appear older than he was.

"Thanks. We'll be discreet." Then, I turned to Hogan, "Grab a map from the side table by the urns. It helps. I'm going to use a back door to get over to Arletta. Meet me in the Casbah in forty-five minutes."

"You do know that's a famous movie line, don't you?"

"Um, not one I've heard recently."

"Never mind. You weren't forced to watch old black and white movies growing up like I was. The actor who said it was Charles Boyer."

"Sounds familiar. Probably some movie heartthrob of my mother's."

"More likely one of your grandmother's."

"Shh. A tour is coming through."

I ducked out and walked across the lawn to the Garden Grotto. Arletta was already seated in one of the Adirondack chairs. Darn it. Why couldn't she have taken a table? I hated those chairs and couldn't figure out why anyone would think they were comfortable. Especially her. She was a heavy-set woman with tight reddish curls and she kept pulling her cardigan closed around her like a mummy.

"Hi!" I said. "Sorry to keep you waiting. I'm Marcie Rayner. Thanks for agreeing to meet with me. Um, maybe we'd be more comfortable at one of the tables."

Arletta stood up. "Fine with me. I'm not sure I understand what all of this is about but I don't want it to be said that I wasn't being helpful. Which is more than I can say for this place. Not a bit of help whatsoever when they let me go. I had to do my own legwork for COBRA health insurance and had to keep bugging Anna Gainson for a letter of recommendation. If I didn't get that ten thousand dollar check from Helena's lawyers, I really would've been in a mess."

"I'm sorry to hear that. Losing a job, especially under such circumstances, must be really tough."

"I'll manage for now. My husband's got his disability checks and I've got un-employment. Of course, that will dry up soon enough so I've got to find something else pretty quick."

Arletta placed her handbag on top of the table and sat back. It gave the appearance of blue leather but it didn't look synthetic. It did, however, look new.

"I was hoping you could answer some questions for me regarding Helena's death," I said. "There seem to be some inconsistences and that's why my firm was hired. Unfortunately, I'm not at liberty to divulge more information than that."

"What inconsistences? What do you mean? All I know is that I walked into her office expecting her to be at her desk and when I didn't see her, I went into her living room figuring maybe she was reading or relaxing. I knew she wasn't downstairs in the day room because she had stopped going there a while back. She had to have been in her bedroom and that's when I walked in there and found her. Those eyes! Those awful cloudy blue eyes staring straight up at the ceiling. It was awful. I must have screamed my head off."

"If you don't mind my asking, where were you before you walked into her residence?"

"I was running an errand for her. She sent me to the Truffle Palace downtown because she was having a hankering for 'some real chocolate and not that miserable waxen stuff.' Said it was bad enough she couldn't enjoy taffy anymore."

"So, she wouldn't eat anything like say... a Tootsie roll pop?"

"Goodness no. Too chewy. Those things are for children. Hmm, I think the last time I had one of those was when I was a kid. Anyway, it was one of the nights the chocolate shop was open late. She gave me a twenty-dollar bill and told me to buy her a pound of the mixed truffles. Said to bring back the receipt and the change. I did, you know. Brought back the receipt and the change. Only eighty-eight cents. I was bringing the box of chocolates to her when...when...well, you know."

"And the chocolates? What happened to them?"

"Now don't take this wrong or anything, but seeing as Miss

Heatherbrae had already passed on, I put them in the pantry and took them home when I left. It wasn't as if they were going to do anyone else any good."

"I'm not worried about the chocolates," I said. "Would you have any idea who else could have been in her residence during the time in which you were gone?"

Arletta shook her head. "No. Minerva was the only other person in the house and she was in the main kitchen downstairs. Helena had wanted chicken pot pie for dinner and all the special spices were in the big kitchen. Minerva told me that as long as she had to be downstairs making the pot pie, she'd go ahead and prepare the next day's breakfast for Helena - a frittata. Said she'd heat it up the following morning."

In my next life I'm hiring my own cook.

"That kitchen is two floors below Helena's apartment. How did Minerva hear you scream?"

"Because I went running out of the place. I was screaming and screaming. All the way down the grand staircase. Minerva must have heard me because next thing I knew she was running up the stairs asking me what was going on."

"And no one else was in the house?"

"No, only me and Minerva."

Arletta shoved her handbag aside with her elbow and leaned forward. I could see the bag's cross-shaped gold clasp and the small letters – Fendi. My God. I was staring at a blue leather Fendi bag, something I'd only seen in fashion magazines. Unlike Gucci and some of the other designer bags, Fendi bags weren't usually targeted for knock-offs.

"Miss Rayner? Miss Rayner? Were you going to ask me anything else because I have things to do this afternoon."

"What? I'm sorry. I was just thinking. When you walked into Helena's room with the chocolates, was anything out of place? Anything look odd to you?"

"What was odd was the way Helena was lying on her bed. She always slept propped up with a wedge cushion or she'd have a gastro attack. I had to prepare the bed special. It was awful seeing her there. Dead, I mean. I guess I lost it and screamed myself silly."

"That's understandable," I said. "Um, did you happen to notice if anything looked out of place anywhere else? Like her desk?"

"Honestly, I don't remember looking at her desk. But her dressing table was fine. Everything was the way she liked it. Hairbrush and comb on the right, along with her facial lotions. Easy for her to reach."

"So, she was right handed?"

"I hadn't thought of that, but now that you mention it, I suppose she was right-handed. It would've been a nuisance to reach across the dressing table for a brush or comb. Why? Does that matter?"

Only if there was a reason the computer mouse was off to the left.

I shook my head. "It's probably inconsequential. At this juncture in time, we're more interested in her behaviors. Were you aware of anything at all that upset Helena in the past few months?"

"Do you mean annoyed her, or really, really upset her?"

"Really upset her. Something major."

"I can't think of anything like that. I know she'd get flustered at the bank accounts and had a few conversations with her attorney about the castle business but that kind of stuff had been going on for years. I really think poor Miss Heatherbrae was suffering from some sort of cognitive disorder. That's what they call it these days, right? I guess senility would be considered a bad word to use, huh? Anyway, there were times she imagined someone wanted to poison her or gas her to death. Very sad really."

"Did anyone have a reason to harm her?" I asked.

Arletta reached for her bag and held it close to her chest. "Harm her as in kill her?"

"Yeah. That."

"I don't want to point a finger at anyone but if I were you,

I'd keep an eye on Sydelle."

"What makes you say that?"

"She almost poisoned Miss Heatherbrae."

The words came babbling out of my mouth. "What? When? How?"

"It was a long time ago and I've got someplace to be. Maybe another time. Just saying. Keep an eye on that one."

Arletta stood up, glanced at her wristwatch and shoved her blue leather bag under her arm. I was still staring at the side of the bag when she stepped off the porch and walked straight to the parking lot.

CHAPTER NINE

Hogan seemed to be mesmerized by the giant Hookah in the middle of one of the Casbah rooms. He immediately turned as soon as he heard me. "If we have time I wouldn't mind taking another look at the grotto. I would've loved that place as a kid. All those skeletons. And decked out, too. Hell of a wedding, huh?"

"I suppose. In a macabre kind of way. I'll stick to beachfronts and mountain tops."

"You're not giving me any ideas, are you?" He winked and I could feel the heat in my cheeks.

"What? No. No way."

"Whoa. You're going to hurt my feelings."

"You'll survive. Come on, let's see if we can sneak upstairs. And by the way, how does someone almost poison someone else?"

"On purpose or accidently?"

"I'm not sure. Arletta dropped that bomb on me as she was leaving."

I was about to explain when a small tour group of eight or nine people crowded into the Casbah section. Hogan took my hand and we wedged our way into the foyer.

"We have to go through the tomb room to get to the back stairs," I said. "They're hidden behind a burgundy curtain. If someone's in the room when we walk in, pretend to be interested in the big sarcophagus."

"I don't have to pretend. I am interested."

Fortunately, no one was in the tomb room or anywhere near it. No voices. No footsteps. No nothing.

"It's now or never," I whispered as I shoved the curtain aside and reached for the key Minerva had given me. Hogan held one panel apart to let in enough light for me to see the lock. A quick turn and the door opened effortlessly.

"Hurry. Let the drape go." I flipped on the light after fumbling around to find the switch. "Watch your step or you'll fall down the stairs to the kitchen."

Hogan closed the door behind us and we tiptoed up the stairs. I felt a giddy kind of excitement that was hard to explain.

"I thought it would be darker in here," he said as we walked through the butler's pantry. "And all that dust. It's really noticeable with the sun coming through the windows."

"Yeah. The glass panels are huge and none of the curtains are drawn. No one's cleaned this place since Helena died. Anna was deciding whether or not to open it for the public. But I imagine that would be after someone went through Helena's personal effects."

"Someone like who?"

"I don't know. Her attorneys maybe. I'm not sure if her will designated an executor. It didn't sound as if she had any living relatives. But she did have a will. That's how her staff got their token checks for ten grand. Anyway, it's something Max and I have to look into this week."

We walked through her kitchen into the small office. Nothing looked as if it had been disturbed since the last time I was in there with Max. The computer was off and only the modem lights were visible.

"Minerva said Helena kept a floral datebook in this desk."

I pulled the front drawer open and prayed to the gods she was right. "Yep, this is it. Easier than I thought."

Hogan glanced at the desk and then sauntered past the office into the elegant Russian living room. "For someone who was having her food tasted and her windows kept open, she was awfully trusting about her valuables and documents. I'm surprised her desk wasn't locked."

"Maybe she thought the only thing anyone wanted to take was her life. I'm going to sit here and start reading this datebook. Something must have happened between February and April. Why don't you look around the place and see if anything out of the ordinary jumps out at you?"

"Careful how you word that. In this place, I wouldn't be at all surprised."

I could hear Hogan quietly walking around Helena's apartment as I turned the pages of her datebook.

"Interesting arrowhead collection," he said, "among other stuff."

"Knock yourself out. I haven't gotten past the second week of February."

For a woman in her nineties, Helena's cursive was amazingly legible. Her notations of doctors' appointments and beauty parlor appointments dotted the pages. So far, nothing that screamed, "This is the date when it all went down."

I turned to March and stared at the date blocks for the first week. A beauty parlor appointment for Friday and a luncheon on Saturday. Sunday, like all the other Sundays, was blank. Or maybe if she did attend a church service, she didn't feel the need to write it down. I suppose if I was that interested I could compare it with the chauffeur's log. But I wasn't looking at her schedule. More like a change or shift in it. Or if I was really lucky, a notation. I kept browsing. Over my shoulder I could see Hogan scrutinizing one of her showcases. Even her inner sanctum was a museum.

My fingers moved to the second week in March when I heard the footsteps. Hogan must've heard them, too, because he put his index finger over his lips as he walked toward me. "Someone's on the stairs. How do you want to play this?"

"I don't. Quick. The nesting dolls. Green and gold. Hurry."

Hogan had no idea what I was talking about but he didn't question me. Another reason I think I may be in love with this guy. I raced to the bookshelf, eyeballed the doll and shoved it aside. My free hand reached frantically for a release mechanism while my other hand clutched the datebook.

Damn it, Max. You'd better be right about this.

I felt a slight bump and pushed on it as hard as I could. The entire panel moved forward without as much as a creaking sound. Behind it was a small windowless room. Or at least it appeared to be that way. I reached for Hogan's hand and we snuck in seconds before I heard a key in the door. The bookcase panel closed automatically and we were left in total darkness. I could feel Hogan's breath on my neck as he whispered.

"Wow. A rotating pivot. How'd you know about this?"

"Educated guess and one hell of a prayer. When I was in here with Max, he pointed out a knot in the wood that he thought was a release mechanism. Turned out he was right."

"Now what? Who do suppose is in there?"

"Everyone's got a key except Arletta. That is, if I believe her."

Suddenly a white flash illuminated part of the room and I gasped. Hogan gave my arm a pat. "Shh. Sorry. Didn't mean to scare you. Figured I'd put this phone to good use. Actually, it's more of a flashlight and camera than a phone. Especially if I'm in Biscay."

Hogan was referring to the fact that cell phone service was iffy at best in Biscay where his brewery was located. Something about the towers being unable to transmit.

I turned away from the light and looked down. "I really don't want to know what's in this room, especially if it's anything like the grotto."

"Don't worry. It's not. More like *ancestry.com*."

"Huh?" I looked up and scanned the place. The walls were

covered with framed photos of what I presumed to be Helena's family. The only piece of furniture was a heavy wooden chair that sat in the middle of room. I was surprised we didn't bump into it when we charged inside. I walked to the back of the bookcase and pressed my head against it.

"Damn it. Can't hear a thing. I wonder how long they're going to be in there."

"From what you've told me, the place is off limits so whoever's in there probably won't be sticking around long."

"Think they're looking for something? Maybe that's what they were doing originally. Snuck in here from a secret passage and wound up killing Helena. I said something similar to Max but there wasn't enough, or should I say, *any* evidence, to support my theory. And now that I look around this room, I can tell he's right. There's no other way in or out other than the bookcase."

"Look up."

Hogan flashed his light on the ceiling and I took a quick breath. "An attic door. One of those trapdoors. Oh my gosh, that's probably why the chair's in here. I mean, other than Helena wanting to sit and look at those old family photos. And she couldn't do that without—"

"This?" I asked.

In that split-second Hogan turned on a small wall sconce that illuminated the room. "There are four of them. Look around. Enough light to gaze at the relatives for hours."

"But why? And why in here?"

"Beats me. Look, since we're stuck here, I have an idea."

"If it has to do with kinky sex," I said, "count me out. I'm telling you right now I'm really not comfortable with the mile-high club or anything that comes close."

"Uh, hate to disappoint you but as much as I'd enjoy the pleasure of your company right now, I'd rather wait until we've got something softer underneath us. Call me an old fart, too. What I had in mind was using my phone to snap pictures of these relatives. It might lead to something."

"I'm such a moron. Hold on, my phone's right— Oh hell no. Not again. I can't believe it. It's in my bag and that's on the floor under Helena's desk. I put it down when I sat to look at her datebook."

The last time I did something brainless like that was about a year ago. I left my phone in the Crooked Eye's tank room when I charged in there to accuse Hogan of killing his partner. Needless to say, it was a long night.

"Calm down," Hogan said. "Whoever's in there isn't going to pay attention to a small bag stashed under a desk. I'll snap these photos, we'll wait a little while longer and then take our chances getting out of here. Okay?"

"Um, you don't think we're trapped in here, do you? I hadn't considered that."

"No. The bookcase rotates on a pivot and the release is on the other side. All we have to do is push from in here and we'll be back in her apartment. Unless of course you'd like to see what's behind door number three."

"You mean the attic?"

"When else are you going to get the chance?"

Before I could say a word, Hogan pulled the chair directly under the trapdoor and pulled on the small dangling rope. "Guess no one here ever heard of an attic door pull or they wouldn't have needed the chair."

He was halfway up the ladder. "We'll snap the pictures on the way back, come on."

"Shine that light everywhere. I'm not going up if the place is riddled with attic rats."

"Relax. It looks fine. Your typical storage attic."

The only light came from Hogan's phone but it was enough for us to see old trunks, racks with vintage clothing and miscellaneous boxes. Unlike the attics I've seen where you have to watch your step for fear of falling into the insulation and unfinished flooring, this one had a solid wooden floor beneath us – tongue and groove. I figured it was probably added when they put in the fold-up ladder door.

"That can't be the only trapdoor." I said, "Not with this size house."

"Oh, I can assure you, it's not. Stay here and don't move. I'll check it out."

"How am I going to move? You have the light."

Hogan walked straight ahead, leaving me standing next to a small table with boxes on it. He waved the light back and forth like Indiana Jones. "Look at this place, will you? The span of it is so large, they've got supporting beams throughout."

"Make it fast. Just because you didn't see any traces of vermin doesn't mean there aren't rats up here."

"Not the four-legged kind anyway."

"What do you mean?"

"Rats don't buy lottery tickets and there's one on the floor. I doubt Helena came up here and dropped it. In fact, I doubt she even bought the ticket."

I raised my voice slightly, not wanting to yell at the top of my lungs. "Stick it in your pocket so we can take a closer look. It could be older than the hills."

"It's got a barcode and a QR code. Hold on a sec. I'll take a closer look."

If it was dark where I was standing before Hogan directed the flashlight beam onto the lottery ticket, it was almost pitch black now. Only a narrow shaft of light was visible from the spot where I stood. Thank goodness the acoustics compensated and I could hear him without any problem.

"Oh, it's recent all right. The drawing is tonight. That means whoever bought the ticket was up here within the past few days."

"Stash it," I said. "Max and I can find out where it was purchased. And I can't believe I'm saying this, but I hope it's not a winner. That would really complicate things."

CHAPTER TEN

———

"Yeah, money will do that," Hogan shouted. "Hang on a sec. I want to see where those other attic doors are. They should be pretty easy to spot unless someone deliberately concealed them, which I highly doubt. Hey, think I'll bump into another one of those family skeletons up here? And I'm being literal."

"No, just corny. And I can't believe I left my phone back there. I swear, I'm never going anywhere again without it in my pocket or my hand. Hurry up, will you?"

I could hear Hogan's footsteps but the span of the attic was so long I lost sight of him. Only a hazy beam of light was visible from where I was standing. I began to tap my foot on the floor, a nervous habit I was trying to break. "Can you hear me? Hurry up."

Suddenly I could hear footsteps headed my way. Hogan's reconnaissance was over.

"Marcie! Follow me. Watch your step. You're not going to believe this."

"If it's something that's going to creep me out, tell me now. I'm not in the mood for surprises."

"You'll like this one. Trust me."

Staying a good three or four feet behind him, I walked what seemed to be the entire length of the building's attic. We passed four sections where giant barn beams supported the structure.

"This better be good," I said.

"It is. Look behind that old rocking chair on your left and tell me what you see."

"Looks like a railing to me. You know, the kind you see on the top of staircases— Oh my God! Is it—?"

"Oh yeah. It's the top of a staircase. Probably the original way into the attic. I'm walking down."

This time I was so close to Hogan I could see everything. It was a narrow staircase framed by walls on either side and it had a full-length door at the bottom.

"Is it locked?" I asked.

"Not from this side. Here goes."

Hogan opened the door to allow the tiniest bit of light through. After a second or two, he opened it a bit more.

"It's a bedroom. Canopied bed. Fancy bedspread. One of those old-fashioned water pitchers and water basin on the nightstand. I think the room's open to the public."

With that, he closed the door and adjusted the flashlight so it wouldn't be in my eyes. "Here. You take this. I'll follow you up the stairs."

The walk back to our original point of entry seemed a heck of a lot faster than I expected. The attic door was still open and we climbed backward down the trapdoor ladder into the hidden room. Hogan held the light for me but it really wasn't necessary. The wall sconces made it bright enough to see clearly.

"There's no question about it," I said. "Someone knew about the opening from behind Helena's bookcase and they had to be familiar with the entrance into the attic. It has to be one of the employees. I mean, who else could it be? All I need to do is figure out who plays the lotto. Maybe there'll be a hint in this datebook of hers. I've got to take it with me. No time anymore to sift through it. Besides, I don't think it'll be missed."

Hogan gave my shoulder a slight squeeze. "You're probably right. At least about the book. Well, we've been out of that apartment for a long time. I doubt anyone's still in there. I'm ready to take a chance. I'll push on the bookcase slowly and at the first sign of noise or conversation, I'll stop. Okay?"

"No. Wait! You forgot to take pictures of her photos. They may give Max and me a better idea of who might've had it in for the old lady. It's light enough in here. Go ahead."

All of the framed photos on the walls were black and white. Probably about fifteen or sixteen in all, and he snapped every one of them. "Done. Here goes. I'm giving the bookcase a shove."

"Don't forget to turn off the wall sconces." I said.

The back wall moved forward and we stepped out into Helena's bright living room. Hogan was right. Whoever had been in there had made their exit. I took a few steps forward and looked around before walking into her office to retrieve my bag from under the desk. The absolute last time I'd leave it anywhere.

Hogan remained in the living room taking another look at Helena's eclectic collection of small art items.

"It doesn't look as if anything's been disturbed," I said. "At least not overtly. And according to Anna Gainson, all of Helena's important documents were stored with her attorney. Her jewelry, too. Anna said only the costume jewelry remained in Helena's immediate possession."

"Yeah. About that…I'm not so sure."

"About where she stored her possessions?" I asked.

"No, about anything being disturbed. Come here a minute, Marcie, and take a look."

I moseyed over to the glass shelves that housed the strange little ivory and gemstone carved figurines. "Looks the same to me. The lapis frog. The rose quartz lion. Those awful petrified pieces of dinosaur dung that Greta pointed out…What are you seeing that I'm not?"

"Working and running a brewery, I've had to learn to pay attention to details. Really pay attention. One small mistake and it could cost us an entire tank of brew."

"What are you saying?"

"When we first came into this apartment, we immediately noticed the dust. Especially in the sunlight. Place hasn't been cleaned since Helena's death. Not that it would really matter in this case because what I'm about to show you isn't the kind of thing that gets dusted all the time. Maybe a few times a year, if that."

"What? What? You're driving me crazy all ready."

"Take a good look at this showcase and tell me what you see. Pay attention to the dust."

Oh my God. The last time I heard anyone tell me to pay attention to the dust was my mother and that's when I was fifteen and she was nagging me to death about cleaning my room.

I bent my head in all directions trying to figure out what he was getting at. Then, I saw it. It wouldn't have been obvious on a cloudy day or any day for that matter unless someone was worse than Monk.

"Some of the figurines don't match up to the dust around them," I said. "There are clear spots where there should be dust underneath. Someone's moved them."

"Not moved them. Replaced them."

"Are you sure? How can you be sure?"

"While you were going over Helena's datebook when we first came in here, I was studying her nifty little collections. The fetishes and arrowheads specifically. One of those Native American fetishes was a large raccoon with babies on top of it and a narrow yellow arrow in the raccoon's mouth. Symbolic, but that's another story. Anyway, it's gone. And in its place is a similarly colored carving of a bear or something and I wager it's made in China or India or anywhere but in the southwest. Let's have a look."

Hogan turned the small key that was still in the showcase

lock and pulled the door opened. Then he reached for the figurine and turned it over.

"Just as I thought. It's ceramic and it says, 'Made in Thailand.'"

"Oh my gosh. How many of these are fake? We can't really see the dust on the top shelves."

"More than the one I noticed from today's escapade, I'd say. Listen, this has probably been going on for a while. With Helena spending a lot of time downstairs in that day room, our little thief was busy pilfering some pretty valuable goods."

I held the figurine in my hand for a second before giving it back to Hogan. "Poor woman never even knew what was happening around her. Martin, the handyman, told me Helena's face touched the computer monitor when she worked. She never would have noticed the switcheroo. Unless...she caught the thief in the act and that's what got her killed. I can't tell anyone about this except Max. None of the staff can be trusted. If I thought they were suspects before your discovery, I'm certain of it now. Hey, what time is it? We really should be getting the heck out of here."

Hogan gingerly placed the replica back in its spot and closed the showcase door. "I'm taking a photo or two of her showcase. For reference in case you need it."

"Wow. I was just about to ask you to do that."

"Goes to show you. Great minds think alike. Say, it may be easier for us to exit through Helena's front door over there by that little foyer. It should take us to the long corridor. Right? No sense going back to the tomb room."

"Good idea. What do you say we check out that bedroom on the other side of the attic door as long as we're up here?"

"Go for it," he said.

We were lucky. No one was upstairs. With the door closed tightly behind us, we meandered down the corridor as if we were taking the grand tour. No surprises in the bedroom. The attic door was a plain dark wooden door and when Hogan tried to open it, the knob wouldn't turn.

"I'm going to see if Minerva's key works. Keep an eye on the hallway."

Like the other locks to Helena's residence, this one was also a deadbolt and the key worked perfectly.

"When Martin changed the locks, he must've changed this one, too."

Suddenly we heard a loud voice coming from downstairs. "All tours will end in ten minutes. Guests, we will be locking up in ten minutes. Please conclude your visit. Thank you."

"That's our cue," I said, "other than my stomach. It's been grumbling for the last twenty minutes."

Hogan put his arm around my waist and guided me to the staircase. "If it can hold out for another forty minutes, there's a terrific sports bar restaurant in Chaska."

"Chaska? Isn't that a bit out of the way? "

"Good food's never out of the way. You won't be disappointed. Too bad it's not early in the day with time to spare. Lots of neat parks and lakes around Chaska."

Hogan was right on the money about the food. The steak was tender, the garlic potatoes were heavenly and the sautéed beans and mushrooms made me forget I was eating vegetables. Maybe we'd get to check out the lakes and parks another time.

"Told you you'd like this place. Too bad we're still on the road or I'd trade this O'Doul's for one of our brews."

"The Crooked Eye's micro-brews are on tap?"

I hadn't looked at the beverage side of the menu, only the appetizers and entrees. Like most sports bars, Hy's Place offered a variety of finger foods and some offbeat specialties. Large flat-screen TVs took up most of the wall space but it was the circular bar, with its maroon and gold chairs that were the focal point of the room. When we walked in, most of the bar was filled with patrons and all but two or three of the booths were taken. We opted for one that was in the corner, away from the noise.

Hogan stabbed a French fry with his fork. "Only the pale ale. We're working on the rest."

I glanced at the bar again and noticed a change in the patrons. A few of the couples were gone but had been replaced by single men. One of them turned and patted his buddy on the back. My mouth dropped open and I quickly turned away.

"What? Were you watching one of the games? I didn't realize you were that into sports."

"I'm, uh...not. Not really."

"Then what?" Hogan was looking at me in the strangest way.

"That guy over there...Don't look. All right, look but don't be obvious."

"What guy? Look where? Marcie, what's going on? Is it your ex-husband?"

"Oh hell no. I'd be tempted to heave one of your French fries at him. No, it's Scott Byrd, fiancé to one of my clients. She hired me to find out if he was cheating on her. Their wedding's coming up pretty soon but she's convinced he's playing around. So far, I haven't been able to substantiate that. Um...until now. Take a look."

Scott and the Justin Timberlake look-alike he was sitting next to were laughing and elbowing each other. I kept my voice really low. "The tall guy with the light blue shirt and sandy hair. Don't stare."

"You think he's a switch hitter?"

"Lots of men get married to cover up the fact they're gay. You wouldn't think it would be such an issue today but apparently it still is for some people."

"What are you doing?" Hogan asked.

"Trying to see if I can make it look like I'm snapping a selfie."

"Just because two men are horsing around at a bar doesn't mean they're romantically involved, you know."

"I know. I know. But according to my client, her fiancé isn't exactly interested in the usual time with her. Um, if you know what I mean. Look, I've been so occupied with Helena's unsolved death that I really haven't been able to focus on this case. And now, I caught a break. A real break that dropped into my lap so to speak. Anyway, I was going to ask you—"

"If we could follow those two out of here?"

"Uh-huh."

"For all we know they could be here until the place closes. That's hours from now."

"Yeah, but tomorrow's Sunday," I said. "We can sleep as late as we want. I'll even make you breakfast."

Hogan gave me one of his adorable smiles. "I thought you were trying to convince me."

"Ha-ha."

CHAPTER ELEVEN

"You know, Marcie, for someone who keeps telling me to be discreet, you haven't taken your eyes off of those men."

We had finished our dinner and were nursing our drinks like two little old ladies at a church social. Hogan had already paid the bill in case we had to hurry. He figured if we wound up staying a whole lot longer, he could start a new tab.

"I don't want to miss it if they get up to leave." I said.

"You won't. One of them is heading for the men's room. It could be a sign they're getting ready to split."

"Or that the drinks are catching up with him."

While we were waiting for Scott and his…his what? Boyfriend? Date? Paramour?.. to make a move, we returned to our drinks.

"So, tell me," I said. "How do you know so much about those Native American carvings in Helena's collection?"

"Hey, you're looking at the all-around American boy. I was totally into arrowheads and all that stuff when I was a kid. Did you know that hunters carved replicas of the animals they planned to kill and inlayed semi-precious stones to form an arrow by the mouth? They would breathe the air out of the mouth before they went on a hunt and if they were successful, they'd breathe the air back in when they returned."

"Wow. I had no idea."

"And those little carvings of Helena's are worth a small fortune. Whoever's been stealing them is probably selling them on eBay or another site."

"About that, I had a strange thought. When I met with Arletta earlier today she had a blue leather bag with her. At first, I thought it was a cheap imitation. But I saw the clasp and I looked carefully at how it was made. It was a Fendi."

"A Fendi? You lost me there."

"Fendi's right up there with Gucci, Chanel, Louis Vuitton, Hermes…"

Hogan shrugged.

"They cost in the thousands. The thousands. And the bag she had was at the high end of the scale. No way could she have afforded it on her salary. And who else had better access to Helena's apartment than her own personal maid?"

"True, but didn't you tell me Helena left all of her staff a ten-thousand-dollar gift? Maybe Arletta decided to buy herself a once-in-a-lifetime thing."

"I'd like to believe you but— Oh my gosh. They're getting up. Scott put some money on the bar and they're leaving. We've got to hurry."

I stood up, grabbed my bag and motioned for Hogan to get out of the booth.

"Calm down," he said when we got outside. "They're walking slowly. In the opposite direction from where I parked my truck."

"I'll tail them. You get the truck. Swing it around, pick me up and let's see where they go."

"You're really eating this up, aren't you?"

"It beats sifting through crime statistics. Now hurry."

I kept a good distance from the two guys as they crossed the street to the next block, occasionally turning my head to see if Hogan was pulling up. The men were moving at a brisk clip. No public signs of affection but hey, this is Chaska, not San Francisco. I heard Hogan's truck slowing down before I actually saw him. Then I raced to get inside.

"They're across the block," I said. "Oh no. The Justin Timberlake guy is getting in that blue Audi. Damn it. I can't get to a pen fast enough to write down the license."

"There's a pen in the glove compartment. And old receipts. Write it on one of those. I'll slow down but I don't want to be obvious. We'll go around the block."

"We'll lose them."

"Yeah, well we can't hang out in the street. If I double park they'll notice something."

My hands fumbled for the pen as we drove past them. It was a short block with no traffic. Hogan got us back just in time to watch the Audi coupe pull out and Scott get in his CX-9.

"Who do you want to follow if those cars go in opposite directions?"

"Scott. I'll run his buddy's license on Monday."

Scott got on the 212 for a straight shot west to Glencoe and then the 15 down to New Ulm. We followed him to his street and watched from a few houses down as he pulled into his driveway.

"Guess the chase ends here, huh?" I said. "You must be as exhausted as I am."

Hogan touched my arm. "Not that exhausted."

I delivered my promise the next morning and made him a pancake breakfast calling it my "Sunday special." With the dishes soaking in the sink, we took a good look at the photos Hogan had snapped in Helena's secret room.

"I thought they'd be blurrier on the monitor but they seem pretty clear." I skootched my chair over so Hogan could have a better look. He clicked the mouse a few times to study each one before he said anything.

"What do you know about her? Or the family?"

"Only what the flyer about the Mystery Castle said and what I read on Wikipedia. Her father, Randolph Harvey Heatherbrae, was a wealthy industrialist and his wife, Margaret Lee Wakefield, came from old money. Helena was an only child."

"Then how do you explain all the photos of that little boy next to her? He looks to be about two or three years younger maybe. Could she have had a brother who died? Childhood illnesses were really common back then."

"I don't think so. Maybe he was the child of someone who worked for the Heatherbraes. You know, like a playmate for Helena."

Hogan shook his head. "Lots of class distinctions back then. Look at his clothing. Other than the fact it looks damn uncomfortable, I doubt the servant's dressed their kids so formally."

"Look at the other photos. Helena appears to be in her teens. No sign of him. Just her and the parents posing in front of the house. Oh, and another one. She's a bit older and they're out back by the Garden Grotto. Looks like it was some sort of greenhouse back then."

"Maybe the kid was a relative. Visiting. Didn't you tell me she had a cousin or something?"

"Yeah. A third cousin from Rochester. Deceased, according to Minerva who did some double checking. I'll put that on my list for the week. Maybe Minerva knows more about it. If not, perhaps Helena's attorney does. Whoever that may be. I mean, I know the attorney's someone from Blair and Lowery or maybe she had more than one attorney from the firm, but so far we've only been in contact with their business manager, Warner VanWycke."

"So, uh, have you decided how you're going to handle the other case?"

"Ugh. I dread it. But I'm going to take a neutral approach. I'm going to see if Loreen recognizes the guy talking with her fiancé. Maybe you're right. Maybe they are just friends. Only…

here's the problem. I can't very well show her that photo. The two of them are next to each other at a bar. It looks, well, compromising."

"Not really. Nothing in the photo indicates it was taken at night. And lots of businessmen grab quick lunches in sports bars."

"I suppose you're right. If it turns out to be someone she knows, like a coworker of his or an old school buddy, then we can cross the guy off the list. If not, I'll pursue it further. By tomorrow I'll have his name and address but that still won't tell me about his relationship with Scott. Only Loreen can do that. Like I said, 'Ugh.'"

We looked at the remainder of Helena's photos but nothing really stood out. I figured Max and I would take another look this week. At a little past five, Hogan left for Biscay. He had a few things to check on at the brewery and probably wanted to sack out at his own place and get some sleep.

"What are the odds of us getting together this week?" he asked gathering up a few of his things.

"Everything's so up-in-the-air with these investigations but I'm aiming for Wednesday. Fair enough?"

"Of course. Gonna miss you, Marcie. Keep me posted and stay safe. Yeah?"

It was one of those long drawn out kisses by the door that was making it harder and harder for me to say goodbye. While our relationship didn't exactly classify as long distance, we were still a distance apart and had to juggle schedules and time. Then there was my mother. No juggling there. Just ducking and running.

And what the heck was the matter with my brother? How could he have let her break him down to the point where he told her I had a boyfriend? No escape now. My mother would want to meet Hogan during her family visit in November. And she'd waste no time hinting about our "future plans." *Better lace up your Nikes and start running now, Hogan.*

Thank goodness my mother was staying with Jonathan and

Gale. I think she felt they could use her help with the baby, and I wasn't going to say otherwise. At some point, I'd have to prepare Hogan for Iris Krum, the epitome of a Jewish mother who balked at the thought of an unwed daughter in her late, very late, twenties. Luckily, that was a good six months away. No rush. Not like the two cases that were driving me batty.

I finished up the dishes in the sink, gave Byron an extra handful of kibble and placed a call to Minerva. The bombshell Arletta dropped on me regarding Sydelle nearly poisoning Helena wasn't something I wanted to put off. I had enough on my plate this week and needed some answers. Minerva picked up on the second ring.

"Hi Minerva. It's Marcie. I know it's Sunday evening but I was wondering if you could clarify something for me." Before she had a chance to answer, I went on. "I had a conversation with Arletta this weekend and she said Sydelle almost poisoned Helena. Were you aware of it? What can you tell me about that?"

All I heard at the other end of the line was Minerva taking a deep breath. "I hope I didn't catch you at a bad time," I said. "Do you know anything about the...the um, incident?"

"I know Arletta can be a fool drama queen from time to time but I doubt Miss Heatherbrae would've succumbed to botulism. Still, Arletta had a point."

"Botulism? That can be fatal, can't it? What happened?"

"It was months ago. Around Christmas I think. Yes, Christmas. I remember now. I was downstairs making a roast and Sydelle was preparing one of Miss Heatherbrae's favorite lunches upstairs – salmon croquettes. You take the canned salmon, add egg and bread crumbs, some seasonings, form nice flat patties and fry them in—"

I'm never going to make them as long as I live. My God! Will she ever get to the point?

"You said botulism. Was it the can? Was the can bulging at the seams?"

"Sydelle was already frying the patties when Arletta walked

into the kitchen and noticed the empty can on the counter. It had a small dent in it. Arletta went ballistic and Sydelle had to take out another can from the pantry and start all over again. She swears the can wasn't swollen and said she didn't even notice the dent. It must've been really small."

"You didn't see it yourself?"

"No, like I said, I was downstairs making a roast. Now, about dents in cans. There are safe dents and unsafe dents. Safe dents can be anyplace on the can except the seam. Unsafe dents are on the seam. Even the slightest nick can pinprick a hole that lets in bacteria. You have to know these things if you intend to prepare food. Most likely, it was a small safe dent but nonetheless why take a chance? Sydelle was so rattled by Arletta she was practically useless the entire week. Double and triple checking everything."

"So, this was an oversight, nothing more?"

"That's what I think but Arletta has her own opinion."

"Which is...?"

"Sydelle knew about the dent and didn't care."

I thanked Minerva for clarifying the matter and made one more phone call before taking a shower and calling it a night. No sense in postponing the inevitable.

"Hi Mom. Hope it's not too late."

"Just tell me this. Your boyfriend. Is it serious? If you're planning to get married any time soon, do it when I come for Thanksgiving. The airfares cost a fortune."

CHAPTER TWELVE

Angie looked up from her computer screen when I walked through the door. "I like to get in early on Mondays to avoid any surprises. So, how was your weekend?"

"Private Investigator 101. I'll need at least two coffees to get rolling. Max in his office, yet?"

"He left a message. He's having breakfast with a buddy of his. Another retired police officer. Anyway, he'll probably be in soon."

"Good. I know he was running background checks on some of the Mystery Castle employees. I'm curious to see what he's turned up."

"Yeah, speaking of which, weren't you going back there on Saturday? You must be getting tired of the place."

"More like frustrated. Makes the *Adams Family* house look mild. I'll tell you one thing, if someone wanted to commit a murder in there, they'd have no problem making an escape. All those secret rooms and hidden staircases. It's a nightmare. Which reminds me, I need to call Loreen Larsen."

"The fiancé case?" she asked.

"Uh-huh. I've got a photo I want to show her."

"Doesn't sound too good."

I shrugged. "We'll know soon enough."

The first thing I did when I got into my office was to phone one of my contacts at the St. Paul Community College Office of Public Safety where I used to work and ask for a small favor. I had bailed out Emily McLoughlin a number of times and she owed me.

"I'll run the license if you tell me the real reason, Marcie. Did the guy ask you out?"

"What? No. Come on, it's for a case."

"Fine. Give me a few minutes and I'll call you back, okay? So, not to be nosey, but are you seeing anyone? Your ex has been spotted with more coeds dripping off his arms than last year but I don't think he's seriously involved with anyone."

"I don't care if he proposes to a three-eyed baboon. I'm glad to be rid of the jerk. Call me as soon as you find out. And thanks, Emily. I appreciate it."

While Emily tracked down the blue Audi coupe's registration, I dialed Loreen. She worked for a travel agency in town so I knew she'd be in. I just didn't expect her to answer on the first ring.

"Travel and Leisure Time, Loreen Larsen speaking. How can we assist with your travel plans?"

Oh, I don't know. Maybe a week in Bora Bora or the Maldives. "Loreen, this is Marcie Rayner—"

"Marcie! Hold on a second."

Dead silence and then, "It's okay. Amber's at the copier and Seth's in back. What did you find out? Is that louse cheating on me? Who's the witch he's been carrying on with?"

"Um, all I need you to do is see if you can identify someone in a photo with him. I took it on Saturday night." I was being careful not to tell her where I spotted him, but it probably didn't matter.

"He told me he was tied up with business. Working real late and that sort of thing. And on a Saturday no less. That liar. Look, email me the photo. I'll give you the address again. It's

LLlady@—"

I wasn't about to email it to her for fear she'd fly off the handle and confront her fiancé in one of those ugly, yet memorable scenes. I should know. I've done it. Only I used most of my phone's gigabit storage since there were so many pictures.

"I can't email it. Can you stop in here for a few minutes on a lunch break or something? Travel and Leisure Time is only a few blocks away."

"Just tell me. What does she look like? Is she thinner than I am?"

"It's not a she."

"Hold on a second." I could hear Loreen's voice even though she wasn't close to the receiver. "Amber, I have a ten o'clock. If they get here early, tell them I'll be right back. I've got to run an errand." Then, she was back to me. "I'm on my way." Click. Just like that, a click. That's one thing landlines have over cell phones – the drama. Sure, cell phone calls can end abruptly but nothing says, "I'm pissed" like a good old-fashioned slamming of the receiver. I prayed Hogan was right about Scott's drinking buddy.

As my emails started to pop up on the screen, the phone rang and Angie got it.

"It's a call for you on line one, Marcie," she shouted from the outer office.

Line one was becoming the standard joke. We only had one line but Angie thought it sounded more corporate to use that terminology.

"Hey, it's me. Emily. Got a pen handy?"

"What did you find? Who's it registered to?"

My God. I was sounding as bad as Loreen.

"The car's registered to a Dayton Ganz who lives in Chaska. Address is 1603 Fairway Court. Oh, and I did you a favor, too. No priors."

"Thanks Emily. You're the best."

I immediately googled the address, and like his car,

Dayton's house and neighborhood were pretty upscale, too. Maybe Hogan was right. Maybe the guy was an investor and Scott was having some sort of innocent business meeting. I figured I'd wait to see Loreen's reaction which, according to the time at the bottom of my computer screen, was going to be any second.

I got up, headed for the coffeemaker and grabbed myself a cup just in time for Loreen's entrance. With her red hair in a French fishtail bun and her tailored top, she looked as if she worked on Madison Avenue and not New Ulm.

"Hi Loreen," I said. "Can I get you a cup of coffee?"

"No, I mean, no thanks. Just show me the picture."

We walked into my office and she took a seat next to my desk. I turned the computer screen her way and didn't say a word. I wasn't about to tell her I knew the guy's identity until I heard what she had to say.

She stared at the screen. "Beats me. Were they with any women?"

"No."

"Are you sure?"

"Absolutely. No women."

"Were they acting…you know…like they were on a date?"

"No." I didn't want to mention the laughing or elbowing because, as Hogan put it, "It's kind of a universal jock thing."

I flipped some fly-away hair off my brow and made a mental note to re-think my longer hair. At least I didn't have to mess with the color. Thank goodness it was naturally blond. "So, do you recognize him?"

Loreen squinted and leaned forward. "Where was this taken? It doesn't look like anyplace around here."

"Chaska."

"Chaska? Who the hell does he know in Chaska?"

"Um, that's what I'm trying to figure out. Your fiancé may be telling you the truth. That he really is tired out from his business dealings."

"His business dealings don't need to take place on a

Saturday night. And he doesn't need to be so secretive about it. After all, if two people are about to get married, they should be open and honest with each other. Don't you think?"

More than you know. "Uh, whatever you do, Loreen, do not say a word about this to Scott." *Yep, there goes the open and honest bit.* "Not right now. Not while I'm in the middle of investigating. It could really muck things up."

"So, now what? What am I supposed to do? Wait and see if he knocks someone up or catches a horrific STD?" Loreen pushed her chair back from the desk. "Well? What?"

"Stay calm. I'll be tailing him on the off times. When he's not with you. Make sure I have your schedule of date nights. If he's up to something, I'll find out."

"Date nights, huh? Yeah, I'll let you know. The way things are going, you'll have plenty of time at your disposal. Call or text me if you find out anything."

"I will."

She got up and walked out of my office. I stared at the computer screen and wondered what Scott and Dayton were really doing together at that bar in Chaska. Granted, they might not have been romantically involved but I doubted it was a business meeting. And if Dayton was a good friend of Scott's, why wouldn't he have been introduced to Loreen? Especially with a wedding in the near future. The Loreen and Scott case was beginning to feel as mysterious as the one at the Mystery Castle, only there were no dead bodies.

A sharp rap on my door and I jumped. "Geez Max, you scared me."

"Concentrating or daydreaming?"

"Both. Hey, I've got a zillion things to go over with you. I don't even know where to start first."

"Start in my office. Finished up those background checks. It pays to have friends on the force. Cuts down on the paper chases. How'd the interviews go at the Mystery Castle? You can tell me once I'm planted at my own desk."

"Be right there."

My coffee had turned cold but I took it with me anyway. Coffee's coffee. Max was at his desk shuffling through some papers when I pulled up a chair. "Other than the retired chauffeur and the new guy, I interviewed everyone on staff."

"And?" Max put the papers down and looked up.

"Strange. Not exactly one of those finger-pointing 'he-did-it' conversations but certainly enough innuendo and some downright accusations about things that make me think anyone on her staff could've been responsible for killing her."

"Give me the abbreviated version."

I took a sip of my coffee and put the cup on the corner of his desk. "No particular order. Arletta accused Sydelle of poisoning Helena but it was an oversight. Minerva accused Sydelle of being a liar but that was an exaggeration. Martin accused Arletta of being up to no good and Ernie pretty much pointed the finger at everyone. Oh, and Helena didn't eat Tootsie rolls so that means someone else was in her room."

"Terrific. It could be anyone. Too bad the preliminary background searches aren't going to narrow things down for us. No one has a criminal background, no one is in the country illegally, and not a single one of her employees has had as much as a parking ticket on file."

"Were you able to dig up anything on past employment?"

Max shook his head. "Not yet. But I was able to expand the search to include Arletta's husband. Hit a dead end there, too. The man worked in a mill, got injured and is on disability. Greta's husband is deceased and Sydelle is single. That leaves Anna and Phoebe. Still casting the net on those two."

"Max, Hogan and I uncovered some creepy stuff when we were in the castle on Saturday. And you were right. About the bookcase in Helena's room. It *is* a hidden door. I'll tell you about it in a minute. I need to email you something from my phone. Wanted to do it first thing but didn't get a chance."

I snatched my half empty coffee cup and darted out the door to upload the photos that were hanging in Helena's secret room. When I returned to Max's office he was already pulling them up on his screen, his index finger taping the top of the mouse. "What am I supposed to be looking for? Where did you find these? And what's so creepy about old family photos?"

"The family. Starting with Helena. She had these on the wall in a secret room behind her bookcase. Hogan and I had to make a quick escape from her apartment when we heard someone coming up the stairs. I remembered what you said about that knot in the bookcase. Thank God you were right."

"I take it you weren't in her apartment officially?"

"As official as it gets since Minerva snuck me a key."

Max groaned and clicked the mouse. "These are family portraits. I'm not seeing a red flag."

"I did some homework on Helena. Mostly Google searches and historical information about her family. The grandfather started a flour industry that was later sold to a number of companies that still exist today. Mother was a philanthropist. Anyway, Helena was an only child. No mention whatsoever of siblings. So, who's the little boy playing with Helena and why weren't these pictures displayed in the main lobby like the other ones of her family?"

"Yeah, I glanced at those photos when we passed through the place but I didn't have time to scrutinize them."

"Well I did. On my way out of the place with Hogan. We had to go through the main foyer. And guess what? Lots and lots of family photos but none with that little boy in it. If that's not a red flag, what is?"

Max wiped his forehead with a crumpled napkin that was still on his desk. "The kid's probably a nephew, a cousin, maybe even a friend of the family…"

"Then why keep those photos hidden? Maybe our circle of suspects isn't the staff. I'm thinking I should be taking a deeper look at Helena's past. Particularly her childhood."

"You said you haven't interviewed the chauffeurs yet. See what you can dig up from them. Those drivers are notorious for hearing all sorts of private conversations. People simply forget someone's at the wheel and divulge all sorts of things to whoever happens to be in the car with them. I had a case a few years back where the driver actually overheard his employer orchestrating a Ponzi scheme."

"Okey-doke. Well, I'd better—"

"Before you go racing off, what else did you want to tell me about the bookcase? You said there was something else."

"Oh my God! I completely forgot! And if it doesn't spell out motive for murder, I don't know what does. You're not going to believe this."

Max leaned back in his chair and pressed his shoulder blades together. "Is this going to be one of those drawn-out sagas?"

"I'll cut to the chase. When Hogan and I got back in Helena's apartment, whoever was in there had left. But they took an expensive Native American carving from her showcase and replaced it with a fake. It was Hogan who noticed the difference. Something about dust. Anyway, it wasn't the only carving that had been substituted."

"Are you thinking Helena caught the culprit in the act and that's what got her killed?"

"It's certainly a viable motive. You always said people kill for love, money, or revenge. Unless they're bat-shit crazy."

"Yeah, I remember. And you're right. The theory makes sense…Native American carvings, huh?"

"Little things. Small enough to hold in the palm of your hand. Turquoise, quartz, semi-precious stones. According to Hogan, who had a childhood fascination with that kind of stuff, it's the carver that determines the value. Some Zuni carvings can fetch thousands of dollars."

"Oh brother. Just what we need to track down. A fence for Native American figurines."

"Don't sound so irritated, Max. If I know you, you probably have a list of names tucked away somewhere in that messy desk of yours."

"Nah. It's on a Word document now."

He minimized the computer screen and pulled up Office

2010. "It shouldn't be too hard to find out what galleries and museums are adding to their collections."

"What about eBay and Craigslist?" I asked.

"Takes too long. And costs too much. Especially eBay. Doris decided to sell some of her grandmother's Carnival glass and it was a nightmare. Between eBay taking a portion of the profits and then the packing and shipping, it was hardly worth it. Well, almost hardly. Don't tell her this, but it didn't break my heart to have all that pink glass leave the house."

I chuckled. "What about Craigslist?"

"I don't think it's the right venue. From what you're telling me about these thefts, we're looking at museum quality acquisitions. Let me make some calls. I think there's enough on your plate at the moment."

"Thanks, Max. And by the way, I won't say a word about that donut you snuck in. The napkin was bad enough but you've got crumbs on your keyboard."

CHAPTER THIRTEEN

Townson O'Neil was Helena's original driver. According to the information Anna gave us, he'd been Helena's driver for longer than I've been alive. If anyone knew what would have prompted her murder, he'd be the one. Unless of course, it was him. I was getting as bad as the staff – more accusations than observations. Then there was Harry Sorenson. He came on board three months before Helena died. Right around the time she started to act suspicious. Maybe he knew something.

After two more frustrating days of getting nowhere with Scott Byrd's possible infidelity, I was hoping for some better luck with Helena's murder. I had called Townson and Harry on Monday to see if they were willing to meet with me on Wednesday and they both agreed.

Townson was having trouble with one of his knees and asked if I wouldn't mind talking with him at his place in Lilydale, a few miles north of the Mystery Castle via Route 35E and Lilydale Road. The guy was in his early seventies so I wasn't particularly worried about being alone with him if he insisted on meeting in his own apartment. Besides, I now carry a Ruger LC9. Max's idea. Actually, Max's directive.

Harry agreed to an interview at a more populated place – the same coffee house where Max and I had first met Minerva. Since the guy had to be at work by nine for his new job at the airport, I was stuck meeting him at the ungodly hour of seven thirty. It was still dark when I left my house and got on the highway.

The aroma of freshly brewed coffee was a salvation when I walked inside the Fischerville Coffee House in Mendota Heights. Harry did a pretty decent job of describing himself so I had no trouble taking a seat next to the red-haired guy with the soft stubble on his face and the brown semi-rimless glasses.

"You must be Marcie. Thanks for getting up so early. I couldn't afford to miss any time at my new job. Let me get you a cup of coffee, you look like you could use it. I'm on my second cup."

"That's okay. I'll get it. I'm already standing. It'll only take me a second."

With a hot cup of extra-cream-hold-the-sugar coffee, I sat myself down across from him and propped my elbows on the table. "As you know, my partner and I are looking into Helena's death. There were some inconsistencies that prompted our investigation."

Harry crinkled his nose, causing his glasses to slide down a bit. "Do you mind my asking who hired you?"

"I'm afraid that's confidential. The Mendota Police Department is aware of our investigation and they've been more than cooperative. Please be assured anything you tell me won't go any further."

"I really don't know what I can tell you. In fact, other than using the sitting room, I've never even been in the Mystery Castle other than Anna Gainson's office when I first applied for the job and then again, when I was hired."

"But you have chauffeured Helena from time to time, isn't that right?"

Harry nodded and I continued.

"I know the driver's log is on file at the office but I'd like to hear from you. Where did you take her? Did she have regular appointments?"

"On Fridays she had a standing appointment at a beauty parlor in St. Paul. I'd pick her up at nine thirty and we were always back by noon. She preferred to have lunch in her own residence. Once a month she'd have me drive her to the Acacia Park Cemetery on Pilot Knob Road in Mendota Heights. If it weren't for the fact there was a sign, I would've thought it was a park. No upright grave markers. Only flat bronze ones. I don't know who she visited but she always made me stop at the small chapel near the entrance so she could sign the guestbook. It was listed by gravestone she said. I imagined Helena was visiting her parents. Strange, huh? A public cemetery. You'd think with all the money the Heatherbraes had, they'd be in a private cemetery."

"Yeah, that's a bit odd. What about other excursions? Restaurants, shows, that sort of thing…"

"Nope. Like I said, she preferred to eat at home. There were occasional visits to her ophthalmologist and her rheumatologist but that's it. She seemed to be in great health if you ask me."

"Was she always alone when you chauffeured her?"

"Most of the time, yes. Like the cemetery and the beauty parlor. Miss Maycomber accompanied her to the ophthalmologist. Probably because it would've been difficult for Miss Heatherbrae to see if they dilated her eyes."

"You said occasional visits to her eye doctor. How occasional?"

"She had a few visits since I started working for her. Said she had wet macular degeneration and needed injections in one eye. Told me her vision was blurry and even though it improved a bit, she still had some trouble with details and depth perception."

"How awful for her."

No wonder Helena didn't notice her figurines were being swapped out. Macular degeneration clouds the central vision so she might not have noticed the change unless she picked up one of the figurines. Funny, no one else on her staff shared that bit of knowledge with Max or me.

"Anything else out of the ordinary regarding her appointments?" I asked.

Harry shook his head and took another gulp of coffee. It didn't appear as if he was going to get me any closer to figuring out who killed Helena. I pushed my chair back and started to thank him when he held up his hand.

"Aren't you going to ask me if I know who might've killed Miss Heatherbrae?"

"I thought you said you didn't know anything."

"I said I'd never been in the castle, but what I do know is that someone cancelled Miss Heatherbrae's ride to the beauty parlor the day she was found dead."

"Someone? What someone?"

"I'm not sure. There was a message on my cell phone that said Miss Heatherbrae wouldn't be needing my services that day. Those were the exact words – 'wouldn't be needing my services.' I didn't think much of it at the time. Figured it was Miss Maycomber and I let it go at that."

"And you never told anyone?"

"There was no one to tell. Until now. Um, I've got to get going. I can't be late."

"Sure. Sure. I really appreciate it. Oh, just one more quick thing. If you had to go back to that cemetery, would you be able to point out the spot where you dropped Helena off?"

"Immediate right from the circular entrance. Then right, left and left again. I dropped her off where the road merged into another one. No real distinguishable features in that cemetery but Helena sure knew where she was going. She always walked west toward the river. I figured the gravestones she visited were somewhere between the road and the Sibley Memorial Highway."

"Thanks, you've been very helpful. If you think of anything else, here's my card. Feel free to call."

Harry walked out of the coffee house and I got a refill. I had at least an hour before my meeting at nine with his predecessor. Thankfully Townson wasn't one of those people who slept late or I'd be really buzzed from all the caffeine.

It only took me a few minutes to drive to Lilydale, a small community that's actually housed inside a national park – the Mississippi National River and Recreation Area. If you're going to retire, this is probably the place. Gorgeous river views. Bluffs. Wildlife. And a decent retail shopping area. All within an easy drive to Minneapolis or St. Paul.

Townson lived at The Villas, a senior retirement community that boasted an active and enjoyable lifestyle for retirees. I pulled into a huge parking lot in front of a courtyard-style complex with a perfectly manicured lawn and carefully tended trees.

We agreed to meet in the main lobby of the complex but the room didn't look anything like a lobby. It was a combination of smaller rooms, each with their own distinct furnishings and decor. For a second it reminded me of the Casbah section of the Mystery Castle and I wondered if the architect for the Villas was inspired by Randolph Harvey Heatherbrae's mansion.

A gray-haired man wearing what my brother referred to as "an old man cardigan" was thumbing through one of those large coffee table books when I approached. He was the only man in the lobby so it was a good guess it was Townson.

"Hi! I'm Marcie Rayner and I'm hoping you're—"

"Townson O'Neil at your service."

He put the oversize Italian art book on the coffee table and reached out to shake my hand.

I smiled and sat down. "Thanks so much for agreeing to meet with me." I was beginning to sound like a game show host with that same line. "Is it all right if we talk right here? As I mentioned on the phone, my firm is looking into the circumstances of Helena Heatherbrae's death."

"Here's as good as any place," Townson said. "Took me by surprise. Miss Heatherbrae up and dying like that. I always thought she'd outlive everyone on her staff. Even if it meant dying well into her hundreds. The obituary said 'natural causes' but what's natural about dropping dead when you're in good health? And unless something took a turn for the worst in the last few months, Helena Heatherbrae managed to skate through life without getting a calling card from the grim reaper. You know…cancer, Alzheimer's, stroke…"

"Um, yeah. That's what Harry said, too. Your successor."

"Nice kid, Harry Sorenson. We worked together for a week or so before I handed over the keys to him. What's he up to now?"

"Working at the airport. He wasn't too specific."

"He'll be fine. The chauffeuring was only temporary for him. He's studying nights to become a medical coder. Had some background in billing from what he said. Anyway, don't let me ramble on and on, what did you want to ask me?"

"You've worked as Helena's chauffeur for fifty years, right?"

Townson nodded and I continued. "And I imagine you're pretty familiar with the staff at the castle."

Again, he nodded.

"So, tell me," I said, "Is there anyone who would have had a motive to kill her?"

"If someone wanted her dead, why wait so long? Unless it was about the estate. The castle. Maybe the money was drying up quicker than anyone thought and they had to donate the old place to the park service sooner than later. Helena always planned on turning over the Mystery Castle to the state national park system when she died but certainly not while she was still breathing."

"You said 'they.' 'They had to donate.' Who's 'they?'"

"Why, her management of course. Anna Gainson for one. She runs the business end of things. Wouldn't surprise me a bit if her greedy little hands were all over those documents."

Anna Gainson. Max wasn't all too fond of her, either. "What makes you say that?"

Townson rubbed his hands together and stretched. "After the recession in 2008 and the economic decline in 2016, the

Mystery Castle wasn't as lucrative a business as it had been in other years. Employees like me saw it in our paychecks and bonuses. I knew I'd be fine. I had a decent IRA and enough money stashed away so the wife and I could retire comfortably. Then she died unexpectedly from a heart attack in 2012. My wife's life insurance policy enabled me to have a more than comfortable retirement when the time came. Not so with Anna."

"What are you telling me?"

"In case you hadn't noticed, there's no Mr. Gainson. Now I'm not saying every woman needs a husband to provide for her, but when the job she's holding doesn't seem as solid anymore, it's time to worry. Or, in Anna's case, to look for an alternative. And that alternative was to have Helena turn over the estate to the park service while she was still alive."

"Please don't take this wrong, but how did you know what was going on?"

"It's a funny thing about household staff. We become fixtures and once that happens, employers forget we're even in the same room. I've heard more than my share of private conversations while I was driving or while I was 'off-duty' in the sitting area."

"'Off-duty? Sitting area?' I don't understand."

"When you're someone's driver, you don't spend the entire day sitting in the town car waiting for a call. You have a schedule, of course, but when that schedule is blank, you're still on duty. Just in case. If I wasn't washing or polishing the car, I was driving Miss Heatherbrae or reading in the sitting room."

"Where's the sitting room?"

"In the same corridor as the main office. It's next to the foyer that separates Anna's area from the rest of the castle. It's got a television, a small refrigerator, and lots of books."

"I must not have noticed it when I took a tour of the place."

Townson laughed. "There's so much to see, it would take half a dozen tours and it still wouldn't be enough. So, have I answered all of your questions?"

"Only one more." I took out my phone and pulled up one of the family pictures from the hidden room. "Do you have any idea who the little boy standing next to Helena is? Judging from Helena's age, the photo must have been taken in the early 1930s."

Townson shook his head. "I'll be darned. I've seen all of the family photos on display. The front foyer is practically a shrine. Never saw one with that little boy. Couldn't've been a brother. Always thought she was an only child."

"That's what I'm trying to figure out."

"You may want to start with the state historical society. They might have something on the family. Sure as hell beats me. And in fifty years working at that place, there was never a mention about any children except for Helena. I'd tell you to check with the local schools but I know for a fact Helena had tutors until she entered high school."

I thanked Townson and wished him well. He promised to contact me if he remembered anything else. On the way out of the Villas, I turned to take another look at the lobby. No doubt about it, the architect must have spent time at the castle.

The state historical society would be a good start but I knew it would take some planning on my part to find the right librarian. No sense wasting a trip to Minneapolis. I'd need to make some phone calls first. Townson never asked where that photo came from, but I was certain if I showed it to Anna, she'd demand to know where I got it. And that wasn't something I was about to divulge to her.

The few cups of coffee I had downed weren't going to hold me all the way back to New Ulm. My stomach was demanding a more substantial filler, and given this area, I'd have plenty of choices. Then something occurred to me. Chaska wasn't all that far away if I went south and took the 494 west. Bartenders talk. Granted, the odds of having the same bartender on duty for the lunch crowd at Hy's Place was slim to none, but if Dayton and Scott were regulars, whoever was serving drinks might be able to serve me some information.

The highway traffic was thick with the early morning commuters but at least there were no accidents to slow things down. I arrived at the sports bar just as they were opening for the pre-lunch crowd. By the time I took a seat at the bar, my stomach was practically screaming, "You got me up before five, don't you think it's time to eat?"

The bartender wasn't the same guy Hogan and I saw. No surprise there. This one was taller and older, maybe mid-forties. He was wearing a navy-blue golf shirt with a Hy's Place logo on the front and khakis. Dark hair. Mustache and small goatee. "What can I get you?" he asked.

"Cheeseburger, fries and a Coke."

"You've got it."

Two middle-aged men walked in and took the first booth by the door as the bartender headed to the kitchen, presumably to place my order. A few more customers came in but none of them sat at the bar.

"Be right with you," the bartender shouted to the men, the kitchen door swinging behind him. "I'm holding the fort for a few more minutes until Marylou gets in."

Marylou. I figured she must be the regular waitress. Good. I'd have two people to question about Loreen's fiancé. When the bartender returned after taking more orders and delivering them, I leaned over the bar and motioned for him.

"Oh, that's right. Your Coke. Hang on."

"Um, actually, I called you over because I need to ask you something." I immediately took out my Minnesota PD license and held it up for him to see.

He smiled and shook his head. "Yesterday it was Alcohol and Gaming Enforcement. Boy, this week just keeps getting better and better. At least you're a lot cuter than the Neanderthal from yesterday."

Marcie Rayner. Cuter than a Neanderthal. Good thing I'm not registered on a dating site.

"Those guys probably have to prove they're checking for

underage drinkers," I said.

"Nope. Not this time. They were checking up on illegal promotional pull-tab games."

I drew a blank. "Pull-tab games?"

"Games that require the purchase of alcohol in order for a pull-tab chance to win drinks. Only state-licensed games are allowed. Guess they've had some complaints so now they're checking all the establishments."

"Um, speaking of checking, do you recognize either of these two men? They were in the other day." I showed him the photo that Hogan sent to my phone.

"You're too young and too good looking to be a private investigator. And yeah, I know them. Scott must have gotten himself into some serious gambling trouble this time. When that happens, he usually gets his buddy Dayton to bail him out. So, what happened? Did someone call in all their markers?"

Just then the kitchen door opened slightly and someone shouted, "Order up."

"Let me get your meal and take care of those other customers. I'm Brad, by the way, and we can chat when you're done eating."

If I was hungry when I set foot in this establishment, I was practically salivating and it had nothing to do with food.

CHAPTER FOURTEEN

I wiped the last bit of juice from my cheeseburger and took another swallow of Coke when Brad returned.

"Hallelujah," he said, "That's Marylou coming in the door."

Twisting my neck slightly, I could see a curvy brunette with gold hoop earrings and a short skirt. She couldn't have been older than twenty. Brad gave her a wave as she walked to the back of the restaurant. "Once she stashes her things, I can concentrate on the bar. So, what was it you'd like to know about Scott and Dayton?"

"How you know them for starters. I mean, do you know them other than as customers here?"

Brad reached for a dishcloth and wiped his hands. "I've known both of them for a few years but only as customers. Customers who live big loud lives. That happens when the alcohol takes over."

"You mentioned gambling markers. I take it they bet often."

"You'd think so, being this is a sports bar, but no, they're poker players. Always a backroom game going on somewhere. About a year ago, Scott got himself into some serious debt but Dayton bailed him out. I imagined that money was repaid or they wouldn't still be paling around."

"Do you know what Dayton does for a living?"

"Ever hear of the Weymer family? Largest timber business in St. Paul, although now it's referred to as the cellulose fiber industry."

"I think so. Sounds familiar."

"Well, that's Dayton's family. The father married into it. And from what I hear, none of them are hurting for money. Dayton included."

"I wonder how Scott fits in."

"That's easy. Wharton School of Business."

"The University of Pennsylvania? They were both students there?"

"Yep. And they both came back to roost in Minnesota. Want another Coke? Looks like you're down to the last ice cube."

"Thanks. Sounds like those two are regulars. Any girlfriends in the picture?"

"If there are, I haven't seen them in here. Hold on a sec, will you? Hey, Marylou, got a question for you."

Marylou, who was on her way into the kitchen, turned and walked toward Brad.

"What? What do you need?"

"Remember those two guys who always pal around together? You know who I'm talking about. Justin Timberlake and his buddy."

I knew Dayton Ganz looked like Justin Timberlake. I knew it. I knew it.

Marylou crossed her arms and shrugged. "Yeah, what about them?"

"Any girlfriends in the picture?"

"My Gaydar tells me they're straight but no girlfriends that I've seen and no wives either. I always check for wedding bands."

Then Marylou took a good long look at me and smiled. "Oh, I get it. Which one of them do you have your eye on?"

"I, uh, um…"

Brad laughed and answered for me. "Neither. She's a private investigator. Very hush, hush."

"Well," Marylou said, "I don't know what stuff they're into, but if you ask me, it isn't drugs or anything like that. Too clean cut. Besides, how would they find the time with all those poker games?"

She made a beeline for the kitchen and I took a swallow from my freshly refilled Coke. "Sounds like I'll have to learn how to play poker if I intend to get any further with my investigation."

"So," Brad asked, "what's the deal with those two? Embezzlement? Money laundering?"

"I'm sorry. I really wish I could tell you but—"

"I know. I know. Just don't tell me the two of them are really undercover for the alcohol and gaming enforcement."

"No worries there. You're safe. Um, one more thing. Do you know where the poker games take place? You mentioned backrooms. What backrooms?"

"It's only an expression. Those guys are high rollers. They play at private houses. Ever hear of Lake of the Isles Parkway in Minneapolis?"

"Isn't that like the millionaire mansion street in the Cedar Lake area?"

"Uh-huh. And that's where your buddy will probably lose his shirt this Saturday if he's not careful."

"How do you know all this?"

"Like I said, people drink and people talk."

"I don't suppose you'd have an address?"

"I don't hear that much but if you're any good at being a private eye, you'll figure it out."

I thanked Brad, left him a generous tip and made it back to New Ulm in time to catch Max darting out the door.

"Don't mean to give you the brush-off, Marcie, but I'm late for another damn dentist appointment. If it were up to me, I've have all of them pulled and get implants. So, help me, if the words 'root canal' come up in the conversation, I might just do that."

"Ew. That bad, huh?"

"Annoying on its way to bad. And while we're on the subject of annoying, we had Doris's brother and his irritating wife over for dinner last night. At least I got to see the first piece of red meat on my plate since Reagan was in office. Anyway, I finally have a handle on those blueprints thanks to my brother-in-law. I'll tell you about it first thing tomorrow morning. Got to run."

Max was out the door before I could say a word so I was left standing there with my mouth open and Angie laughing.

"You might want to close your mouth before the flies get in."

"Very funny."

"So, how'd it go? Your meetings with those chauffeurs, I mean."

"Surprisingly good. But that's not all. Remember me mentioning that sports bar in Chaska where Hogan and I saw Loreen Larsen's fiancé?"

"Uh-huh."

"Well, I had some time so I went back there to see if I could get any information from whatever bartender was on duty."

"And…?"

"Turns out the bartender recognized Scott from the photo Hogan snapped. And that's not all. He knew the other guy, too. From what I learned, I don't think Scott's cheating on his fiancée. Not with another woman anyway."

Angie pushed herself away from her desk and gave me her undivided attention. "So, Scott and the other guy are—"

"No. Not that either. Although it would be easier to explain. Scott, apparently, is a gambler. A poker player to be precise. I think that's where he's spending his Saturday nights. According to Brad, that's the bartender, Scott's had some pretty substantial losses and his drinking buddy has had to bail him out."

"Whoa. Unless Loreen Larsen intends to keep a tight grip

on the purse strings, she'll be in for one hell of a start to her marriage."

"No kidding. Before I dare mention this to her, I really need to be sure. Does Max still have any of those magnetic micro GPS trackers in the safe?"

"He bought two recently so I'd say yes."

"Great. Loreen's going to get her answer whether she likes it or not. Come Friday morning, Scott's car will weigh an extra tenth of a pound."

It was a little past three when I booted up my computer. The state historical society would still be open so I figured I might as well start tracking down that photo of Helena's. For some inexplicable reason, I kept thinking that once I figured out who the kid was in the picture, it would bring me closer to solving Helena's death.

The labyrinth for the state historical society's phone system was worse than the one for cable television. "For English, press one. For all other calls, stay on the line. If you're calling for tax records, call the state assessor's office. If you know your party's extension, you can dial it at any time. For hours and location, press one." At least they didn't tell me to hang up and dial 911 if it was an emergency. Finally, I got to speak with a human – Cynthia Dickerson.

I explained my situation to Ms. Dickerson and she agreed to do a bit of legwork for me. Something completely unexpected.

"This is such a fascinating topic," she said. "I was always intrigued by that Mystery Castle. Can you email me a copy of the photo?"

In less than thirty seconds, I sent the file to her computer and she was ecstatic.

"I'm surprised the clarity is this good, all things considered. I'll do a bit of homework for you and get back to you in a few days. Would that be all right?"

"Oh my gosh, yes. It would be more than all right."

Next, I googled the location for the Lake of the Isles Parkway when I suddenly remembered a commitment I made to Hogan - the shindig in Willmar. It was one of two big festivals the Willmar German Club held. The other being Oktoberfest. Hogan's brewery was one of the sponsors for both events. Damn! I hated to miss an opportunity to finalize a case, but the last thing I wanted to do was finalize another relationship. Especially one that was going so well. I picked up the phone and called him.

"Slow down, Marcie, it's not the end of the world."

Hogan's voice sounded calm and reassuring, unlike mine. "But I feel awful. Last weekend I dragged you all around that castle and this weekend I'm ditching you altogether."

"Not necessarily."

"What are you getting at?"

"I take it you're not all that familiar with poker games. They go on all night."

He emphasized "all night."

"It's a straight run from Willmar to Minneapolis on Route 12. Shouldn't take us longer than an hour and a half, and that's with the speed limit. We'll have plenty of time after the festival. And I'm serving the brew, not drinking it. I know what our beers taste like."

"So, you don't mind driving into the city to do some sleuthing?"

"As long as that's not the only thing I'll be doing, I'll be fine."

"Honestly, Hogan."

"So, we're all set?"

"Sure. What time should I be at the brewery?"

"The festival starts at eleven and I need to set up by ten. So, eight-thirty or nine, okay?"

"Make sure there's coffee."

Ending the phone calls was still tough for us. We weren't at the "I love you" stage so that left "take care," "see ya" or "hang in there." Today it was, "be careful, okay?" Still better than "See ya."

I clicked the email icon on the monitor and waited for the

lineup to appear. Nothing out of the ordinary except for one message. It was titled "I May Have What You Want" and it was sent by a PLeyton@gmail.com I didn't know any P. Leytons and was about to dump it when I suddenly remembered Leyton was Phoebe's last name. I quickly opened it.

"This email is being sent to Max Blake and Marcie Rayner. It is being sent from my home address so whatever you do, please do not call me at the Mystery Castle. I think I may have found the missing pages for those blueprints. This is my home number and I should be in after six this evening. Again, please do not call the office. Thank you, Phoebe Leyton."

My jaw dropped and I read the email again.

CHAPTER FIFTEEN

Poor Byron. I literally gave him the brush-off the next morning as I filled his bowl with kibble, changed his water and rushed into the shower. Usually I spend some morning time stroking his long hair or scratching him behind the ears but I wanted to get into the office before Max decided to take off on one of his pressing errands.

As things turned out, Max and I nearly collided with each other at the office door.

"Angie still beat us in," I said.

He held the door open for me but instead of heading straight for the coffeemaker, I stopped dead in my tracks. "If I get Phoebe fired, any chance we could hire her?"

"What? Phoebe from the Mystery Castle? Anna's assistant? Why would you get her fired?"

Suddenly Angie perked up. "Who's getting fired?"

"Not here." I said. "But feel free to listen in."

With me standing in the way, Max had no choice but to sidestep over to Angie's desk. I stood directly across from him so all three of us could be in the conversation. "I called Phoebe last night. But that's only because she sent me, well, us, an email first. Phoebe found the missing blueprint page. Remember Anna told us there were two original sets of blueprints? And oddly enough, both were missing the page we needed. Well, not any more. Phoebe's sending one of them to us FedEx special delivery. It should be here this afternoon. She's doing it on her own. Anna doesn't know."

Max raised his eyebrows and stepped back. "Whoa. That's a surprise. I wonder where she found it, but more importantly, why she decided to send it to us."

"All she told me was she came across it while straightening out some files that had been archived. I think getting the blueprint back to her is going to be the challenge. I suppose we can mail it to her home address…"

"Let's not worry about that for now," Max said. "But Holy Hell! Another dinner with my brother-in-law's wife."

Angie shoved some papers aside with her elbow and leaned on her open palm. "She can't be that bad."

"Oh no? You try having dinner with her. That high-pitched voice of hers is enough to drive anyone insane. And her endless ramblings about the vacations they've taken, the vacations they planned to take and the vacations they should take are enough to send the most stable person over the edge. I'll tell you one thing, if anyone deserves a vacation after spending an evening with her, it's me!"

The three of us were silent for a moment and then Angie spoke up. "Give me your brother-in-law's number. I'll call him and ask him if he wouldn't mind stopping in here. Where does he work, Max?"

"He doesn't. He's retired."

The smile on Angie's face got bigger. "If you're right about the wife, your brother-in-law will jump at the chance to get away from her for a while. Let me see what I can do."

I poured myself a cup of the fresh coffee Angie had brewed and opened my office door. Max shouted from the other side of the room. "Give me about ten minutes, Marcie, and then come in here. I'll go over the blueprint pages we do have. At least I've got a handle on them."

Six email responses and four gulps of coffee later, I adjusted the extra chair in Max's office so we were both staring at the computer screen.

"To begin with," Max said, "Wallis, that's my brother-in-law, had to piece together all the separate snapshots for each floor and go back and forth. Great idea to use the iPhone but a pain in the butt. Anyway, after listening to his lecture on exterior elevation, structural details and building section specs, he told me it was a matter of figuring out the damn symbols, lines, numbers and illustrations."

"Yikes."

"So, I told him, I didn't need to figure it out, *he* did. To make a long story short, the house was designed with hidden passages. Just as we thought. He made me a rough sketch on a piece of paper but it's only for the first and second floors. The grotto shows two means of access but without the blueprint for the ground floor, we were stuck. That little present of Phoebe's, via FedEx, should pull that part of this mess together."

I took a closer look at the screen but it was gobble gook to me. "We know for a fact Helena had her own secret room and entrance built when she converted some upstairs bedrooms into her residence, making an easy access from the attic. It had to be a major feat, considering she needed to have gas lines installed and electricity. I get it. She wanted her own sanctuary. But why did she really switch those downstairs rooms? And install a new dumbwaiter. Any idea from the blueprints?"

"I asked Wallis the same thing. The first-floor blueprints were the originals. I guess we'll never know. Might as well wait till the FedEx truck gets here. Oh, and one more tidbit Wallis pointed out – the house didn't have electricity when they built it at the turn of the century. Minneapolis didn't have a complete grid back then. They used gaslight. Houses weren't converted to electricity until the twenties or thirties. Yep, that Wallis is a regular wealth of information. Anyway, I've got a few other things on my plate including that background check on Anna Gainson."

"My first appointment isn't for another hour and a half. I'll take that list of fences off your plate if you want. Run me the names and I'll see if anyone is in the market for Native American carvings. The thief may translate to the killer, you never know."

"Don't get your hopes up, kid, but hold on, I'll print it out for you. Maybe you'll have better luck than I did with the historical museums and their Native American collections. No recent acquisitions at the Smithsonian's Museum of the American Indian or the Heard Museum. Angie's checking with some of the smaller ones. Frankly, I think the recipient is a private collector. Try to be discreet with those contacts."

"You got it, boss."

The laser jet printer popped out the list in seconds and I was out the door and back to my own office. After scanning for messages and returning a few calls, I stared at the names on Max's list and laughed. There were nine names and all of them looked pretty ordinary to me. I guess I'd seen one gangster movie too many because there was no "Louie the Shark" or "Vito the Knife" on the list. In fact, it looked more like the men's club list at my mother's community center.

Two names had x's in front of them followed by the word "deceased." That left seven. Next to three of those names Max had typed "electronics only" and next to another, the word "disposable." I knew what that meant. Whatever was stolen had to be a hot ticket item and easily gotten rid of. I didn't suppose Native American carvings fit into that category. With three remaining names, I did a little bit of my own research and learned one of the "purveyors of stolen goods" was serving time. I was down to two possibilities – Arnold Zimmerwald and Marco Gomez.

Max's list had their last phone numbers but chances were slim to none they were in service. I took a chance and dialed Arnold's number first. "Leave your name and number. You know the drill." Like hell I was going to leave him my name and number. Or worse yet, the office's. Instead, I had Angie get me one of our Walmart special burner phones and left him that number instead.

Marco Gomez's number had been changed and luckily, the new one wasn't disconnected. A woman answered on the third ring. "Yes?"

"Um, I'd like to speak with Mr. Gomez please. It's regarding a business matter."

"You damn collection agencies will stop at nothing. How many times does my family have to tell you he's dead. Let me spell it out for you. D.E.A.D."

And then, silence. I put another x on the list in front of his name.

Midday, Angie ran out for subs and the three of us ate in the office. Max was mired under with background checks and I was finalizing a few reports when the FedEx delivery came.

"Your map to *The Treasure of the Sierra Madre* just arrived," Angie announced. I walked to the outer office to see her hold up a long tube and grin. "And that's not the only good news. Wallis should be here any minute. When I called him, he was getting his hair cut a few blocks from here. Talk about good timing."

"His wife better not be with him, is she?" I asked.

"Gee, I didn't ask but it didn't sound that way."

Max stepped out of his office and eyeballed the door. "I heard that. So help me, if Camila walks in I'm heading for the restroom and I don't expect to leave any time soon."

"I'll keep her occupied if she does come in," Angie said. "Honestly, I've never seen a grown man hide from a woman."

"You haven't seen Camila. Anyway, hand me that mailing. We might as well open it and spread the blueprint out on the workroom table."

I grabbed a paperweight from my desk and one that was sitting on a shelf in the workroom. I also took the tape dispenser from Angie's desk and my stapler. "This should be enough weight to hold it down. No unused coffee mugs like the ones we found in Anna Gainson's conference room. Those worked really well."

The blueprint slid out easily from its container and Max wasted no time positioning it on the table. I arranged the weights so they wouldn't obscure our view.

"Hey, hey, don't start the fun without me."

It was Max's brother-in-law, Wallis, and apparently Angie told him to go straight to the workroom. Wallis appeared to be in his late fifties or early sixties, tall with carefully trimmed sandy brown hair. Then I remembered that he had just come from a barbershop or hair salon. Max quickly introduced me and peered out the door.

"Camila went to the movies with a girlfriend," he said. "You don't have to be on high alert."

Max cleared his throat and looked at the blueprint. "I wasn't—"

"It's all right," Wallis said. "She drives me crazy, too. So, let's take a closer look at the missing link."

For the next fifteen minutes, Wallis poured over that blueprint as if it was the original Declaration of Independence.

"I've never seen anything like this," he said. "I'll be darned."

Max leaned over the table and rubbed his chin. "What? What will you be darned about?"

"It's not surprising the downstairs kitchen takes up the entire floor. They had to have room for storage that didn't require cold temperatures. That explains the pantries. Everything looks perfectly normal on the left-hand side of the blueprint. Including the dumbwaiter. The dining room was right above it if I recall correctly."

"It was before Helena had the rooms switched," I said, "but what about the right-hand side? What aren't you telling us?"

"Here. See for yourself."

Wallis pointed to what appeared to be a small drawing of a cylinder adjacent to the doorway that led into the root cellar. "Do you know what that is?"

"Oh, for heaven sakes, Wallis, just tell us," Max blurted out.

"We haven't got all day to play Twenty Architect Questions with you."

"That cylinder is a hidden staircase. It's built on a pivot. It only appears as a cylinder on the blueprint but from the kitchen itself it would look like an ordinary door. Open it and you've got the back of the stairs. Unlock it and you've got the steps. Actually, more of a ladder. Enough of an angle to make access fairly easy."

"Unlock it how?" I asked.

Wallis stretched and made a slight groaning sound. "I didn't mean 'unlock' in the conventional sense. I meant find the release button or whatever mechanism they designed. Very clever. Very clever indeed."

Just then, the burner phone I had stashed in my pocket began to ring.

"I've got to take this. It's important."

I stepped out of the workroom and made it to my office before the third ring.

"Hi," I said. "This is Marcie."

"This is Arnold. How'd you get my number?"

The list of fences was sitting face up on my desk and I grabbed it. My eyes went to the first name.

"Um, yeah. I usually deal with Bennie, but unfortunately, he passed away. I had your number stashed somewhere in case Bennie couldn't, um, secure the items I requested. I think he was the one who gave me your number in the first place."

"Sounds like something Bennie Delgado would do. Look, I don't know you and I don't do business over the phone. You in New Ulm?"

Closer than you think.

"Uh, I can be there."

"Know where the German Park is?"

"I'll find it."

"Good. Meet me at the fountain in an hour. That going to give you enough time?"

"Yeah, it'll work. How will I recognize you?" I asked.

"I'll be the only one not ogling or taking pictures. That doesn't help, I'm wearing a black Vikings jacket."

"Okay. See you in an hour."

Max and Wallis were still talking when I returned to the workroom.

"Wallis thinks the kitchen staircase leads to a series of hidden passages. I was right all along. About those gaps in the walls." Max pointed to something on the paper.

"Fascinating, huh?" Wallis said. "Don't know why anyone would bother doing something like that...Yeah, sure, it was commonplace in all those old European castles and don't get me started on the ones in Russia. One bedchamber led to another if you know what I mean."

I looked at the blueprint and bit my lower lip. "Hmm, I don't get it. Only Helena and her parents lived in the Mystery Castle. Not a whole lot of need to go bedroom hopping, so why all the secret passages?"

"For the fun of it, for crying out loud," Max said. "They had money. Lots of money. As far as Helena's parents were concerned, it must have been like building their own funhouse."

"Too bad Helena was an only child. She didn't have any siblings to enjoy it with or— What am I saying? She did. She had that little boy in those photos. Whoever he was."

"I don't know what you're talking about," Wallis said. "I got an earful from Max about the castle the other night but he didn't mention any little boy."

"That's because your wife was too busy mentioning weekend retreats."

"Fine. Fine," Wallis said. "So, what's the story about this little boy?"

Max turned to me. "You're faster on the computer. Can you pull up those photos at your desk?"

"Sure thing, boss."

Five minutes later, we had rolled up the blueprint and put it back in the cylinder. I clicked open the file that had Hogan's photos from the other day and pointed to one of the frames that showed Helena and the mystery boy.

"I've seen that photo before," Wallis said. "Not all of it, but the kid's face. Trouble is, I can't remember where or in what context."

CHAPTER SIXTEEN

Wallis left but promised to call us if he remembered where he'd seen the photo.

"I've got to head out in a little while, myself," I told Max. "I'm meeting Arnold Zimmerwald at the fountain in German Park."

"Name sounds familiar."

"It should. He's on your fence list. The others were either dead or only dealt with electronics or highly disposable stuff."

"You've got your gun with you, right?"

"Uh-huh. Look, we're meeting smack dab in the middle of New Ulm's most frequented park. I seriously doubt the guy's going to abduct me."

"I could always follow you."

"Max, I'm not going to be much use to you if you have to babysit me. I'll be fine. I'll be back in the office before we close."

"Got a plan as to how you're going to get information from him?"

"I'm pretending to be a buyer. We'll see where it goes."

"Hey, before I forget, I got a phone call from Warner VanWycke, the business manager for Blair and Lowery. I meant to tell you yesterday. Helena's attorney is a woman by the name of Elizabeth Chesney and we've got a meeting scheduled with her for tomorrow at ten. I'll drive if you want. I've got to start writing these things down. Anyway, if you've got other appointments, see if Angie can rearrange them for you."

"Don't worry about it. I think my schedule's pretty clear tomorrow."

"Good. Let's leave around eight thirty."

"Sounds good to me. I'd better get a move on."

FORTY MINUTES LATER, I WAS smack dab in the center of German Park. I tried a few scenarios in my head before settling on the one I planned to use with Arnold. Having never dealt with anyone who fenced stolen goods, this was going to be a first. Sure enough, the guy was easy to spot. He was the only one standing at the base of the fountain who was an adult.

Children were everywhere. Reaching in the water to splash each other, chasing each other around the fountain or, for some inexplicable reason, crying. I shouted to Arnold and he turned around.

"I thought you'd be older," he said.

"I am. Just compare me to the kids in the park."

We walked over to an empty bench underneath one of the big park awnings. I took a breath and stared straight at him. He looked to be in his late fifties or maybe early sixties. The slight stubble on his face accentuated his jowls but he had relatively few wrinkles or crow's feet.

"I'll try to make this quick, Mr. Zimmerwald," I began. "I work for a private collector of Native American Art and we understand some old Zuni carvings have become available. We're not talking museum shop souvenirs or even recent art. My employer is interested in carvings that go back at least eighty or ninety years. Precious and semi-precious stones."

Arnold clapped his hands and shouted. "What the hell is it with those damn Indian carvings? All of a sudden everyone wants old Zuni carvings."

"What are you saying?"

"Look Marcie, or whatever your real name is, I handled one transaction for a client who was into that same stuff. Darn right crazy what people collect these days. We have a standing agreement and I have what you'd call a retainer of sorts. So, if I were to, let's say, get my hands on some of those carvings, I already have a buyer."

I could feel my hands trembling slightly so I rubbed them together and didn't budge. "You may have a buyer, but we may offer you a better price. Before you make that deal, call me. You've got the number."

I stood up and started to walk. This is always the part on those TV shows where the other guy yells, "Stop!" or "Wait!" Arnold didn't say a word. At least not right away. I was halfway back to the fountain when I heard him.

"Hold on. Hold on a second, will you?"

I turned and walked toward him. "Yes?"

"How do I know I can trust you?"

"Oh, come on. You can't be serious. How many law enforcement officials are conducting stings on Native American carvings? Drugs yes. Diamonds maybe. Electronics for sure. But figurines? Give me a break. Like I said, I work for an eccentric collector, that's all."

"I may have something coming available this weekend. I'll call you."

"Great. Nice meeting you."

My heart was pounding so fast I thought it could be heard by anyone within a five-foot radius. To be on the safe side, I didn't go back to my car right away. Instead, I strolled through some flower gardens that were partially obscured by huge columns with overgrown vines. After a good five or six minutes feigning interest in Mother Nature, I got in my car and drove back to the office.

"She's back in one piece!" Angie shouted when I got in the door.

"Don't tell me he was really worried. It was a public park,

not a hotel room."

She smiled and shrugged. "You know Max. Very protective."

I nodded and knocked on his doorjamb. "I'm alive and well."

"Good. Did you get anywhere?"

"Let's put it this way, how much money do we have to buy stolen art?"

I told him about the conversation I had with Arnold and how I persuaded him to put us on his buyer list.

"That's not all, Max," I said. "I think someone's about to go back into Helena's apartment for another acquisition. That *has* to be where the stash of those figurines is coming from. No museum thefts. No other notable thefts or we'd hear about it."

"Yeah. Got to agree with you on that one. Whoever's doing it is doing it piecemeal. He or she doesn't want to raise any suspicions."

"I'm still thinking the thief and Helena's killer are one and the same. Whoever it was, she probably took them by surprise and fought back."

"The medical examiner would have noticed signs of a struggle. Those things are pretty obvious. I've seen the report. You've seen the report – natural causes. Given the absence of any bumps or bruises and the fact she was in her nineties, the ruling on her death was cut and dry. But there is one thing. One nagging thing that's been under my skin since we first took the case."

"What's that?" I asked.

"Helena might've been scared to death. Not attacked. Not strangled. Not suffocated. Terrorized. I remember reading an article about an elderly woman who dropped down dead when a masked man entered her bedroom. The guy was charged with murder even though he never laid a hand on her."

"But encountering a burglar in your apartment doesn't rise to the level of terror that would result in dropping dead, would it?"

"I know. That's the only fly in the ointment, so to speak.

If someone did terrorize that woman, it begs the question –
How?"

"Or why?"

"Something personal, maybe? What if someone on her
staff really had it in for her? Or perhaps it was the very thief in
question."

"Geez, about that… Arnold practically told me someone's
going to be rooting through her apartment. I'd offer to stake
out the place this weekend but I'm already tailing Loreen
Larsen's fiancé."

"Staking out the Mystery Castle wouldn't do you much good
anyway. Chances are, someone's getting in there as a regular
visitor and then finding his or her way into the apartment. You
and Hogan already figured out how that could be done."

"What do you propose?"

"The minute Arnold calls to tell you he has a carving for
you, we notify the police. We've got two photos of Helena's
showcase thanks to your boyfriend. If the carving matches up
to something in there, we've caught our thief. Or, in this case,
our thief's middleman, but it's a start."

"Let's hope he calls."

"Oh, he'll call all right. If he wasn't interested, he wouldn't
have taken you up on the offer. For all we know, he could be
in cahoots with the museum's director. Something really fishy
going on there."

"Huh?"

"While you were meeting with Arnold, I finished that
background check on Anna Gainson."

Max reached across his desk and handed me a few printouts.
"I'll save you some time. Everything looks hunky-dory for the
past nineteen years, eleven of which she was employed by the
Mystery Castle. Before that, eight years working for a now
defunct business in Mankato, and before that, she didn't exist."

"What?"

"You heard me. No record of her whatsoever. No marriage
licenses, no divorce papers, her driver's license was originally

issued nineteen years ago and her payments into Social
Security began that time, too. It was like she materialized out
of nowhere."

"A stolen identity?"

"Quite possible. With references from the company she
did work for, and her knowledgeable background in museum
management, I imagine she walked into her position at the
Mystery Castle without too much trouble."

"Hmm, I wonder if she's walking out with a whole lot more.
What about the other employees?"

"No red flags. Not yet, anyway. And while we're on the
subject of walking out, I don't know about you, but I'm glad it's
about time to close up. Angie's probably turning off the copier
and coffee machine."

Sure enough, Angie was packing it in for the day. The three
of us were out the door with Max giving Angie last minute
instructions for "holding down the fort" since he and I would
be in Minneapolis tomorrow morning meeting with Helena's
attorney.

"Last I knew, Blair and Lowery's office is by the College of
St. Catherine, not on the Oregon Trail," Angie said. "I'll be fine
and so will our office."

She gave me a wink and locked the door.

The next morning, I arrived at a little past eight with two
coffees to go from Backerei's Coffee Shop and two cinnamon
rolls. I figured Max would appreciate anything that didn't
smack of flaxseed or whole grains.

"Thank God. Coffee. I can barely function. Wallis called
me at three in the morning. Three in the morning. I thought
someone died. I hate to ask you this, Marcie, but do you mind
driving? All I can see are the insides of my eyelids."

"Sure, no problem. Why did your brother-in-law call you
at that ungodly hour?"

"Because he had an epiphany. That's what he called it. A
damn epiphany. He remembered where he'd seen that photo of
the kid standing next to Helena. It was in some article he read

in an architectural journal for one of his college classes. Hell. I can't even remember what I had for dinner the night before. Anyway, all he could remember was that the article had to do with dumbwaiters and improper installation."

"Why was that boy's picture in it?"

"Beats the hell out of me. Wallis said he was going to look into it further. I told him the next time he gets a stinking epiphany to do it during the daylight hours."

I laughed. "Want to take the 169 and hit the city from that direction?"

"I'd just as soon go to Mendota Heights and cut across than deal with all that downtown traffic. And if you don't mind, forget the GPS. I'm sick of those things shouting 'Recalculating.'"

"That's fine with me. Out of curiosity I googled Elizabeth Chesney. She's been with Blair and Lowery for at least a decade. Graduated right here, from the University of Minnesota."

"Let's hope she's been with Helena that long," Max said. "I'd really like to get some answers about the will and the estate. Especially any beneficiaries who might have motives for murder."

Max and I made decent time and arrived at Blair and Lowery in downtown Minneapolis at a quarter to ten. The office was housed on the ground floor of a brick three-story building that looked as if it had recently been refurbished along with some of the other old stately buildings on the block.

"Welcome to Blair and Lowery" were the first words out of the receptionist's mouth when Max and I entered the office. The man looked to be my age. His closely cropped mustache and beard couldn't conceal the fact he was young. If my mother were here, she would poke me in the arm and say something like, "Why is it women try to look younger and men insist on looking older?"

"Hi!" Max said. "Max Blake and Marcie Rayner here to meet with Elizabeth Chesney."

"Yes, welcome. I see you're on her schedule. Can I offer you anything? Coffee? Water?"

I shook my head "no" and Max responded, "Thanks, but we're fine. We'll take a seat over there and wait."

"Over there" was the section in the outer office with large leather chairs as opposed to another area that had a small bistro table and not-so-comfortable metal chairs. Framed abstract paintings added the only splash of color to the otherwise drab room.

Out of habit, I took out my iPhone and scanned for emails. Max picked up a magazine from the coffee table and looked at the cover. "At least it's recent," he said, "and not recycled from someone's family subscription."

"Mr. Blake? Miss Rayner?" The voice caught us both off-guard. "I'm Elizabeth Chesney, won't you please step into my office?"

We stood up, shook her hand and followed her down a small corridor into her office. Max thanked her for agreeing to meet with us and took a seat at her desk. I pulled another chair over.

"I'm sorry it's taken so long," she said, "but my schedule's been a bear. At least I'm back to looking like my photo on the wall in the hallway."

I halfheartedly shrugged and Max sat there wordless.

"The auburn hair. I finally had time for a beauty parlor appointment. I was beginning to look like Grandma Moses. Anyway, I understand you're here regarding Helena Heatherbrae's estate."

"That's right," Max said handing her his business card. "We've been hired to look into the circumstances surrounding her death."

Elizabeth brushed some strands of hair from her face and stared directly at my boss. "Yes, that's what I've been given to understand but I thought she died of natural causes. My client was in her nineties."

"She may have been in her nineties but there were some discrepancies Miss Rayner and I are looking into. That's where

Helena's will comes in."

"I see," Elizabeth said. "Helena was very specific about drawing up her will and providing for her household staff. She had no surviving relatives. Since I've been her attorney for over four decades, she felt comfortable appointing me as the executor of the will. I'm in the process of carrying out her wishes as we speak."

"Um, can you backtrack for a minute?" I asked. "You said something about providing for her staff. I thought her household staff each received a check for ten thousand dollars. Are you saying there's more to that?"

Elizabeth clasped her hands and nodded. "Those checks were simply some immediate monies to tide over the employees until their actual inheritance could be finalized."

Max made a weird shuddering movement as if someone poked him. "You mean to tell us her employees were in the will?"

"That's right. With the exception of Harry Sorenson, Helena's staff had been with her for years. She certainly wanted to be sure they had some sort of a pension. Let's see, I can give you some rough estimates. Hold on for a moment, won't you?"

Elizabeth typed something on her computer and waited for the screen to pop up. I mouthed the word "wow" to Max and he gave me a nod.

"Yes, here it is," Elizabeth said. "Townson O'Neil, Arletta Maycomber, Sydelle Alridge, Greta Hansen and Minerva Watson will all be receiving the equivalent of their yearly salaries effective the first of the year and retroactive to the date of Helena's death. In addition, those salaries will receive a three percent increase each year to compensate for the cost of living."

"And those pensions or whatever you call it, go on indefinitely?" Max asked.

"As long as the annuity she set up remains solvent, and I have no reason to believe it won't, then yes. But once her immediate beneficiaries pass, the money is to go to certain charities she selected."

"If I understand correctly," Max went on, "her employees would receive their salaries for life."

Elizabeth Chesney nodded. "As I said, *if* the annuity remains solvent. Investments are always at the whim of market fluctuations."

I was practically jumping out of my seat. "Do her former employees know this?"

"They should be receiving detailed information within the next two weeks."

Max placed his hand on my arm and faced Elizabeth. "So, up until now, her employees think the only compensation they got was for ten grand, right?"

"I suppose so."

He made a grunting sound and continued to speak. "They're not the only ones. The director of the castle itself, Anna Gainson, had no idea either. That's probably why she added some of them to the Mystery Castle staff, but not on a full-time basis. Seems your office dropped the ball somewhere."

"Mea culpa. I'll direct our business manager to send them a letter regarding their pensions and a cc to Miss Gainson. Thankfully their employment was in the private sector so there's no issue of 'double dipping.' Is there anything else I can answer for you?"

"Oh yeah. You mentioned the household staff. What about the employees of the Mystery Castle? I'm talking specifically about Anna Gainson and her assistant, Phoebe Leyton. Not the hourly tour guides, the handyman or the gardener."

"I can respond to all of those names. The Mystery Castle itself is a separate business. Completely removed from Helena's personal estate. The castle operates on its own funding. Donations, events, admission, etc. No doubt you've spoken with Miss Gainson who probably informed you they've been in the red for quite some time and that's why—"

"Helena agreed to sign the papers and turn it over to the National Park Service," Max said.

"You've done your homework, Mr. Blake. Actually, it was

Miss Gainson who expedited that matter."

"You mean *pressured* Helena into transferring the castle while she was still alive."

Elizabeth pursed her lips. She opened them slowly and swallowed. "It appeared to be a mutual understanding."

"Um, the employees from the Mystery Castle business are now employees of the National Park Service, is that right? And does that mean they weren't in Helena's will, one way or the other?" I asked.

"Right on both counts." Elizabeth leaned back and stretched. It was a signal I recognized and Max did, too. The meeting was over.

We thanked her again and left the building.

"My God," I said. "My head is spinning."

"Well, let it spin over to the nearest pizzeria. This is a college area, so the pizza shops are bound to be good. What do you say?"

"I'll take mine with pepperoni."

CHAPTER SEVENTEEN

$\mathbf{M}$ax was like a homing pigeon when it came to food. He found a fabulous pizzeria in a matter of minutes and we placed our orders as soon as we sat down. The lunch crowd hadn't arrived yet but by the time I was on my last slice of pizza, clusters of giggling girls had taken up the entire restaurant.

"I'll get the check," Max said. He stood up and walked to the cashier just as my phone rang.

"Marcie! This is Loreen. Scott just cancelled our Saturday night plans. The SOB is on his way back to his office. Surprised he could even find time to have lunch with me. Said some business matter came up and that he'd call me on Sunday. The hell! Find out who's getting into his pants and where! I almost threw the ring back in his face but it's a 2.5 carat Leo diamond."

"Um, that's good. That's good. No sense throwing the diamond back yet. Look, I can't get into details but I promise I'll have some news for you by Monday."

"I'd follow that jerk myself but that's why I hired you. Besides, I might be too tempted to run him over or cut off his cajones if he got out of his car with another woman."

"Keep an open mind, Loreen. It may not be a woman."

"Oh hell."

End of call. At least she wasn't a screamer. I'd had one or two of those in the past few months and it wasn't pretty.

"Ready to go?" Max asked.

"What? Oh, sure. Loreen called. I don't have the heart to tell her Scott may turn out to be a compulsive gambler who's so far over his head in debt the national trust wouldn't be able to save him. I'll know more Saturday night. Good thing you sprung for the long-life battery on that GPS tracker."

"Yeah, it should last about seven days and not seven hours. Sure you know how to use it?"

"Uh-huh. I already inserted the SIM card before I attached the device to Scott's car. All that's left is to call the number for the real time coordinates and use my iPhone to track him on Google maps."

"Much more fun than managing crime statistics, huh?"

"I don't think I could ever go back to my former job, but don't you ever wish you could see the end results right away?"

"If I wanted to do that, I'd mow the lawn. Come on, if one more coed walks into this place, it'll be standing room only."

On the walk back to my car, Max reiterated his stance on my carrying a gun. He was insistent I keep it on me at all times, especially tomorrow night when Hogan and I track down Scott's whereabouts.

"Don't do anything foolhardy or risky," he said. "That bartender you spoke with gave you a general idea of where he expected your buddy to be. The GPS tracker will pinpoint the spot. But then what? Do you plan on bursting into one of those million-dollar homes on Lake of the Isles Parkway?"

"No, of course not. That's the last thing I intend to do. Hogan and I will try to remain inconspicuous and hopefully pick up enough incriminating conversation when Scott leaves the place after a night of poker. Men talk too, you know. At the very least, I'll have the address and I can find out who owns the house. Also, Hogan and I can snap photos of the other players. Loreen needs to see it's not an affair her fiancé is having, it's—"

"A gambling addiction? We're detectives, not counselors. Because if we were in the life coaching business, I'd say it's all the same – gamblers, cheaters, boozers, druggies… We can't tell our clients what to do but we sure as hell can shove the facts right at them."

"Ugh. That's not going to sit well with Loreen," I said.

Max moaned. "Those things never do. Sure your boyfriend's okay spending his evening sleuthing?"

"Hogan's a man of many talents and brewing beer is only one of them. Besides, I think he likes the excitement."

"There's a lot to be said for boring, too, you know. Like staying alive."

"Come on, Max. We're tailing a gambler, not Al Capone."

We made good time getting out of Minneapolis and back to the office. Angie said it was a quiet morning with a few calls for Max and only one pressing phone call for me to return – Cynthia Dickerson from the state historical society.

"Oh my gosh, Angie. This could be it. She might be able to tell us who that little boy in Helena's photo is. Oh my gosh."

I raced into my office, grabbed Angie's original note and made the call. My fingers were tapping on the desk while I waited for her to pick up. At least I didn't have to go through the maze of connections this time. Cynthia left me a direct line, and she answered the call right away.

"I'm not sure this will help you," she said, "but it may bring you closer to finding the answer you wanted, Miss Rayner. I was able to come across a photo that was taken when the Heatherbraes added the Garden Grotto to their estate. Helena and a little boy are seen on the wrap around porch with lollypops in their hands. The photo appeared in the local newspaper of the day and the caption reads, "Little Helena Heatherbrae and friend enjoy their candy pops at the newly constructed Garden Grotto at the Heatherbrae estate."

"Does it give a name? Does it say more?" I tried to keep from shouting.

"It's dated October 10, 1935. I'm sorry, that's all I could

find."

"The newspaper. The newspaper. You said it was from a clipping in the paper. What paper?"

"The Minneapolis Tribune. It later merged with the Minneapolis Daily Star to form the Star Tribune. The photo is on microfiche and you're more than welcome to visit the historical society and take a look for yourself. Call me anytime."

I didn't think a trek to the Minnesota Historical Society was going to bring me any closer to identifying the mystery boy but I thanked Cynthia and kept the option open.

Two things plagued me as I sat at my desk and ran my fingers through my hair. The first of course, was not knowing who that little friend of Helena's was. At least the newspaper clipping ruled out any possibility he was Helena's brother or even a relative. The second was the juxtaposition of the original dining room with what is now the day room. Sydelle brushed it off when she gave me the quick tour of the main kitchen. Something about rich people doing whatever fancied them. It seemed an awful lot of work and expense for a mere fancy. Then again, I was never rich.

I pulled up the snapshots Max and I took of the blueprints when we were in Anna's conference room. Resting my head in the palm of my hands and leaning into the computer monitor, I stared at the section containing the dining room. That was where the original dumbwaiter was. Granted, it needed new ropes and perhaps a whole new pulley system according to Greta, but still, that's a whole lot cheaper than sealing it shut.

According to Greta, and Minerva, too, Helena loved the location of the day room with its fabulous view. Maybe it wasn't all that crazy for her to have it switched with the old dining room and have a new dumbwaiter installed. Still, something about that bothered me but I couldn't quite explain what it was. Max was no help either.

"Yeah," he said when I moseyed over to his office, "The blueprints we have are the originals. There's nothing on file about the remodeling. Maybe we're trying to read more into it. Lots of old homes were refurbished for all sorts of reasons."

"I suppose. Hey, when you spoke with your brother-in-law this morning or whatever ungodly time it was, he mentioned seeing that picture of the mystery boy in an architectural journal. Some article he read when he was in college. When was Wallis in college?"

"Heck Marcie, I don't even know when Wallis was in a taxi the last time, let alone college. Fine. Fine. He's younger than Doris by two or three years so that would make him close to my age. I do know he enlisted in the Navy to get out of the draft. A three-year enlistment that felt like thirty according to him. And the only action he saw was in a barroom in Naples. I'm guessing he was in college sometime between 1970 and 1977 before going into the building trades. Why? Why the sudden interest in Wallis?"

"Max, don't you see? I can narrow things down. The librarian at the historical society had an archival photo dated 1935. All I need to do is google architectural journal articles between 1970 and 1977 that had something to do with dumbwaiters. That's what Wallis said, right? Dumbwaiters. If I can find that article, it may shed some light on the kid."

"Unless the article was historical in nature and then, who knows when the hell it was written. But if you've got the time—"

"Got it and using it."

I was back at my desk in a matter of seconds with a new burst of energy and had no problem isolating articles written in that time frame. It was mind boggling. Who knew that something as simplistic as a simple service elevator could be so darn complex? My eyes scanned from one topic to the next. Alignment issues. Counterweight issues. Guide rail issues. It was overwhelming. I was about to give up altogether when I glanced at the words, "Developing and Designing Safety Mechanisms for Otis Dumbwaiters."

Greta mentioned the old dumbwaiter as being an Otis model. I didn't pay attention at the time but I pulled up the article. No photo but that didn't matter. It was written in

1937 by a team of engineers proposing locking doors to avert such tragedies as the one that took the life of a Minneapolis youngster in1936.

"This has to be it, Max," I shouted. "This has to be it!"

Angie looked up from her desk as I stormed into Max's office. The words gushed out of my mouth. "I think I know who the boy is. Or was. I think I found it. Oh my God! I think I found it."

Max was shouting "slow down" while Angie was at my heels yelling "What? What? What did you find?"

I was literally panting as I spoke. "I think I know why Helena had those rooms switched and it had nothing to do with that view of the lake."

Angie leaned against the file cabinet adjacent to Max's desk and the two of them listened to my explanation without uttering a word. Finally, Angie took her glasses off, rubbed her nose and said, "I think that was a movie I saw on *Netflix*."

Max was more diplomatic. "Interesting conjecture. Very interesting. We have no evidence whatsoever to prove that boy in the photo fell to his death in a dumbwaiter, let alone to have Helena responsible. Even if it does beg the question. Beg. Not prove. Did the article happen to identify the mansion in question?"

I shook my head. "Not exactly. That was my next move. To pull up old news articles from that year. Okay Max. Okay. I'll start pulling. But I'm telling you, I think I'm right. And not only that, but it may be a motive for murder if someone was seeking revenge."

Angie started to laugh and I shot her a look. "And don't tell me you saw that on *Netflix*, too."

I left Max's office and returned to my desk. It was four thirty-five and in less than a half hour we'd be packing it in for the day. Funny, but I felt energized and deflated at the same time. I ran my fingers through my hair, forgetting for a minute that it made the ends stand up, and immediately went to the Minneapolis Newspaper Index. It was something Cynthia had mentioned. All I needed to do was identify subject headings and cross reference them.

It was easier than I thought until I realized it meant taking those references and running them through the old catalogues in the reference room at the University of Minnesota's Wilson Library. There had to be another way. Cynthia Dickerson told me I could call her anytime but I seriously doubted she meant twice in the same day let alone the same hour. Still, I picked up the phone and held my breath.

CHAPTER EIGHTEEN

———

"A 1936 house tragedy in Minneapolis?" Cynthia's voice was clear and direct. "Sure, it won't take me very long to bring up archival information. Not with a subject, date and place. Give me twenty minutes and I'll call back."

I shoved my chair away from the desk and sauntered into the main office. "I'll lock up," I said. Angie had just turned off the copier and her computer. "You sure?"

"Yeah. I'm waiting for a phone call. *Netflix* my you-know-what."

"Couldn't help it, Marcie. Your theory had a better plotline than most novels. Will you be in tomorrow? I know it's Saturday but Max said something about finalizing background checks. I asked if he wanted me to come in but he said he'd manage."

"I'm supposed to drive to Biscay tomorrow and go with Hogan to the German Festival in Willmar. The Crooked Eye Brewery is serving beer. From there, it's off to Minneapolis. Loreen Larsen's fiancé doesn't know it, but we're tailing him. She needs some answers and I expect to have them before the night's over."

"Be careful, will you? Last time you did something like that you nearly got killed."

"Last time I was tracking down a murderer. If Scott's guilty of anything, it's gambling. I'm not too worried. Besides, Hogan will be with me."

"Not that it's any of my business, but if he's going to keep company with you, he may want a pistol permit, too."

"Oh my gosh. My brother said the same thing the other day. Hogan doesn't even own a gun. Of course, things might change if we keep this stuff up. Besides, most of the cases I deal with are benign. Only a few—"

"A few is a few too many. Anyway, see you on Monday. And good luck."

Angie snatched her bag from the top of her desk and headed out. In that instant the phone rang and I made a beeline for my desk. I could hardly catch my breath as I spoke.

"Miss Dickerson? Did you find out anything?"

"You're in luck. Here goes. Very sad. Very tragic. On Christmas Eve, 1936, two children were playing in the dumbwaiter. Apparently, there was a house party going on and no one was paying much attention to them. Anyway, they must not have realized the cart was no longer on their floor and when the boy stepped in, he fell to his death."

"So that's what prompted those engineers to re-design the dumbwaiters so that safety mechanisms were in place. Did it give the boy's name?"

"It was the Williston Family. A prominent Minneapolis family. Their son. Six-year-old Kent."

"Williston Family? Are you sure?"

"I'm sorry, Miss Rayner. I know you were trying to find some information about that photo with Helena Heatherbrae. I'm sure your leads were promising. So sorry this didn't yield you the information you needed."

"You've been so helpful. And so willing to take time out of your day. I really appreciate it," I said.

"That's what we do at the historical society. Have a nice weekend."

I stared at the phone receiver and sighed. Nothing like hitting a dead end. And other than the Willmar German Festival, the closest I'd come to a nice weekend was to chase down a gambler. I took a deep breath and plodded back to Max's office. He was pouring over some papers when I walked in.

"I guess I jumped the gun about Helena being responsible for that boy's death. Heck, for all I know, he could still be alive. But I was right about the dumbwaiter. Some other poor kid died horsing around on one of those. Same time frame – 1930s. Anyway, how are you coming along at your end?"

Max massaged his temples and groaned. "I'm stymied by Anna's background check. Nothing a good fingerprint wouldn't cure. Like I said before, nothing in anyone else's information even raised an eyebrow but I'm still digging for connections. As for Anna…"

"I know that look of yours. You're serious. About the fingerprint."

"Yeah, too bad it isn't as easy as pulling up someone's driver's license. Since Phoebe was so willing to share those blueprints with us, I gave her a call and asked for a favor. Told her I'd reimburse her for the wax paper."

"She's going to get Anna's fingerprints? How's she going to do that? And more importantly, why?"

"In case you hadn't noticed the body language, there's no love lost between them. I think Phoebe would do anything she could to work for another boss. But something tells me it goes deeper than that. Anyway, it doesn't matter. She's going to help us out."

"Won't Anna be suspicious?"

"It's not as if we're sending Phoebe in to dust the place for prints. Anna is obsessed with lint on her clothing. I noticed that little trait as well. She used transparent tape to remove the particles. Phoebe's going to catch her in the act, distract her and get her to drop the dispenser. When Phoebe picks it up, it'll be minus a piece."

"You really should hire her, Max, if she loses her job. She's got amateur sleuth written all over her. And don't look at me like that. I'm a real detective. At least according to the state of Minnesota. So, you think it will work? The fingerprints?"

"We'll know in a few days. Phoebe will mail us the tape using wax paper so it won't stick. Meanwhile I'm going to give Minerva a call and keep her posted. I know she didn't want investigative reports but I figured it wouldn't hurt to update her."

"Boy is she a far cry different from her cousin. Alice Davenport gave me nightmares when I had to send her those chronological and thematic reports. Now I'm getting frightening day messages from my mother. Calling to ask, 'Did you solve it yet? Did you solve it yet?' She stopped nagging about my social life since my brother opened his big mouth but now she's relentless about my work life. Whatever we do, Max, let's never ever take another case that originated from Iris Krum."

"Good luck with that, kid. Your mother's like a tsunami. There's no stopping her. I don't know about you, but it's time to get out of here. I'll finish up in the morning and I'll see you on Monday. Don't look so despondent. Just because one lead didn't work, doesn't mean we won't have some better luck. Have fun at that German festival before you start that surveillance. Life's not all work, you know."

"Right. Coming from the guy who's going to be here all weekend."

"Hey, I never said that pertained to me."

I turned off my computer, shut the outer office lights and locked the door behind me. "Finish up in the morning" my you-know-what. Unless Doris was planning to cook a brisket or anything with red meat, Max was probably going to be at his desk for another few hours.

Byron started meowing the minute I set foot in my apartment. His bowl still had plenty of kibble but I think he really craved the company. He immediately began to crunch those morsels as I changed his water. It was going to be a long thirty or so hours for him without having me in the house. For a brief second, I thought about getting another cat so he wouldn't be alone, but if my relationship with Hogan got more serious, Byron would have Foxy and Lady to contend with.

Granted, it's only been a year that we've been together, but given how we both feel, things may get serious enough for us to take the next step. I still laugh when I think back to having first met him. Met him and placed him on a suspect list. Yeesh!

"I'll only be gone overnight, Byron boy," I said stooping down to pet his head as he ate. "And I'll leave you lots of food and extra bowls of water. I'm sure you'll get plenty of entertainment looking out the courtyard window."

Of course, he'll be entertained. The Bayberry Apartments are a never-ending source of action from late night fist fights in the courtyard to women screaming from the window for their kids to get inside.

My stomach was rumbling so I made myself a grilled cheese sandwich and chomped on an apple before changing into sweats and giving Hogan a call. He answered right away.

"I can't wait to see you tomorrow. Look, you really need to be here by eight thirty so we can make it to Willmar before the set up at ten. I also promised to take the first shift at the beer flight tasting. I know how you hate to get up early, but it'll be worth it. Honest. Oh, and just throw on any old T-shirt. I got you an official Willmar German Festival shirt to wear."

"Wow. That was really nice of you."

"No, it wasn't. It was a freebee. It says 'staff' on it but the logo is cool with dark red letters against a black background. I thought you'd like it."

"I'm sure I will. Thanks. And thanks for agreeing to drive me to Minneapolis. I never actually tailed someone using a GPS device. This is kind of new for me. Max and I went over it a few times so I should be all set."

"Yeah, about that…If I understand correctly, all we're doing is tracking the guy to the house where the poker game is going on. Short of looking into basement or ground floor windows for any action, we'll have to find a hidden spot near the front door so we can overhear the conversation as he leaves the place. Does that sound right?"

"Uh-huh. That's it. Very boring. Most surveillance is. We have to plant ourselves outside that front door or we'll never be able to listen in on the conversation. Not like I could walk up to the guy and ask, 'Did you enjoy a lovely evening at our casino?'"

"What if we don't hear anything?"

"We continue to follow him. If it's not that late, he'll probably end up at a bar. We're bound to pick up enough incriminating evidence to give his fiancé her money's worth."

"Make any headway on the Mystery Castle case?"

"Zilch. I'll share my frustrations with you tomorrow. After the festival. Max told me to have good time and I intend to do just that."

"Great Marcie, see you in the morning."

I took a long shower, ate a bowl of chocolate chip ice cream and crashed on the couch to channel surf before calling it a night. Byron was already on my pillow when I got into the bedroom. With the alarm set for an obscene wake-up time, I turned off the lights and after rolling back and forth from my side to my back, I finally fell asleep.

It was an awful night's sleep. There was some sort of commotion in the courtyard downstairs and the flash of blue and red lights woke me up. Byron was already looking out the window. All I could see were shadows moving about. I tip-toed to the living room and made sure my door was locked. Even though the situation had nothing to do with me, I took my gun from its usual spot in my nightstand and held it for a few seconds before putting it down.

Wide awake, I watched the shadows move about in the courtyard. Four of them. Finally, they all seemed to gather by the police car and next thing I knew, the car drove off. Lights still on but no siren.

Whatever it was, it was over. I put my gun back in the drawer and got under the covers. It took me longer to fall asleep this time and when the alarm went off, I was sweating as if I was in Belize and not New Ulm.

All I could remember were fragments of a horrible dream in which I was trapped between the walls in a house and no matter how hard I tried, there was no way out. Then, if that wasn't enough, I had that throat clutching falling feeling and I could hear someone yelling "Help! Help me, Helena!"

I was still sweating even after brushing my teeth and pouring myself a bowl of cereal. I gave Byron a tad of milk along with his regular kibble and water before making up my bed, getting dressed, and gathering a few items for my overnight bag. Forty minutes later I was on the road to Biscay and the Crooked Eye Brewery.

A number of five-gallon beer kegs and a few cartons of growlers were visible in the back of Hogan's truck as I pulled into the parking lot of the Crooked Eye Brewery. The little place in the middle of Biscay, along with the Triangle Diner, was the only real sign of civilization in that tiny hamlet nestled between Glencoe and Hutchinson. I glanced again at the truck and remembered Hogan telling me he had to buy mini-kegs for the beer flights so customers could sample all the varieties.

With a quick look at the visor mirror, I hurriedly fluffed my hair with my free hand and checked my eye makeup. Only a tad of eyeliner was needed. Hogan was out the door and on the porch before I could even moisten my lips and put the car in park. He was holding a brown paper bag and balancing two coffees.

"I had to practically hide these from the guys," he said. "Fresh pastries from the diner and coffees to go. I figured you wouldn't have time for breakfast."

"I barely had time to get dressed but I made it."

"You look fine. Oh, before I forget, your T-shirt's on the front seat. You can change into it when we get there."

I was relieved to have someone else do the driving for a

change. Not that I really minded the back and forth trips to Minneapolis, but each one of them seemed to get us nowhere. I hated to use the word 'stalled,' but that's what it felt like.

"I was so close," I said. "So damn close. Only to find out the tragedy I thought happened to Helena's household actually happened to another wealthy family whose house had a dumbwaiter. I may never pose another theory again."

Hogan laughed and gave my thigh a squeeze. "Right. And I'll never brew beer again. Seriously, what does your boss think about the case?"

"Max is as methodical as can be. He reviews every little detail and double checks before he takes the next step. I think he likes working with me because I'm like his polar opposite."

"Nothing wrong with that."

"Anyway, Max is fixated about the castle's director. And he may be on to something. Ann Gainson has only existed on paper for nineteen years. He's hoping to nab a fingerprint and go from there. And we're both close to nailing the thief whose been stealing those Native American carvings from Helena's apartment."

"No kidding."

Hogan listened without saying a word as I told him about Arnold Zimmerwald and my impromptu acting role at the German Park. "So you see," I said, "the guy all but assured us his source would have something for us. If it turns out to be one of Helena's pieces, then Arnold will be in possession of stolen property and the police may be able to find who our thief is. That's the good news. Maybe. Sure, there's a chance the thief is our killer but I'm not too sure. Anyway, that's where we are with this thing."

"Whoa Marcie. You didn't even stop for a breath. Look, I know you're frustrated, but just listening to you I can tell you and your boss are gaining ground. You said he was really methodical, right? Let it play out."

"I hope you're right about getting closer to figuring it out. I hate to say it, but I think I'm turning into one of those people with a really strong closure element."

"A what?"

"A closure element. That's a nice way of saying 'in a hurry to get things done.'"

CHAPTER NINETEEN

Miller Park in the southwest corner of Willmar, a small city west of Minneapolis whose claim to fame, according to my mother and her trivia games, was a bank robbery by Machine Gun Kelly's gang in 1930, stood a stone's throw away from Biscay where the Crooked Eye Brewery was located. It was also the site of the festival. I'd been to the downtown area a few times, mostly when Max and I were dealing with the awful accusation that the victim of a shooting was responsible for an arson that destroyed two businesses. It was a gut-wrenching investigation that seemed to take us everywhere in Willmar except the one place Hogan and I were headed for this morning.

Unlike Mendota Heights with its sweeping views of Minneapolis, Willmar was more low key with its tree-lined streets and Colonial Revival houses. No wonder I was flabbergasted at the sight of large blue and white stripped tents when Hogan pulled off of Route 12 and drove a few blocks south to the park.

"My God! You didn't tell me the festival was ginormous. I sort of pictured a tent with some beer tasting and maybe an outdoor seating area for eating and dancing."

"That's kids play. Welcome to the big time. This festival draws people from all over the state. I'm surprised you haven't heard of it. One of your breweries in New Ulm, Schnell Brewery, is also a sponsor."

"What about the giant companies, like Longfellow?"

"Nope, only small companies and micro-breweries but there are enough of us so the beer won't run out. We're in tent three over to the left. I'll park in front and get someone to help me unload the kegs. That's the other good thing about this festival – lots of volunteers."

"Anything I can do to help?"

"Not right now. Why don't you find a place to change your T-shirt and scope out the other tents? Lots of vendors with all sorts of things. You can get an idea while they're setting up."

"Sounds good to me if you're sure."

"I'm sure."

With the T-shirt tucked under my arm and my bag flung over my shoulder, I took off for the largest tent. It had an enormous stage and an even larger area for dancing. Long rectangle tables were set up to accommodate all the drinking and eating. A few musicians in lederhosen were tuning up and two stocky men were hoisting a large sign indicating the band schedule.

Dieter's Oompah Band, The Alpine Wanderers, Polka Magic Musicians and The Tyrolean Tinders immediately caught my eye. I felt as if I had been living under a rock all these years not to know about this festival. Suddenly, I caught a whiff of roasted meats and immediately stepped out of the tent.

With an event of this magnitude, there had to be a food tent and I was determined to find it. I wandered from vendor area to vendor chastising myself for not being able to zero in on the exact spot where the aromas were emanating. I gave up momentarily and ducked into the park restroom a few feet from where I was standing in order to put on the festival

T-shirt Hogan had gotten me.

Thankfully, I had the place to myself. I knew once the festival opened, the restrooms would be impossible along with the circular band of blue porta potties. The T-shirt I was wearing was so old and worn I was able to scrunch it up and put it in my bag. The thought did cross my mind about throwing it out but that was something we never seemed to do in my family, thanks to my mother.

"You can still get a few more uses out of that. When it gets real bad, I'll turn it into a rag."

Nothing ever seemed to make the transformation from clothing to rags. They disintegrated before that ever happened. Out in the open again, I lifted my head in a vague attempt to isolate the source of those amazing aromas.

"Miss Rayner, is that you? Miss Rayner?"

I turned my head to find myself face to face with Greta. One of the last people I expected to see in Willmar.

"Um, er, Hi! Hi Greta! You caught me by surprise. I guess I didn't expect to find anyone from the Mystery Castle at this German Festival."

"Yes, the same could be said for you as well. Are you on a case?"

"No. I'm with my boyfriend. He's one of the owners of the Crooked Eye Brewery in Biscay."

"I've never tried those beers. I'll have to put it on my list. I come here every year for this festival. My family's in Willmar. It's funny that I've run into you because I've been meaning to call your office."

"Really?"

"Remember when I showed you Helena's apartment and you asked me if she was having trouble with anyone?"

"Uh-huh."

"There was something. But it seemed so insignificant I didn't want to waste your time. Then I got to thinking about it. Especially since—"

"Since what?"

Greta darted her eyes in both directions and spoke. "First of all, it wasn't Miss Heatherbrae's imagination."

"What? What wasn't?"

I was beginning to feel as if Greta would never get to the point.

"Miss Heatherbrae insisted she detected the scent of bayberry in the room."

I paused and bit my lower lip for a second. "Bayberry? Like that Christmas smell?"

"That's the one. Kind of woodsy and sweet at the same time."

"But you never smelled it when you went in there to clean?"

"Not until recently. Not until a few days ago. Miss Gainson sent me in there to do some serious cleaning. Said the place would be thick as dust and smelly as a tomb if we didn't wipe every surface clean and vacuum. Since the police never declared it a crime scene she wasn't about to wait until you and Mr. Blake completed your investigation."

"What about the bed? The linens?"

"Those were washed and the bed was remade in case Miss Gainson decided to open the residence up for visitors."

"And that aroma? The bayberry?"

"Yes, I was getting to that. Strangest thing. I opened Miss Heaetherbrae's figurine cabinet to gently dust around all those little breakables and the scent of bayberry came at me like a freight train. Miss Rayner, I'm not one to exaggerate, but I caught a whiff of that sweet pine aroma the second I opened the showcase door. It dissipated almost immediately, but I smelled it all right. I most definitely and assuredly did."

"Um, uh, I believe you."

Greta shook her head and looked down. "All this time Miss Heatherbrae was acting as if she thought someone had been in her apartment. She never came right out and said so, but she sure acted that way. Well, maybe someone was in her apartment. Maybe they were snooping around that trinket cabinet of hers. Of course, nothing's missing. All those little knickknack animals are still there, but it begs the question. If someone was in her room, why on earth would they be doing a thing like that? No wonder she was nervous."

"Bayberry."

"Yes, that's what I said."

"And you're certain it wasn't the smell from some cleaning solution? There are lots of those new green cleaners out there."

"No one cleans except me and I use Lysol and Windex. No, it wasn't a left-over cleaning smell."

"Greta, do me a favor and don't say a word about this to anyone else. You have my card, don't you? If you notice anything or smell anything out of the ordinary when you go back to work on Monday, please call me."

"I will. I haven't told anyone about this except you, and I don't intend to. I can't help but get the feeling someone's up to no good. Hope you get some answers soon."

"Yeah, me too."

At that moment, I heard a screeching yell followed by laughter. A little boy raced over to us.

"Auntie Getta! Auntie Getta! Look! Cotton candy!"

Greta bent down and gave him a big hug. "You're a regular sugar monster."

The boy giggled and bit off a piece of the spun candy.

"This is my great nephew Cooper," Greta said, making sure the cotton candy was nowhere near her hair. "And this is Miss Rayner."

I extended my hand and smiled. It wasn't hard. The kid was adorable. Pink sugary smudges all over his face. "Nice to meet you, Cooper."

"And this is my niece, Tilda. She's Cooper's mother. I don't get to see her that often. Only when she's in Minneapolis and we almost missed each other the last time. Ridiculous miscommunication. I thought we were meeting at my house but Tilda thought it was at my work."

I was so taken by Cooper I hadn't noticed the tall muscular woman who was a few yards behind him. She was making sure the backs to her earrings were firmly in place. I watched as she pushed her short dark hair behind her ears. With minimal make-up, she reminded me of a poster girl for healthy living or paid up gym memberships.

"Hi Tilda, I'm Marcie."

"Oh, you'll have to excuse me," she said. "I lost one of my favorite earrings not too long ago so I've become obsessed with checking them all the time."

Greta took her niece by the arm as she spoke. "Marcie's an investigator from New Ulm. Her company's looking into Helena Heatherbrae's death. I didn't mention that to you, did I?"

Before her niece could respond with more than a shake of the head, Greta looked directly at me. "Tilda used to work at the Mystery Castle in the summers. As a tour guide. Of course, that was before Cooper was born."

Tilda's eyes darted back and forth from her aunt to me. "Seems like a long time ago. I loved that place. We all did. The tour guides, that is. I was sorry to hear Miss Heatherbrae passed away. She used to invite the tour guides into her residence from time to time. I always thought that place was more interesting than the castle itself. All those weird collectibles. If he was older, Cooper would have a field day in there. Anyway, the papers said it was natural causes. Her death. I mean, a woman in her nineties…"

Tilda's words sounded rehearsed. Maybe it was my imagination. I watched as Cooper continued to take large bites from his cotton candy, oblivious to our conversation. "Um, yeah," I said, "that's what the medical examiner wrote, but there were inconsistencies. That's why my company was hired. It's a private investigation. The police are cooperating but they're not directly involved."

Tilda bit her lip slightly and took a breath. "Inconsistencies? What does that mean?"

"I can't really say much, but in general, inconsistencies mean the evidence at the scene doesn't match up with the circumstances."

"Are you saying you think someone might have killed her? I thought she died peacefully in her bed. In her sleep."

"I don't know. Not yet."

Greta took Cooper's hand and gave Tilda one of those neck rolls that meant "let's get moving." Sure enough she spelled it out.

"Tilda, we need to get seated in the tent before the entertainment starts and we find ourselves behind a bunch of tall people in those feathered hats. We won't be able to see anything. Marcie, it was nice running into you. Enjoy the festival."

"Thanks. By the way, Cooper's adorable. How old is he?"

"He'll be five next month," she said. "But to see him around computers people would swear he was fifteen. I imagine when he does get older, we'll be spending a fortune on electronics."

I laughed. "Maybe by then the prices will come down. Oh, before you leave, can you or your aunt tell me where the food tents are?"

Tilda gave me explicit instructions and I all but ran.

Fifteen minutes later I returned to the Crooked Eye Brewery tent with a large brat for Hogan and one for me. The festival wasn't about to officially open for another twenty minutes but when the food vendor saw my T-shirt he assumed I was a worker and never questioned me.

"I come bearing gifts," I said handing Hogan his lunch. "Hope you like mustard and sauerkraut."

"Love it. Thanks, Marcie. So, did you get to see lots of neat vendors?"

"I did one better. I got to have another conversation with Greta Hansen. She's got family here in Willmar. Comes to the festival every year. Go figure. Listen, she thinks someone has been getting into Helena's apartment. She smelled bayberry when she went to clean Helena's showcase."

"Hmm, I opened that showcase and didn't smell anything. But an odor can really get trapped in there. It's such a small space. That's why we have to be so careful about ventilation in the brewery. If she's right, it means someone had been in that apartment shortly before she got there. Our thief, most likely."

"Yeah, that's what I thought. Now we know something about him. At least I think it's a him. We know his cologne of choice is bayberry."

Hogan stepped away from the counter where his beer flights were lined up and gave me a hug with his free hand, careful not to drop the bratwurst he was holding in his other hand. "See, I told you not to worry. You're one clue closer."

"I'd better let Max know about this. Give me a few minutes and I'll be right back."

I stepped out of the tent and spotted some empty benches a few yards away. I had already hit speed dial for the office and waited for Max to pick up. I knew he'd be there working but I forgot he never answered the phones. Scanning my contacts list, I re-dialed. This time to his cell number.

"Marcie, is everything okay?"

"Your phone identified me?"

"Hey, you're not the only one who can use technology. What's up?"

"I'm in Willmar. At the festival. The housekeeper from the Mystery Castle is here, too. Greta Hansen. Can you believe it? The minute she saw me she marched right over and told me something weird. Said Helena detected the aroma of bayberry in her apartment once in a while. Greta didn't believe her until she smelled it herself a few days ago. Anna sent her in there to clean the place."

"Wonder why Greta waited so long to tell us. *If* she planned on telling us."

"She could've avoided me but she didn't. So yeah, I think she would've called."

"Okay, I'll give her the benefit of the doubt. If she's right, then we've got a sweet-smelling thief on our hands. I'm crossing my fingers our fence comes through. That'll give us solid evidence for the police. Meanwhile I've widened the net regarding the employees."

"Anything promising?" I asked.

"Not sure. We know Greta's a widow. She's got a sister in Willmar who has a grown daughter with a child of her own."

"I know. I met the kid. Adorable little boy. So, what did you find out?"

"Greta's clean. No priors. No traffic tickets. No nothing on any of her family for that matter. Oh, and real easy to track down. The sister and niece are teachers in the area so their prints were on file with the state. But get this, the niece used to work during the summers at the Mystery Castle as a tour guide. That's when she was teaching in Minneapolis. Now she's back in Willmar. Hasn't worked at the castle for at least four years."

The Oompah band got louder and I raised my voice. "I know. She told me when Greta introduced us. I think there's more but I'm not sure what. Anyway, we know Arletta's husband is on disability and Sydelle is single. What about Phoebe? Gosh, I hate to think Phoebe is scamming us somehow."

"You don't have to yell. I can hear you fine."

"It's the music. Driving me crazy. Do you trust Phoebe?" I asked.

"She wouldn't take the risk to get us the info if she was using us. Get this – Phoebe's single too. I'm beginning to think it was a requirement for those jobs."

"What?"

"I was kidding. I also ran credit checks on all but one of those employees. I'm working on that right now."

"And?"

"So far, they have better scores than I do. Looks like we'll need to wait this out on Anna's fingerprints and Arnold's latest acquisition. Oh crap. Hold on a second. That idiotic weather alert is beeping on my computer."

"Rain in the forecast?" I asked.

"A severe thunderstorm watch for the entire Minneapolis area late tonight. Maybe you'll want to re-schedule your after-hours surveillance."

"Max, it's a watch, not a warning. Those things change every hour. Does it give a timeline?"

"Hold on. I've got to scroll through the hourly forecast. Darn this thing. They've got the stupid sunrise and moonrise times. Who cares about those? Wait, here it is. Scattered and severe thunderstorms beginning at midnight."

"Hmm, we should be fine. The festival ends at five. We'll have everything loaded up by six and the drive to Minneapolis shouldn't take us more than two hours tops. We should be back on the road well before that first raindrop falls. Stop worrying."

"Don't take any chances, okay? If you don't catch that guy gambling tonight, I can guarantee there'll be another opportunity."

"I'll be fine, Max. I'll give you a call tomorrow."

"Go have fun at the festival, will you? I can smell the Weiner schnitzel from here."

"Want me to bring you back a pretzel? It'll keep till Monday."

"Nah, I'll live."

CHAPTER TWENTY

A line of seven or eight people was already forming in front
of the Crooked Eye Brewery table when I walked back to
the tent. Hogan had everything arranged for the tastings.

"I can give you a hand," I said. "I've watched you do this a
zillion times. Pale ales first and then the darker varieties."

"I'm taking you up on your offer. The midday shift was
supposed to be another brewery but they cancelled at the last
minute. Good thing we brought enough brew. Sorry, Marcie.
You'll be exhausted."

"Relax. I'll be fine."

"Here's the rundown. Customers will either have a yellow
ticket or a red ticket. Yellow is five tastes and red is eight. They
purchase the tickets at that center booth just outside the beer
tents. That's where they check for ID, too. Saves us the hassle."

The next three hours were a blur as customers went through
the beer flights and I made small talk with them. I used words
like malty, smoky, sharp, spicy, musty, and my personal
favorite – complex. My head felt like mush and judging from
the expression on Hogan's face, he wasn't doing much better.

At two thirty Hogan turned to me and said, "Why don't

you take a short break? I can manage. Besides, I'm starving. Maybe they've got some of those huge pretzels somewhere. If not, I'll eat another bratwurst." He handed me a twenty and I shook my head.

"I can pay for food once in a while, you know."

"Fine as long as you don't make a habit of it."

I smiled as I headed over to the food tent. After my disastrous and short-lived marriage, I was amazed there was someone decent out there. And relieved I didn't have to face the dating scene with a list of eligible men courtesy of my mother's friends.

With a plate full of brats and pretzels, I returned to our tent and managed to scarf down the goodies while serving beer flights. Hogan took a ten-minute restroom break and returned to tell me I'd be better off trying to find a park restroom than a blue porta potty. Something I already knew.

The next two and half hours moved quickly. Maybe I was getting used to the pace of serving beer flights. Sometime around four Hogan darted out and returned with two huge funnel cakes coated in powdered sugar. We devoured them like vultures. By quarter to five everything was winding down including the Oompah music from the adjoining tent.

When the last customer, an elderly man with a long handlebar mustache, finished the final drop of his beer, Hogan turned to me. "Whew, it's over. I'll probably be pouring beer in my sleep."

"And I'll have Bavarian music playing in my ears all night. Especially 'Der Singvogel.' They must've played it a dozen times."

"Last year it was 'The Merry Wanderer.' That thing stayed in my head till Thanksgiving. I can still recite the lyrics."

I caught a whiff of my shirt and tugged on it. "I smell like a brewery."

"Yeah," he said. "I should've mentioned that. Those heady odors kind of take over. The good news is we both smell like beer. It'll dissipate in a while. At least we don't have to put glasses on racks for washing. Even though I like to be environmentally conscious, this is one of those times I'm glad we used plastic cups."

"What now?"

"Now, I go get the truck and we load up and head to Minneapolis. Those five gallon kegs are just about empty. I'll deal with them when we get back to Biscay."

"They'll be all right until late tonight?"

"Hell yes. Think of all those frat parties. Sometimes they don't even drain those kegs for days."

"What about the growlers?"

"In case you hadn't looked, we sold all of them. That's what I like about the return trip from one of these events, it's a lighter load."

We made it all the way to Wayzata, north of Minnetonka, before stretching our legs and grabbing coffee at a fast fill gas station. Driving on a two-lane freeway after dark is mind numbing. I probably would have enjoyed the greenery and small knolls had it been daylight but then again, my mind would have been too preoccupied with the case.

"I don't know about you," Hogan said, 'but if I don't see food until tomorrow, that'll be fine with me."

"No kidding. I think I ate enough to last me until Monday. I can't believe we're almost in Minneapolis. I'd better get that GPS APP going."

Thankfully Max showed me how to use the real time tracking when I first started working for him. "Like those big delivery service companies who need to monitor their drivers, these little devices come in handy in our line of work," he said. "Too bad we didn't have one when our kids got their drivers' licenses. Of course, the threat of what Doris would do if she found out they didn't go where they said they were going was enough to keep them in line."

Hogan reached over and gave my shoulder a squeeze. "While you're at it, check the weather APP and see how far away those storms are."

"Southwest. They haven't even reached Minnesota yet."

"Good."

I opened the GPS APP and followed the instructions Max had given me.

"Oh my gosh! It works! Not that I thought it wouldn't but wow, so fast!"

Hogan laughed. "Where's Wild Bill Hickok now?"

"Huh?"

"Didn't you know Wild Bill Hickok was fanatic about poker? That's what got him killed. Well, that and the fact he made many enemies trying to abolish slavery."

"I don't think Scott Byrd is that honorable. Hmm, according to this APP, he's on Lake of the Isles Parkway just as we thought. Give me a sec and I'll see exactly where."

Hogan didn't say a word while I continued to look. "Got it. I've pulled up a satellite image and it's the first house on the west side of the parkway over the bridge from Cedar Isles. Looks like there's a pull-off near the lake. We can park there and walk to the house without being seen."

"I don't think that'll be a problem. It's getting dark now."

My hands began to shake slightly and I instinctively starting tapping my foot on the floor of the truck.

"You okay?" Hogan asked.

"Uh-huh. Just getting antsy. I know all we have to do is snoop without being seen and spot the poker game from one of the downstairs windows. It's the 'not being seen' part that's giving me the jitters. I'll be fine."

"We should be getting close to that parkway in about twenty-five minutes."

I clasped my hands together and focused on breathing slowly. "We never talked about what we'd do if we got caught."

"You show them your ID and apologize for trespassing. Most people won't want any trouble. Especially if they're conducting an illegal gambling operation."

"If I didn't say it before, I'll say it now. Thanks for coming with me."

"Hey, I should be the one thanking you for doing all those beer tastings today. You must be exhausted."

"I'm too wired to notice."

Illuminated by spectacular outdoor lighting, each mansion on Lake of the Isles Parkway outdid the one before it. The Minneapolis skyline across the lake seemed to glisten like a holiday postcard, and for a moment I wondered what it felt like to be so affluent as to enjoy this view day after day. I wasn't alone in my thoughts.

"This is really mega mansion city, huh? I've always loved those Victorian homes but when I think of all the work that goes into their upkeep, I keep that love platonic," Hogan said.

"Yep. If you can't vacuum it in twenty minutes, the deal's off. And houses better be the only thing you keep platonic."

Hogan gave my shoulder another squeeze. "I'd give you a demonstration but I think you're already familiar with the product."

"I— Oh geez, we're here. Quick. It says to pull off on the right. On the lake side."

"Forget the APP, Marcie. Take a look to your left. Mercedes and Audis must be the vehicles of choice tonight."

With my eyes glued to the iPhone, I wasn't paying attention to the actual road. When I looked up, I saw what Hogan was saying. Cars were parked directly in front of one of most opulent houses I've ever seen. I imagined it was even more breathtaking in daylight, but with the lights coming through the large bay windows in front and the subtle illumination on the smaller upstairs windows, it was like looking at a fairytale.

"My God, the house even has one of those turrets. That's what they're called, aren't they?"

Hogan had pulled off the road and shut the engine. "Forget the turrets. Check out the driveway. There's a delivery vehicle parked in it. I can't tell what kind from here. Guess we'll find out soon enough."

I closed the door behind me. "Think your kegs will be safe in the truck?"

"In this neighborhood, no one's interested in stealing five-gallon empty beer kegs."

"Yeah, guess you're right."

Knowing that we'd be sneaking around in order to catch Scott in the act, I planned ahead of time. I put my ID and major credit card in a small wallet that I tucked into my jeans along with my iPhone. My gun was safely holstered to my hip where it had been all day. No way was I going to take a chance and leave it in the truck. I stashed my bag under the front seat and joined Hogan as he walked across the road toward the house.

"Remind me, what kind of car does our guy drive?" Hogan asked.

"A Mazda CX-9. Jet black to be precise. Do you see it?"

"Yeah, I think that's it behind that silver Mercedes. Come on, let's creep along the driveway and let the delivery truck hide us until we can get situated behind those bushes in front. The trees can only do so much."

It wasn't until we were directly to the side of the delivery truck that we were able to read what it said. Hogan gave my wrist a little shake and whispered, "This poker game isn't for the faint of heart if they've got the Wildflower Gourmet Food Caterers taking care of the refreshments. They're the most exorbitant caterers in Minneapolis."

"Too bad we won't get to taste anything. Not that it matters. I'm still stuffed from all that bratwurst."

We rounded the front of the catering van and were just about to duck behind a row of bushes when we heard a voice. A loud man's voice. He was coming out the side door of the three-car garage. Given the exterior lighting, it was impossible to miss us. Or him, for that matter. He was tall, heavy-set and appeared to be in his late forties or fifties. Like us, he was wearing a black T-shirt and jeans.

"That was damn good timing," he said looking straight at us. "I didn't think they'd be able to send replacements so soon. Zach and Andi will be pleased they don't have to work their butts off. When Linda got sick and Tom offered to drive her home, I thought we were really up the creek. Anyway, hurry up, the guys are rotating the hors d'oeuvres. In case no one told you, this set-up is different than what we're used to."

Hogan and I gave each other a look and the man continued.

"Not a regular meal. Not the usual table service. These are some hardcore poker players. They're got their own bar set up and two bartenders so we don't need to mess with that. All we're supposed to do is keep rotating the appetizers. We're on the clock for another two hours and then clean-up. I'm going to have myself a smoke in the truck. Oh, and whatever you do, no smoking in the house or on the grounds, understood?"

"No problem," Hogan said. "We don't smoke."

"Good. Use that side door. It'll take you into a utility room and then a pantry. Surprised I haven't seen either of you before. Then again, I usually wind up closer to St. Paul. Same deal with Zach and Andy. I'll catch up with you later."

The man kept walking, and we heard the door to the delivery truck slam shut.

"Unbelievable. Absolutely unbelievable. Remind me to thank the Willmar German Festival committee for designing T-shirts that look like the caterer's. Unless someone gets up close and personal, all they'll see are the giant WGF letters. Talk about luck, Marcie. You just stepped into it."

"Talk about mistaken identities. Wow! I never expected something like this. But we can't go in there, snap pictures, turn around and leave. We'll have to do some work and be subtle about taking out our phones. Both of us should really take pictures just to be on the safe side."

"No problem."

Hogan and I walked past the utility room, which was larger than my entire apartment, and into the pantry. A tall blond woman about my age, with her hair tied up in loose bun, was standing over a sink. Like the man from the truck, she was wearing a black T-shirt with the WGF logo on it.

"Hi! I'm Andrea. Call me Andi. You must be the replacements Wildflower sent over. Didn't think they'd find another crew so fast. Have you been working with them for long?"

I managed to answer without lying. "No. Not long. Not long at all. I'm Marcie and this is Hogan."

No sense giving fake names. I figured I had enough to worry about if someone called out my name and I didn't respond. Hogan gave her a wave and smiled. Just then, Zach came in. Also in his twenties and blond. He quickly explained that we needed to take the platters of oysters Rockefeller from the kitchen, where they were cooling, and bring them into the downstairs game room.

"The staircase is plenty wide," Zach said. "You won't have a problem. Hey, and in case Ronnie forgot to tell you, we're supposed to keep our mouths shut about this job. As far as anyone is concerned, we're catering a dinner party."

"Understood," Hogan said.

Zach scratched his head and leaned on the counter. "They've got a pretty good deal going from what I know. They host enough dinner parties so when they have poker nights no one in the neighborhood gets suspicious. Good news for us is that these affairs usually begin around six and end before eleven."

Andi shook her head in agreement. "Yeah, if they did go all night, some nosey buttinski would be bound to call the police. Mum's the word. Besides, they're good tippers. Especially if they've had a winning night."

I waited until we were out of earshot before talking. And then it was only five words.

"Hallelujah. We hit pay dirt."

I'd seen game rooms before but I wasn't prepared for what appeared to be a mini Las Vegas in some guy's basement. Four octagonal poker tables were centered in the room, each illuminated with its own Tiffany style chandelier. And each table was filled to capacity. I tried to scan the area for Scott but the dim lighting coupled with the fact that no one appeared to be looking up, made it difficult, if not impossible. With the exception of a fiery redhead who was older than my mother, I didn't see any other female players. And the only reason I spotted her was because she put her hand down and leaned back for a second.

The guy from the caterer's truck was right about the drinks. There were two bartenders who worked a circular bar that reminded me of those old, old reruns of *Cheers*. Hogan and I placed the platters of oysters Rockefeller on a long buffet table that spanned the length of the room and brought some empty platters upstairs.

"Thanks," Andi said. "They should be rinsed off before we put on new doilies and fill them again. Meanwhile you can carry the teriyaki beef sticks and orange ginger chicken downstairs. Zach just took them out of the oven."

I looked across the kitchen and could see Zach preparing some sort of puffed pastry.

He noticed me staring and immediately explained. "That's the crab Rangoon. Lump crabmeat. Fresh. Not that horrible pasty stuff they serve in Chinese restaurants. I don't know why I'm telling you this, I'm sure you're familiar with Wildflower's commitment to fresh organic foods."

"Uh-huh," I mumbled. Hogan was already at the staircase with his platter of beef and chicken and I wasted no time grabbing mine and following him.

"Is this what we're supposed to be doing all night?"

"Your guess is as good as mine, Marcie, but now's our chance. Look around. There's our guy. On the left. At ten o'clock. Next to the man with the goatee."

I wrestled my iPhone from my pocket and wedged it between my chest and the platter as I zeroed in on Scott. One click after another. My eyes moved to the phone and I froze. Damn! I must've tapped the icon for a selfie because when I looked down all I could see was the logo on my T-shirt.

"Don't move, Hogan. I've got to re-do this."

"We can't just stand here."

"I know. I know. Walk slow. Real slow."

Now my fingers were shaking and either the platter was going to hit the floor or my phone was. I felt as if I was back in the middle school cafeteria carrying my tray to the table with everyone watching.

"Just do it," Hogan whispered. "No one's looking."

Somehow, I positioned myself by the buffet table and maneuvered the phone so that I snapped a few pics of Scott without as much as batting an eyelash. Hogan, however, outdid me. He actually pretended to be taking a selfie but instead took a few photos of our culprit as well.

With our phones safely stashed in our pockets and the platters positioned on the buffet, we walked to the stairs.

Two steps up and someone tapped me on the shoulder. It was Ronnie. He must've come down the stairs while we were near the table. "Giving you two a heads-up," he said. "No photos allowed. And that selfie of yours better not appear in Facebook or Instagram. Got it?"

Hogan gave a nod and smiled. "No worries. I'll delete it as soon as I take a break if it'll make you feel better."

"You do that," Ronnie said. "Last thing we need is to lose this account. It'll probably cost us our jobs."

I opened my eyes wide and bit my lip. It's a tact that usually works when I want to fool someone into thinking I'm more innocent than I am. "We didn't know."

Ronnie stood there, arms crossed. "Now you do. Come on, we need to go back to the kitchen. The small canapes should be ready by now. Grab a plate and work your way around the room. And keep moving. Remember, no eye contact with these guys and no talking unless they ask you something. And believe me, they won't."

I'd been to enough weddings and bar mitzvahs so when I heard the word canape I pictured pigs in a blanket, crackers, cheese, and stuffed mushrooms. Instead, Hogan, Ronnie and I carried plate after plate of Indian samosas, palmiers, smoked salmon, shrimp with avocado, sausage rolls and prawn skewers.

Ronnie knew this crowd well. No one uttered a word to us.

It was as if they had a third eye somewhere that enabled them to reach for an hors d'oeuvre while clutching their cards close to their chests.

I made it a point to serve Scott's table first. My knowledge of poker was right up there with fly fishing and scuba diving but I knew if the pile of chips in front of a player was slim to none, things were not going well. That was the case with Scott. White, red, blue, green, yellow and black chips were stacked in neat piles in front of the other players but Scott was down to a handful of red chips.

I said something to Hogan about it when we walked upstairs to get more canapes but he had a different take.

"It might not mean anything until we can figure out the denomination for each color. I'll try to sneak a look."

Two more rounds, this time with assorted bruschetta, and Hogan came through. Apparently, his eyesight was better than mine.

"Red's twenty, blue's fifty, green's a hundred, and black's five hundred."

"How could you tell?"

"These are custom chips. The amount's on the front. Oh, and I saw one purple chip. It has to be for a thousand."

"No fives or tens?"

"Not in this game, honey."

CHAPTER TWENTY-ONE

I wasn't Mother Theresa but I was damn sure I was going to save Loreen Larsen from the likes of Scott Byrd. While Hogan traipsed downstairs again, this time with mini cheesecakes and mint ginger brownies, I ducked into a small guest bathroom and emailed my photos to the office. When no one was looking, I cornered him and asked if he'd do the same thing.

"Relax," he said placing his hands on my shoulders. "I already forwarded mine to your email address and Max's. I don't trust Ronnie or anyone else in this house for that matter."

"Why don't we just leave? We've got what we want. We can sneak out and make a run for your truck."

"Believe me, I'd like nothing better than to do that, but I'm afraid people will get suspicious. Maybe even think we've stolen something. It's almost eleven and the games are winding down."

"How can you be sure?"

"Caterers don't serve desserts until the party's about to end. Hang in there for a while longer and we'll walk out of here without raising any eyebrows."

"Aren't you totally exhausted?"

"Technically I'm dead on my feet but that second wind keeps me propped up."

I gave him a quick kiss and hurried into the kitchen for a dessert platter. I got a good look at Scott's buddy, Dayton Ganz, when I returned. His table was diagonal from Scott's and given the relatively small stack of red chips in front of him, his night wasn't going much better than his friend's.

Twenty minutes later, the players were folding up for the night and a few of them had already left the room.

"Yo! Marcie!" It was Zach and he elbow bumped me from behind. "Start bringing all the platters upstairs. We want to get them washed and get the hell out of here before that storm comes blowing in. I already told Hogan and he's one step ahead of you."

The storm. I had completely forgotten about the storm until he reminded me. "Um, when's that supposed to happen?"

"Not for an hour or so according to the news. Ronnie was listening from the catering truck. But hell, this is Minnesota. Anything can happen and I don't want to get stuck here. I told Andi to hustle her butt off, too."

Hustle, we did. Plates and platters to the kitchen and pantry sinks where Andi and Ronnie rinsed them. Baking pans washed by Zach and Hogan who actually looked as if they were enjoying it, and me drying everything off and running it to the truck. That's when I overheard Scott and Dayton. I was at the back of the truck, having placed two giant platters in there, when the two of them skirted by me.

"How much are you in for tonight?"

"Seven or eight. And you?"

"Half that."

"We'll recoup."

"A month's a long time."

"I don't plan on waiting that long."

"So, you're going to—"

Going to what? What are you going to do?

"Don't worry about it. I was planning on doing it anyway."

"Want me to go with you?"

"No. Easier if I do it myself. I can do it blindfolded at this point."

The voices faded and I had no idea who was saying what. I only knew what I had seen firsthand. Both of them lost a heck of a lot of money tonight. I figured one of them was on to another gambling venue. Poor Loreen. Better to find out about it now.

As the guests filtered out of the house, the Wildflower catering crew crammed all of its stuff, including the uneaten canapes, back in the truck. With the dishes done and the kitchen cleaned, Ronnie, Andi and Zach piled onto the front seats.

Ronnie leaned out the driver's side window to where Hogan and I were standing ."You did good tonight. Maybe we'll see you on another gig. Where are you parked?"

"Down that way," Hogan said pointing in the opposite direction.

"Yeah, fine. Make sure you email your hours to the office. I'll verify them when I get in this week."

"Sure. No problem."

We stood in the driveway and waited until Ronnie backed out of there, driving east on Lake of the Isles Parkway. Wiping my hands on my jeans, careful to avoid jostling my hip holster, I let out a long sigh. "I never had to work so damn hard spying on someone!"

"Talk about pulling double duty tonight. But what the hell. I may be in the wrong business. A few of those high rollers slipped me cash as they were leaving."

Hogan reached in his pocket and pulled out a handful of twenties and fifties. "What about you?"

"Only two people gave me tips. I'll probably have enough money for a cup of coffee." I reached in my pocket and pulled out two hundred-dollar bills. "You're right. We *are* in the wrong business."

Off in the distance I could hear the slight rumbling of thunder. I made a mad dash for the truck with Hogan inches behind me. As soon as we were safely inside and buckled up, he spoke.

"Guess your gambler extraordinaire is long gone, huh?"

"Yep, along with all the other high rollers. You know, I never did find out who the owner was. Did you?"

"No idea whatsoever but if you need that info, I'm sure a quick search of tax records will pull it up."

"I won't need. I'm not the police and I'm not planning on busting those guys. Got everything I need right here on this little phone." Then, as if to prove my point, I pulled up the snapshots I took. "Oh yeah. Loreen's going to pitch a fit all right."

As Hogan headed west for Chaska and then Glencoe, I fiddled around with the phone. "Remind me to take that GPS tracker off of Scott's car on Monday. I didn't want to risk it tonight."

I'm not sure if it was idle curiosity or something else, but for some reason I couldn't quite explain, I pulled up the global map to see where he was going. "What the heck. Scott's heading east on 94. He should be going west like us."

"Maybe he's going to go south on 35. That'll take him to the 494. He'll probably cut over on another road."

"No. He's not. He's heading south all right but straight to Mendota Heights on the other side of the river."

"The guy's probably on to another poker game."

"I suppose. At least Loreen can make up her own mind about him."

A light drizzle made the windshield wipers greasy but so far, the storm hadn't arrived. Leaning back in my seat I closed my eyes for a few minutes, the iPhone still clasped in my hand. When I opened my eyes, we were almost at the Chaska exit. I looked down at the phone and decided to check for any messages or emails. First, however, I wanted to know where Scott's next "casino" run was taking him.

"Oh my God, Hogan! Turn the truck around! Head east. To Mendota Heights!"

"What? What's going on? When I looked over, you were sleeping."

"Well, I woke up and Scott Byrd's headed to the Mystery Castle."

"Are you sure? That doesn't make any sense. Not the Mystery Castle. Maybe a card game in a neighboring house."

"Not a neighboring house. He's literally turning off on the only road that leads to the place. And before you say anything, I know. I know. There's absolutely no connection between him and the Mystery Castle. So why on earth is he going there?"

"Got to admit, I'm on your side as far as thinking goes. Why so late at night? And with a storm coming?"

Hogan got off the nearest exit and headed east. The rain was picking up a little but not much. That changed, however, when we reached Richfield, just south of Minneapolis. The drops on the windshield weren't sporadic anymore and the wipers kept a steady rhythm. Hogan gave me a nudge. "Want to sing a chorus of "Der Singvogel?" I think it's the same beat as the wiper blades."

"Very funny. I was hoping to forget that song. I'm keeping an eye on Scott's GPS in case he turns around or something."

"Good idea."

The map indicator showed his position and it didn't budge.

"If there's a damn poker game going on in that place, I swear I'll bite my own nose," I said.

"Don't do that. It's way too cute. If the rain doesn't get any heavier we should be there in a half hour. Traffic's real light. We're the only knuckleheads out here."

The rain got a bit heavier but the winds were holding off. With any luck, that storm would either skirt us or simply turn into an annoying nuisance. I stared at the iPhone again. Scott hadn't budged.

"Seriously. What *is* that guy doing there?"

Hogan made a grunting noise and shrugged. I looked

down at the phone again. "Geez, a missed call. Max. No voice mail. Honestly, he's getting worse than my mother with the worrying. I told him I'd call but I'm not doing it so late at night."

"You're the daughter of his best friend. I imagine in some ways you're like family to him."

"Yeah. I feel the same way, too. But I'm a gun-toting licensed private eye, not some silly little debutant."

"Face it. You're only carrying a gun because he insisted on it. And as for a debutant...wouldn't know."

"Heck. I wasn't even a cheerleader."

A sudden gust of wind moved the truck toward the guardrail and I jumped. "Maybe that storm *is* getting closer."

"That's okay. We're getting closer, too. We should be in Mendota Heights in about fifteen to twenty minutes, give or take."

"It's really unlikely. Absurd even. But what if there really is some sort of a card game going on? I doubt we'll pass for caterers this time. We'll have to see if Minerva's key works and sneak in. If not, I'll be stuck taking photos of the license plates and working with Max to ID the owners."

"Whoa. Backtrack a minute. Minerva's key? I thought it was to Helena's apartment," Hogan said.

"It was. I mean, it is. It might also be a master key. Minerva wasn't sure."

"I'll say one thing, Marcie. Dating you has been anything but boring. Check that APP again, will you? Has our guy made a move?"

"Nope. He may be playing poker after all. The indicator hasn't moved."

The more I thought about it, the more I was convinced someone was using the Mystery Castle as a casino. It made sense in a way. The place was secluded. Especially at night. And there'd be no neighbors to complain. The first and only name that sprung to mind was Anna Gainson. She was so scared of the financial future of the castle that she convinced Helena to turn it over to the National Park Service and not wait to leave the request in a will.

By the time Hogan turned onto the castle's long driveway, I had tried, convicted and sentenced Anna. Unfortunately, I was a lousy prosecutor.

Not a single car was in view when we drove to the front of the Mystery Castle. The only thing the beams from Hogan's headlights picked up were the sheets of rain as he slowed to a crawl.

"Maybe everyone's parked around back by the Garden Grotto. I'm staring at the GPS tracker and that CX-9 is definitely here."

"If you say so. I'll keep the truck on low beams and pull around back."

I held my breath as Hogan slowly followed the circular driveway to the rear of the building. At first, I didn't see anything. The rain was too heavy. Then, off to the side of Garden Grotto, a few yards from a large tree was Scott's jet-black Mazda CX-9. I shut my phone and reached for Hogan's arm.

"I know this is ridiculous, but please drive over there to make sure Scott isn't lying dead in the car."

"And to think, most people are happy going to the movies or bowling when they're dating. I get to scope out sports cars for dead bodies."

CHAPTER TWENTY-TWO

"There's a flashlight in the glove compartment," Hogan said. He pulled up behind the Mazda and got out of the truck. I watched as he peered into the vehicle, the flashlight beam moving back and forth. Then, of all things, he opened the driver side door. Scott had left his car unlocked. The truck lid popped open (Hogan's doing) and he shone the light in there before plopping his soaking wet body back in the front seat of the truck.

"No dead bodies. You can relax."

I wasn't cold but I rubbed my arms, hands crossed over my chest. "None of this adds up. I really expected some sort of covert card game. Instead, Scott Byrd is what? Breaking and entering a national park service museum? We can't turn around and drive back. Not now. We've got to find out what he's up to. For all we know, there might've been a game here and it ended or got cancelled because of the storm."

"You told me the place has a security system. If there was some sort of gambling operation going on, it had to be orchestrated by someone very familiar with the castle. Familiar enough to know the code to disarm the system. And you're right. I can't imagine how your little gambling buddy fits in to all of this."

A sudden flash of lightning followed by an enormous crack of thunder jolted me and I gasped. Hogan reached over grabbed my wrist. "It's okay. We've had worse storms. So, I suppose you're hell bent for leather to get in there, huh?"

"Uh-huh. It's too dangerous to be driving anyhow. I just hope I'm holding a master key. Unless we want to kill ourselves going down that embankment to the grotto, we need to park around the other side of the building and use the kitchen entrance. That's how Sydelle and I got in."

"What if the alarm goes off and the police arrive?" he asked.

"I explain who I am and tell them I'm investigating a possible homicide. I tell them I got a tip and followed Scott to this location. Don't worry. I seriously doubt we'll hear any alarms or they'd be going off by now."

"And to think, only a day ago my biggest concern was whether I had enough beer for the tasting. Uh, what if your key doesn't work?"

"We'll wait it out by Scott's car. I doubt he plans on camping out in that place for the night."

Hogan parked the truck as close to the kitchen entrance as possible and we made a run for it. The wind was at our faces and the rain was relentless. At least the timing between the lightning and thunder meant the major part of the storm was still a ways away.

Small coach lamps on either side of the door gave off enough light for me to try the key. It was a modern dead bolt lock made to look like one of those old Victorian ones, and my key opened it on the first turn. I stood like a statue waiting for an alarm in case Scott had re-armed it. Five or ten seconds went by and no sound.

"Now what?" Hogan whispered closing the door behind him.

"I need a minute to think."

"Now you need a minute? You've had the entire drive over

here since we left Chaska."

"I'm still new at this."

"Okay. Didn't mean to upset you. Take a minute. I don't think anyone is in this kitchen."

The only light in the room came from a small fixture above one of the sinks. There were also a few nightlights at ankle level. I tiptoed lightly as I moved about.

"I'm all right," I said. "My eyes are getting used to the semi-darkness."

"Guess they wanted to be sure the mice would find their way around."

"Ew."

Hogan took a step toward me. "If we knew what the heck Scott was doing in this house, we might have a better idea where he is. It might as well be Buckingham Palace; the place is so big."

"Big, but not impossible. Wallis, Max's brother-in-law, studied the blueprint Phoebe sent us and he found a hidden cylindrical staircase in the kitchen. We can get upstairs without making any noise. The regular staircases are bound to creak."

"Do you know where the hidden one is?"

"Wallis said it was behind a door but the only door I see goes to the root cellar and grotto."

Hogan turned on his flashlight and waved it around the kitchen. "Some of these cabinets go all the way to the floor. Let's start opening them."

One by one we opened cabinets to reveal dishes, linens and dry goods. Finally, we found one that opened to a plain wooden wall. I grabbed Hogan's shoulder and shook it.

"That's it. That's it. Wallis said to look for a release mechanism."

"You mean like this?"

Hogan pushed a small button on the inner frame and the wall spun around revealing a very steep ladder.

"Staircase my butt," he said. "This night keeps getting better and better."

I wondered, after this Nancy Drew-ish escapade, if he'd still want to keep dating me. I swiped the hair from my face and shoved that thought to the back of my mind. "Um, I'd rather go first. I have a creepy feeling about being the last one up the stairs. Like something's going to grab my leg or ankle. Truth is, I watched too many horror movies as a kid."

"Whatever you do, don't freak out and reach for your gun. Unless…oh never mind. Let's get going."

I turned to say something to Hogan but instead stared at the lightning strikes visible from the small basement windows that were level to the ground. The storm was definitely getting closer. Maybe it was because we were below ground or maybe it was because this castle was so well built, but I never heard the thunder and any shaking that I may have felt came from my own body and not the sonic thunder boom.

The beam from the flashlight was bright enough for me to see the rungs of the ladder. I reached up, gripped the one over my head and began to climb. In seconds the light had turned into a strobe. Hogan was moving right behind me. The air was stale and the odor was musty as I grasped the next rung.

"You okay, Marcie?"

"There's no way out. We'll have to go back down. Maybe the stairwell was in the blueprints but it was never completed."

"Take the palms of your hands and feel the sides of the wall for any indentations. Then push."

I felt like the jerk of the century. If there was a release mechanism to get in, there had to be one to get out. Sure enough, I pushed and the ladder began to spin. "I don't like this at all. Not at all. The next case I take better be a lost dog or cat."

Hogan chuckled. "This is ingenious. Absolutely ingenious. The cylinder seems to cut in half and has two separate pivots."

Why is it men are so fascinated with mechanical devices?

"We're on the first floor. In a foyer, I think."

The wooden paneling looked familiar as I stepped off the ladder. Dimly lit wall sconces cast an eerie light on the dining room, a few feet from where we were standing.

"The Casbah rooms are to the left and the day room is on the other side," Hogan said. "I've got a good picture of this place in my mind."

"Me, too. Like 'Der Singvogel.' One of those things you can't get out of your mind. Shh! Do you hear that?"

"It doesn't sound like footsteps. Probably the house settling."

"The house settling? It's had over a hundred years to do that."

"Joints and floorboards creak all the time. Tree roots, water, anything can add to a house settling, or worse yet, sagging."

The light show was still going on outside and sudden flashes blinded us momentarily. Rumbles of thunder came in waves. We decided to walk through the day room and adjoining corridors before venturing into the Casbah section. Was Scott meeting someone here? And if so, then where was their car? In a bizarre sort of way, the Casbah rooms would make great venues for clandestine poker games. Each one perfectly equipped with its own table, or in this case, rug.

"I don't hear anyone moving about, do you?" Hogan asked.

"No."

We kept walking.

The wall lamps in the Casbah rooms were illuminated in different colors. Red, orange and yellow. A soft pounding sound made us both freeze on the spot but it was only rain from one of the outside gutters. We went back to the main foyer barely making a sound.

"He must be upstairs." Hogan leaned against the wall and sighed. "Want to flip a coin? Heads, the main staircase, tails the back one."

"You're kidding, aren't you?"

A series of lightning flashes illuminated the foyer, the dining room and the small corridor to our right. Seconds later, everything went black.

"The power's out, Hogan. The lightning must've hit a

transformer. Can you turn on your flashlight?"

There was no answer. "Hogan, your flashlight. Turn it on. I can't see anything. Hogan? Hogan?"

A second flash of lightning. And a third. All within nanoseconds. I whipped my head around to see if Hogan had moved from his spot against the wall but all I saw was an empty foyer.

"This isn't funny, Hogan. Where are you?"

I wanted to scream his name loud enough to be heard in the next county but I knew better than that. I clasped my hands together and tried to process what was going on. He was leaning against the wall and…And what? The paneling. Damn it. The paneling. What was it Max said about secret passages in this place? Discernable from the gaps in the paneling.

Like a madwoman, I reached for my iPhone, turned on the flashlight and shone it against the walls. Then I began to tap, press and thud, forgetting momentarily that I was supposed to be quiet. At that moment I didn't give a hoot about Scott or his gambling impulses. All I wanted to do was find my boyfriend before he got trapped somewhere.

My hands began to shake and my right foot was tapping involuntarily on the floor. I felt for my gun, more out of habit than need, and I forced myself to take slow deep breaths. I knew this wasn't a horror movie, or worse yet, a sci-fi where he'd be sucked into another dimension never to be heard from again, but that was little consolation with the house creaking, the wind and rain hitting the windows and Scott Byrd in here doing God-knows-what.

With my hand pressed firmly against the holstered gun, I walked to the dining room. That's when I heard footsteps. Loud and clear. Not creaking. Not settling. Footsteps. Footsteps above my head. Somehow Hogan must've stumbled upon another stairwell behind the paneled opening and it was his only way out.

I forced myself to walk toward the main staircase. He was bound to be on the second floor. The footsteps were still overhead and I moved quickly. The little flashlight on my iPhone was surprisingly bright and I focused the light on the wide wooden steps. The upstairs corridor strobed with lightning flashes visible from the bedroom windows since the doors to all those rooms were wide open. Up until now the flashes were sporadic, coupled with rain and wind. Then, in an instant, I thought I'd lose my vision permanently.

A flash so bright lit up the area like a thermonuclear blast. The phone fell from my hand and made a dull thud on the floor. I immediately bent down and reached for it but instead my hand rested on the top of Hogan's shoe.

"Oh, thank God!" I whispered. "You had me scared out of my wits. Turn on your flashlight. I dropped mine."

As I stood up, two hands pressed into my shoulders and I caught the faint aroma of bayberry.

CHAPTER TWENTY-THREE

We were standing inches from the staircase. The lightning was flickering and we could see each other without any need for flashlights. One solid shove and I'd be the next Scarlett O'Hara. Only this staircase wasn't circular and I wasn't laden down with a heavy dress to prevent me from making a move.

I kicked Scott's knee with all the force I could muster and positioned myself against the wall. "If you know what's good for you, you'll tell me who you are and what you're doing here," I said.

Yikes. I think that was a line in some movie. Probably the Hallmark Mystery Channel.

"Why? What do you think you're going to do? Yell for your friend?"

"No. Aim in the dark for your chest. But I'm warning you, I tend to aim low."

By now I had my Ruger LC9 drawn and I wasn't budging. Neither was Scott.

"Hey, Hey, calm down. I'm not armed. Look! I'll even put my hands in the air if that'll make you feel any better."

What'll make me feel better is for Hogan to show up but apparently that's not happening any time soon.

"Stand absolutely still and answer my question."

"What kind of lunatic are you?" he asked.

"The kind with a gun." *And the kind who's watched so many B movies I could write the script.* "Now answer my question."

"Scott. How's that? My name's Scott. Scott Byrd."

"And you just happen to be poking around the Mystery Castle late at night? What happened? Did you lose your tour guide?"

"I happen to have a connection with someone who works here. What's your excuse?"

So that's the link. But who? I should've spent more time helping Max with those background checks.

"I'm a private investigator. Tell me, were you in on it together? You and your connection? Did you plan this together?"

"Plan what?"

"Don't be smug. Helena Heatherbrae didn't die of natural causes."

"And you think I killed her? That's what you're investigating? Helena's death? The woman was as old as Methuselah."

"Not quite."

The hallway sconces began to flicker and for a moment I thought the power was about to come back. Unfortunately, it didn't. But it did allow me to see where my iPhone had landed. Directly underneath Scott's feet.

"Listen carefully," I said. "Gently, and I mean 'gently,' kick that phone toward me."

He looked down and gave the phone a nudge. It moved slightly and he nudged it again until it was within my reach. I bent down slowly, still aiming the gun at him, and retrieved my phone.

"Are you calling the police? Because if you are, maybe we can talk."

I wasn't planning on calling the police. Not yet or maybe

not at all. I wasn't sure. I'd have to explain why I was trespassing, too. Even if the police believed me about investigating a possible homicide, they'd want to know what tip I had gotten. That's where it gets blurry.

I swallowed whatever moisture was in my mouth. "Okay. Talk. Tell me what you're doing here. I'll find out anyway, you know."

"Do you have to have that gun pointed at me?"

"I don't have to, but I'm going to."

Because the minute I lower this gun you'll probably charge at me.

"Fine. If you must know, I was taking a few inconsequential items."

"Is that the politically correct way of saying 'stealing some irreplaceable valuables'?"

"Nothing that was going to be missed. And nothing from the Mystery Castle itself. I had no intention of going after any of that artwork or those fine arts pieces. I took small little things from Helena's apartment."

"Like what?"

As if I didn't know.

"Helena collected really weird stuff. Her showcases were crammed full of crap – pins made out of people's hair, dead beetles all painted up and posed, all sorts of things no one would give a rat's ass about."

"But you did."

"Look. She didn't even know anything was missing. The woman couldn't see a foot in front of her. And it wasn't as if we're talking priceless heirlooms for her family. She had no family."

"And you thought that entitled you to take some of her possessions?"

"Know what's ironic? I friggin' lost money doing that. Bought two lottery tickets and one of them turned out to be a five-thousand-dollar winner. Lost the winning ticket somewhere between her living room and the attic. The attic's was how I got in. Like I told you, I have a relationship with someone who knows every inch of this place blindfolded. And I know my way around here pretty well myself."

"What was it you were after?"

"I know a guy who knows a guy. Old story. But this one collects those Indian carvings. Indian like cowboys and Indians. Not the other kind. Anyway, some of those things are worth a bundle. That's all I've ever taken. And that's why I'm here tonight. I can prove it. Here, see for yourself."

The intermittent flickering from the wall sconces gave off enough light for me to see him reaching into one of his pockets. I moved closer, this time pointing the gun right at his chest.

Scott opened his fist and held out something. With my free hand, I clicked the iPhone and beamed the light into his palm. Sure enough, he was holding an intricate carving of a bison. I couldn't tell what semi-precious stone it was, but it didn't matter. I had the answer to more than one question tonight.

I hate to break it to you, Loreen, but your fiancé's a gambler and a petty thief. Better not let him loose with those credit cards.

I took a breath and didn't take my eyes off of him. "It's a Saturday night. Late. In the middle of a storm. You mean to tell me you came out here just to steal that little trinket?"

"This little trinket's worth more than most people's cars. And why'd you come out here? Same could be said about you."

I stood still and didn't say a word. It was a technique I remembered from one of my criminal justice classes. Stay silent and the perpetrator will keep talking. Darned if my instructor wasn't right. Scott groaned a few times and continued.

"Oh hell. Don't tell me. You got a tip the murderer was in here. Well I'm not him. I had a good thing going. Helena spent most of her time scaring the daylights out of the visitors. The way she sat on that couch in the front room. It was a wonder they let visitors in at all. Now with her gone, it's only a matter of time before they open up her sanctum to visitors. No more easy daytime looting. Don't you get it? I had no reason to knock her off."

The lights flickered on again and I swore I heard a noise from the far end of the hallway. Scott heard it, too.

"I hope to God it's your friend, lady, and not the damn killer."

"It's the house settling," I said, certain Hogan had finally found his way out of whatever passageway he stumbled into.

"Sure. Like it hasn't had a century to do that."

I tried not to laugh. At least I wasn't the only one who poo-pooed the idea of an old house settling. "I want to know how you got in here to begin with. Which employee gave you a key?"

"Sorry, I'm not about to nark on anyone and you're not about to shoot me in cold blood for an answer."

Prissy little know-it-all. He was right. Self-defense, yes. Inquiry, no.

"You're not really worried about that noise being the killer," I said. "Because you know who the killer is – the person who gave you the key."

"What? No. No one gave me key. I—"

The noise got louder and more recognizable. Someone was walking toward us. Only they were coming from the opposite direction from where I last saw Hogan. I gripped the Ruger tighter and turned my eyes to the far end of the hall.

"Tell me the damn truth now, Scott. Who else was in the car with you? Who else is in here with you?"

"Geez! No one. No one but me. If you must know, a friend of mine offered to come with me but I told him no. He went his own way and here I am."

That had to be the conversation I overheard while I was standing next to the catering van a few hours ago. Maybe the guy was telling me the truth after all.

"All right. Move against the wall opposite the staircase and don't make a move."

Scott did as I said. My gun was now pointed at his side and both of us held still as the creaking sounds got closer.

"Footsteps." I whispered.

I stared past Scott and waited. If it was Hogan, he'd say or do something. Unless he didn't realize who we were. Then, as audible as the footsteps were, they ended abruptly. I aimed the beam of my flashlight directly at the hallway but it was completely empty.

"I agree with you," Scott said. "It's the house settling."

Either that or Freddy Krueger's found a new playground.

All of sudden, I heard another noise. The humming sound Hogan makes when he's driving. He stepped out from one of the bedrooms and charged toward us.

"Marcie, are you all right?"

"You don't need to take out your gun, too," Scott shouted before I could answer. "Rizzoli over here is making sure I don't budge."

Hogan's flashlight was in his pocket and his hand was resting over it. In the semi-darkness Scott figured it was a gun. I wasn't about to change that.

"Yeah, it's okay, Hogan. You can keep your gun right where it is. Meet our resident thief, Scott Byrd. He's been pilfering valuables from Helena Heatherbrae's apartment. And why he chose tonight of all nights beats the hell out of me."

"I told you," Scott whined. "I had a deal with a guy. Look, why don't you just take this carving and call it a night."

"If I make any calls," I said, "They'll be to the police. And let me remind you, we're investigators. Not thieves. And you're still not off the hook regarding Helena."

"Look, I was just as upset about her, uh, passing as the next guy. Maybe more. I didn't want to see my secret cache go under lock and key for some tourists. And getting me arrested isn't going to get you any closer to digging up the dirt on her death. I'll put that carving back where it came from if it makes you feel any better."

I had to admit, the guy had chutzpah. And what Loreen saw in him I'd never know. Of course, I'm hardly the one to make judgment calls since my ex could probably hold a world's record for cheating. Then again, he didn't commit any robberies.

Hogan leaned over and whispered in my ear. "It's our best bet. We don't need to spend the night at a police station. We got what we needed."

I gave Scott a kick with my foot and cleared my throat. "Fine. Since you know your way around here blindfolded, lead us to Helena's apartment and put that thing back. No tricks. Wouldn't want to be off with my aim tonight."

"Easy. Easy. It's just down the hall."

Minnesota storms usually unleash their fury and disappear within an hour or so. This one decided to camp out for the night and continued to give us a lightning show as we made our way down the corridor and into Helena's apartment. The only good news was that the flickering stopped and the power came back on. At least for the time being. Scott unlocked her door and we all stepped inside.

"Smells like cigarette smoke in here, doesn't it?" he said. "Got news for you. I don't smoke."

CHAPTER TWENTY-FOUR

Hogan and I watched as Scott approached the showcase in the living room, opened it up and returned the bison along with a few other treasures he had lifted.

"You mean to tell me that when you were in here to snatch that carving you didn't smell anything?" I asked.

"Uh-huh. Just stale old lady smell."

This guy has absolutely no couth.

"It's not cigarette smoke," Hogan said. "It's the ozone from the storm. Sometimes it's a sweet smell, sometimes foul."

I was no longer pointing my gun at Scott but I didn't holster it either. "You said you usually got in through the attic. Someone had to show you. Which employee was it?"

Scott clasped his hands together and bent his head. Finally, he looked me straight in the eye. "I never said anything about an employee. You want to have me arrested, go ahead. What can you really prove? Petty theft? I'll own up to taking a few things that weren't worth a dime and who'll know the difference? You're not interested in me. You said so yourself. You're interested in finding a killer. And like I told you, I'm not your guy."

I knew he was right. I also knew I was in as much of a trap as he was. My only way out was to bluff him, but exactly how I was going to fool an experienced poker player was anyone's guess.

"So," he said. "Am I free to go or what?"

"Not exactly." Hogan's voice was sharp and cold. I don't know about Scott, but it made me shudder for a second. "Here's what you're going to do. Come Monday morning, you're going to walk yourself into the Mendota Heights Police Department and confess to that petty pilfering. Tell them you had a change of heart after hearing a good sermon on Sunday. Tell them you were feeling guilty. Tell them whatever the heck you want, but so help me if you don't admit to what you've done, we'll do it for you. Only we'll have a neat little spreadsheet with the information and monetary values of all those items. Even if we have to fabricate it. By the time the police get through with their investigation, you'll be growing gray hair."

"If I don't go and you try to have me arrested, I'll deny everything."

I smiled and waved my iPhone. "Not likely. Not only can I aim a gun, I'm pretty darn good with the camera. And this one has night settings."

If Scott didn't look ghostly in the dim lighting, he certainly looked it after I put the phone back in my pocket.

"And one more thing." I said. "We're all leaving here together. We'll go out the way you came in. And since you disarmed the security system, making it a whole lot easier for us, you can rearm it in case another thief decides to go for some finer art."

"Okay. Okay."

Scott looked worn out and annoyed as we left the apartment. I made sure Helena's door was locked before the three of us proceeded down the main staircase.

"I came in from the side door, through the kitchen," he said. "The security panel's located there but you don't need me to tell you that."

"No," Hogan replied. "We don't. But what we do need is for you to tell us the code you used. You see, these systems are set up with more than one code. Like residential houses. You know, baby sitter codes, pet sitter codes…some are scheduled to run a week, others can run for months at a time. Don't expect to be breaking in here any time soon. Our office will be calling the alarm company and cancelling your free entrance to the castle."

Scott didn't say a word as we returned to the kitchen. This time via the normal route. It was only when we got to the outside door that he spoke.

"Nineteen thirty-six. Must've been a hell of a year."

Hogan and I watched closely as Scott punched in the numbers. Nineteen thirty-six. The alarm started to beep its warning. Outside the rain was coming down steadily but the lightning and thunder had moved further east. I grabbed Scott by the wrist and waited.

"What? You heard the code," he said.

"Um, actually there's something else. Your choice. Hand over the key to the police or give it to us. If you don't choose to do either, we'll have no choice but to offer up evidence regarding your thefts."

Scott reached in his pocket and slapped the key in my hand. "How do I really know you're not thieves as well?"

Hogan laughed. "Because we'd be after those priceless tapestries in the hallways."

"Here," I said pulling out a business card from my jeans' pocket. "I always keep a few of these with me."

Under the coach light, Scott was able to read the card.

"New Ulm. Are you serious? I live in New Ulm."

"Really? What are the chances of that? Maybe we'll run into each other. You never know."

"I don't suppose you're going to follow me home, are you?"

Hogan shrugged. "Depends on the route you take."

"Chaska to Glencoe and south. I don't need to be eyeballing my rear-view mirror wondering if the two of you are on my tail."

Hogan's voice was surprisingly gruff. "No need to wonder. We're taking another way back."

Scott turned and walked to his car.

"Wait!" I shouted. "I have one more question for you. Do you like Tootsie roll pops?"

"Tootsie roll pops? That kid's candy? Why? Are you offering me some for the ride back? Save yourself the trouble. I already have one dental implant. Don't need another."

The conversation ended right there. Hogan and I watched as Scott got into his car and headed out the driveway. I gave Hogan's arm a slight shake.

"That answers one nagging question Max and I had. Scott wasn't the one who dropped the Tootsie roll pop in Helena's bedroom. Whoever did, was right by the bed and it wasn't our gambler turned thief."

"So much for that clue. What a hellish night. I still can't believe it. One minute I'm talking to you and the next minute I'm in the passageway from beyond. Talk about being freaked."

"What about me? I'm still shaking from having you disappear in front of my eyes," I said.

"But I re-appeared right in time."

"I'll say. You pulled off an Academy Award winning acting scene."

"Let's keep our fingers crossed Scott doesn't ever wind up in Biscay for a micro-brewery beer tasting."

Hogan held the door to his truck open and I got in. "How did you stay so calm?" I asked. "My knees were rattling and I was scared the gun was going to go off."

"You could've fooled me. You seemed pretty darn composed yourself."

"I wasn't. I literally bumped into him on top of the staircase and thought it was you. Where were you? What happened? I was going out of my mind figuring you were trapped behind a wall or something."

"It was like I wound up in one of those old Abbott and

Costello movies. The ones where Lou Costello vanishes behind walls or bookcases. Anyway, the last thing I remembered before finding myself in a very narrow passageway, was stepping on some sort of release button on the floor next to the wall. That portion of the wall was on a pivot, too. Like Helena's bookcase. I stumbled back, lost my balance but didn't fall. The wall closed in front of me and I was wedged in a long narrow space. Good thing I had a flashlight. I tried to find another release button but couldn't so I followed the passage down a ways where it ended at another ladder. That took me to one of the bedrooms upstairs. Holy hell! What diabolical architect built that place!"

I reached across the gear shifter and gave his arm a squeeze. "I'm glad you're in one piece. All kinds of awful thoughts were going through my mind and I couldn't stop them."

"It's okay. We're both fine. And like I told you back at the castle, you got what you were looking for – proof of Scott's whereabouts for his fiancée."

"His soon to be ex- fiancée, I imagine. Um, do you believe him? About not being the one who was responsible for Helena's death? I think he told us the truth. Helena would've had to catch him in the act and there was no way he could have killed her without leaving some evidence on the body. Bruises, cuts, you know. And besides, it was like he said. He had a good thing going and her death would've put a stop to it eventually."

"Yeah, I don't think he's your killer either. From what you told me, Arletta and Minerva were the only ones who were in the castle at the time of her death. Scott admitted to sneaking into the apartment during regular hours when the tourists were moseying through the place. Sure, he had a key and probably used it once he verified Helena was in the day room. But he could only use the key when there was no one on that second floor. Otherwise, he had to unlock that attic door and traipse through there."

"If you ever get tired of running a brewery, I know a great detective agency that would hire you in a heartbeat."

"No thanks. I'm totally worn out from all the suspense. You

must be exhausted, too."

"I'm going to need toothpicks to keep my eyes open," I grumbled.

"About that, it's still raining and we're two hours to my place. How about if we find a decent hotel and call it a night? The airport's pretty close so we won't have any trouble."

"You won't get any argument from me. As long as it's not cucaracha heaven."

"Don't worry about that. I like my creature comforts and that includes not getting bitten by bed bugs."

We drove a short distance south and sure enough found a Courtyard by Marriott. They had a few cancellations due to the storm so we were able to get a standard room with a king size bed a few doors down from the lobby. It had a minibar with assorted snacks and a variety of beverages including three choices of bottled water.

"I'm dying to tear off my clothes and get under the covers but I absolutely reek," I said. "The beer, the brats, the sweat, the rain…I've got to take a shower."

Hogan tore off his T-shirt and waved it under his nose. "I smell like the Minneapolis city dump, so don't feel bad. Want to share that shower?"

It was by far, the best part of the day. And night. The warm water washing over us and the aroma of lemon sage soap on our bodies instead of stale beer. When we tucked ourselves under the covers we were asleep within seconds of Hogan turning off the lamp.

I woke the next morning to the sound of someone coming in the door and before I could let out a scream or reach for my gun in the nightstand drawer, I realized it was Hogan. He was juggling two coffees and a paper bag. He also had something under his arms.

"Morning, Marcie. I thought you might want a cup of coffee. Also got the breakfast bag to go – bagels, donuts and apples. Oh, and before I forget, look what I bought!"

He held up two T-shirts with a map of the state that read,

"Minnesota, The Land of 10,000 Lakes."

"I don't know about you, but there's no way I could put on my T-shirt from yesterday. If they sold underwear, I would've bought that, too. We'll have to rough it as far as that goes. At least we won't offend anyone within close range."

We ate our breakfasts, got washed up and headed back to Biscay, stopping only for gas and a snack near Eden Prairie before getting on the 212 to Glencoe. The rain had ended sometime after our arrival at the hotel and before late morning when we woke up. The roads were still wet but nothing that slowed down traffic.

"I'm still reeling," I said, "about tracking Scott to the Mystery Castle. I thought our night was over when we walked out of that house on Lake of the Isles Parkway."

"Yeah, me, too."

"Max is going to have a conniption fit, you know. Insisting I should've called the police and sent them into the castle. But then I would've had a tough time explaining to the police why I was following Scott in the first place. You know how they verify everything. Scott would've found out Loreen had hired me. This way, she'll have the evidence and she can decide what to do."

"I'm sure Max will understand."

"Speaking of Max, I've got to remind myself to call him when I get home later today. Maybe he was able to dig up more info on those background checks. Too bad I couldn't get Scott to fess up and tell me who his connection was. And there's something else. He mentioned losing a lottery ticket so we can assume the one you found in the attic was his. Only that one wasn't a winner."

Hogan stretched out his arm gave my neck a quick rub. "I was thinking the same thing. He must've dropped another one somewhere between the attic and Helena's apartment."

"Oh my gosh. Arletta! It might explain Arletta's blue leather Fendi bag. I'll bet anything she came across that lottery ticket, knew it couldn't've been Helena's and when it turned out to be a winner, she went and bought herself something extravagant. Never bothering to mention someone might've been in Helena's apartment."

"It doesn't matter, Marcie. Not really. You know *who* that someone was. It's the Tootsie pop someone you need to find."

"Nate checked that lollipop for prints, you know. Nothing useable."

"Figures."

Even though I had gotten a wonderful night's sleep at the hotel, I dozed on and off until we got to Glencoe. Hogan was humming that silly Der Singvogel tune and I opened my eyes.

"Where are we?"

"A few miles from the Crooked Eye."

"Already? I can't believe I slept all that way."

"You're more tired than you realize. When I'm done at the Crooked Eye, I'll probably crash until morning. Too bad you can't stay the night."

"I know. Byron's probably pacing all over the place by now. He's usually fine for a day without me but it feels like I've been gone for weeks."

"I'm off next Sunday and Monday. He won't have to be alone next weekend. At least Foxy and Lady have a good pet sitter. Isn't there anyone in your complex that you trust?"

I started laughing and couldn't stop. "My complex is a revolving door. Seriously. Every day there's a new U-Haul pulling up to load or unload."

Hogan was about to say something when my phone rang, catching us both by surprise. In retrospect, I should've realized who it was. It was a Sunday morning and the unofficial check-in time with my mother.

"Marcie! I wasn't about to wait for you to call me or I'll be in my grave. It's afternoon already. What are you up to?"

"Um, hi Mom! I'm actually coming back from breakfast (not quite a lie) with Hogan. Can I call you later?"

"Is everything all right? I heard there was a storm up your way. It was on the Weather Channel."

"Everything's fine. Just your average run-of-the-mill Minnesota storms. I'll talk to you tonight. Promise. Love you."

There were at least seven or eight cars in the Crooked Eye parking lot when Hogan pulled in. He leaned over, put his arm around me and gave me a long, tender kiss. "I wish I didn't have to unload this stuff and start working."

"I could help, you know."

"Nah, you've got enough on your plate. We'll talk tonight and next weekend will be here before we know it."

"I've still got a murderer to catch. This was just the warm-up act."

"Don't remind me. Be careful, will you?"

We kissed again before I headed to my car and back to New Ulm. At least I was able to close one investigation this weekend, but finding Scott at the Mystery Castle only left me with more questions.

CHAPTER TWENTY-FIVE

I handed Max a small paper bag with a French cruller in it when I got to work the following day.

"Before I tell you what happened this weekend, I thought I'd better bring you a peace offering."

"Uh-oh. Don't tell me something went wrong on that stake-out of yours. After my phone call to you, I got your text. You know how I am about those things. I can never figure them out. At least I recognized the word 'Okay' so I stopped worrying. I knew I'd find out more when I saw you on Monday. So, what awful catastrophe are we looking at?"

"Oh no. Nothing like that. In fact, parts of the evening were quite humorous. Hogan and I followed the GPS tracker, which, by the way, I removed from Scott's car before I came to work today. It was still parked at his house. Thanks for buying the good kind."

"Any time. So, go on."

"That tracker led us straight to the location of that high stakes poker game on Isle of the Lakes Parkway. You should've seen the place. Remind me to be rich someday."

"You got inside?"

"Oh yeah. We were mistaken for the catering crew and wound up serving hors d'oeuvres all evening. The good news was that I took lots of photos of Scott Byrd gambling his money away. Loreen Larsen's going to have second thoughts about her fiancé when she sees the evidence."

Max took a giant bite of the cruller and wiped his lip with the side of his hand. "So why the peace offering?"

"The second part of the evening was a little more dramatic."

"You're killing me. Get to the point."

"Scott's the one who's been stealing those Native American carvings from Helena's apartment at the Mystery Castle."

"What? How on earth did you find that out? Was he soused so bad he told you?"

"Not exactly. Hogan and I were on our way back to Biscay when I noticed Scott's whereabouts on the tracker. He was at the Mystery Castle."

"So, you followed him."

"I had to. I mean, I—"

"It's okay. I would've done the same thing myself. Only not in a dangerous storm. It was all over the news."

It was weird but I felt as if I was back in the tenth grade explaining to my parents why I broke curfew.

"It was only drizzling when we drove to Mendota Heights. The storm didn't actually hit until we were in the castle. Minerva's key turned out to be a master key after all."

I went on to tell Max every single detail from Hogan getting trapped in the wall to Scott offering to bribe me with a carved bison.

"This really was worth two crullers," he said.

"Very funny. And there's more."

Max motioned for me to take a seat. "It's like watching a recital. Sit down already. I've got a feeling this could take a while."

"Scott's not our Tootsie roll guy. Someone else was in there. Oh, and did I tell you he agreed to turn himself in to the Mendota Heights Police Department today?"

"I'll believe it when I get a call. You were lucky, you know. You could've been injured or much worse in that castle. And don't think because you carry a weapon, it means you can take chances. He might not have been alone."

"I know. I know."

"And Hogan? He must not have been too thrilled with the entire adventure."

"Believe it or not, I think he enjoyed it. It was a real change from brewing beer and working the festivals. I swear if I hear Der Singvogel one more time I'll go out of my mind."

"Der Singvogel? I remember that catchy little song from school. 'Der singende Vogel singt der ganzen Tag. Der singende Vogel singt eine gluckliche Melodie. The singing bird sings all day. The singing bird sings a happy tune.' Funny how those songs stay with you all these years."

"The singing bird? That's the name of the song? 'Vogel' means 'bird'? Darn it all. I should've taken a German class in school."

"Yeah," Max said. "Vogel means bird. And no matter how you spell it, bird is bird." He tilted his head back and clapped his hands. "No wonder that conniving little stinker was able to find his way all around the castle. I'll bet dollars to donuts Byrd isn't his given name. At least not the English version. Scott Byrd has to be Martin Vogel's son. Martin Vogel as in the Mystery Castle's handyman."

"My God, Max. That explains how he knew about all those secret passages and the attic leading into Helena's apartment. He probably spent hours in that place while his father was doing all sorts of maintenance. No wonder Scott was mum when it came to telling us his connection with the Mystery Castle. How fast can you find out for sure?"

"As fast as Angie can get through the Minnesota Office of Public Records."

"Do you think Martin knew what his son was up to?"

"I'd like to say no, but anything's possible. Look, let's see if Scott really is Martin's son, then we'll go from there."

"Son or not, he's still a gambler and a thief and I've got to break the news to his fiancé."

"Maybe you should've gotten yourself a cruller."

I smiled. "Where do you think the other one went?"

I could've kicked myself for having that information served up to me in four catchy stanzas but how was I to know what 'Vogel' meant? I walked back to my desk and picked up the phone. No sense in delaying the inevitable.

"Loreen? It's Marcie Rayner. I've got the information you requested."

"I want to know the name. Who's he sleeping with?"

"He's not. That isn't what he's doing when he's making excuses not to be with you. Um, maybe you should come in here. It might be easier if I was to show you—"

"Show me what? What did you find out? Tell me now. I'm paying good money for your services and I want to know now. Right now."

Loreen's voice was at a fever pitch and there was no sense stalling. "Scott isn't cheating on you, he's too busy immersed in high stakes poker games."

"What??? He's a gambler? That's how he really makes a living? You have *got* to be kidding."

"Um, I wouldn't exactly call it 'making a living.' More like losing his pants. So to speak."

"Where? I would've known if something was going on right around here."

"Not here. Minneapolis. Lake of the Isles Parkway to be precise."

For a second, I thought I had lost Loreen on the line. I supposed she was simply trying to process what I had told her, but I was wrong. She dropped the call altogether. Or maybe she hung up. Hard to tell. In any case, I prepared for the worst. I stood up, walked to the front office and called out to Angie.

"Loreen Larsen may be on her way over here. I don't think she's in a good mood."

Angie half choked half giggled. "What did you tell her?"

"Only the truth about her fiancé."

"Oh, *that*. Max gave me the rundown a few minutes ago. I'm going through the department for vital statistics, and if that doesn't work, then I'll check with the county courts. People request name changes all the time. I had a girlfriend whose last name was Farht. She had it legally changed to Farley."

"Yikes. I'm surprised her family didn't change the name years ago. But Vogel isn't that bad. If Scott really did change his name to Byrd, he must've had his reasons. Let me know if Loreen walks in here, will you?"

"I think you'll know without me telling you, but okay."

I went back to my desk and pulled up my notes on Helena Heatherbrae, hoping to find something I might have overlooked. It was as if every page had an unwritten title that read "Dead End."

Twenty minutes later, I heard Loreen's voice from the front room. "Marcie's expecting me. And don't bother looking for an appointment. I don't need one."

I took a deep breath, walked out there and motioned for her to follow me back to my office. Angie ran her thumb across her neck when Loreen's back was turned.

"Have a seat," I said to Loreen. "It's not the end of the world."

The end of the world is when you find out your husband is screwing every coed in his class.

"Show me the evidence. I want to see for myself."

I nodded and pulled up the photos on my computer, turning the monitor slightly so it would be fully visible from where she was seated.

"That's him all right. You weren't kidding about high stakes poker. Look at the labels on the booze bottles behind him. Is that Remy Martin cognac?"

"Um, I didn't really take a good look at the liquor."

"It doesn't matter." Loreen twirled her diamond engagement ring around her finger, then held out her hand and stared. "If he thinks I'm giving back my 2.5 Leo, he can kiss my you-know-what. Last thing I want to do is spend my life with a gambler.

I've listened to enough of those country western songs to know how it'll turn out."

Oh yeah. Nothing like a little Shania Twain or Carrie Underwood for advice about one's love life.

"Not that it's any of my business, but you're breaking off the engagement?"

"That's what I just said. Look, Scott's a hunk all right, and he's no slouch in the sack either, but I have no intention of wondering if and when our house will be foreclosed or our cars repossessed. And don't bother telling me that maybe I should talk to him about Gamblers Anonymous. As far as I'm concerned, it's over. You can send me the bill or I can give you my credit card right now."

"Whoa. Okay then. Um, Angie, our office secretary takes care of billing. I'll need to put the invoices together and she can take it from there. You can give her your credit card information and that way, when the bill's prepared, she can run it."

"Sounds good to me. I'm glad I found out about this now and not after the fact. Well, at least he didn't get arrested or anything. What a nightmare that would've been. He'd have to change his name again."

"Change his name again?" I felt as if someone had poked me with a pitchfork. "Name? What name?"

Loreen shook her head and sighed. "He had this old German last name – Vogel. Had it changed to the English translation when he started his wealth management business. I guess he thought Byrd sounded more promising to clients. It wouldn't've mattered to me because I had every intention of keeping my own last name. Face it, Loreen Larsen sounds a whole lot better than Loreen Vogel or Loreen Byrd."

"Uh, will you excuse me for one second, Loreen? I'll be right back. Can I bring you some bottled water or coffee?"

"No, I'm fine."

I hustled over to Angie's desk and whispered, "Forget public records. Loreen gave me the answer. Didn't want you to waste your time. Tell Max."

Angie mouthed the word "thanks" and I returned to Loreen.

"Sorry about that. I suddenly remembered something Angie needed to do."

"No problem. I should get going."

"I'm sorry things didn't work out for you. I imagine your family and Scott's will be disappointed, too."

Loreen shrugged. "My family will be elated. They keep telling me I'm too young to make a lifelong commitment. I tell them that's what divorce lawyers are for and my mother practically hyperventilates."

"What about Scott's family? Do they feel the same way?"

"I wouldn't know. I only met his father once. I think he may be a widower. Nice man. Name's Martin Vogel. Scott says he works for some large conglomerate in Minneapolis but plans on retiring soon."

Loreen picked up the purse she placed on my desk and walked toward the door. Then, she turned and faced me. "At least that's over with. I don't need any more surprises."

Oh no, honey. That's just the first shoe. The second one's about to drop and I hope it doesn't make a resounding thud on the floor.

"Out of curiosity, does Scott have an attorney?"

"I think so. Why? He's not going to need one, is he? I mean, the place wasn't raided or anything."

"No, no, nothing like that. But having an attorney is always a smart move. Especially if you're in wealth management… or perhaps caught stealing a few items."

"My God! What else did that SOB do? Did he steal something from that mansion on Lakes of the Isles Parkway? That's all I need!"

My cheeks felt warm and I wondered if I was making the right move but it was too late. I pretty much told Loreen her fiancé was a thief, now all I needed to do was fill in the details.

"Uh, maybe you should sit down again."

"I'll stand. Nothing's going to faze me at this point."

I clenched my teeth. "When Scott left that mansion, he drove to another one. A famous one. Actually, it's now a state park."

"What? I'm all confused."

"Look Loreen, Scott broke into that Mystery Castle in Mendota Heights because he's been stealing Native American art carvings from a private residence in the castle. There. I've said it. My, um, er, partner and I caught him in the act. He confessed to everything."

Loreen let out the longest, slowest breath I ever heard. "I got a text from him yesterday. He didn't say anything about being arrested."

"That's because he wasn't arrested. We didn't want to make a scene. Besides, it was raining like hell out on Saturday night when all of this took place."

"Geez. This really beats the end all, doesn't it? Boy can I pick 'em. Ugh. I wonder when he was going to break the news to me. Or maybe I should say *if*. *If* he was going to fess up."

"I'm sorry," I said. "I really am."

"Don't be. I'm done."

CHAPTER TWENTY-SIX

L oreen might have lost a fiancé but Max and I gained a suspect. Granted, Scott pretty much had me convinced he had nothing to do with Helena's death, yet he did score two out of three on the motive, means and opportunity test.

Then, there was his father. Martin Vogel. What did we really know about him? And could he have been the brains behind the thefts? I was mulling over the possibilities as I drove to work the next day. Max had arrived early and flung the door open for me.

"Were you standing there waiting for me?" I asked.

"Nah, I'm waiting for my coffee. Can't help it if I looked up and saw you approaching the door. Listen, I've got news for you. I almost called you last night but I figured why bother you at home. Another twelve hours wasn't going to make a difference."

"About what?" I put my bag on Angie's desk and took a coffee mug from the shelf.

"Wallis called me at a little past eight. At least he didn't wait till two in the morning. He located the article he remembered seeing in an architectural journal. Said he was right all along.

That boy's picture was in it."

"You mean to tell me your brother-in-law spent hours and hours of research to find it? Sifting through all that microfiche?"

"Good grief, no. The only thing Wallis sifted through was that attic of his. Or maybe it was his basement. Guy's a regular packrat. He never throws anything out. The man has stacks and stacks of architectural journals dating back to 1964. We must've hit a nerve because he was adamant he remembered the boy's face. Turns out he was right."

"Oh my gosh. That's fantastic. Who was the boy? And what was he doing in an architectural journal?"

"Coffee's ready. Give me a second. Wait. Better yet, put your stuff away, and join me in my office."

I grabbed my bag, tossed it on my desk, raced back for my coffee mug and threw myself into one of Max's chairs just as Angie came through the front door.

"Good morning," she shouted. "I'll leave you alone for your early morning meeting."

We shouted back "Good Morning" and Max yelled, "Hold my calls."

"Hurry up," I said, "I'm dying to know the details."

Max leaned back in his chair and raised his eyebrows. "According to Wallis, the article was about improper installation of dumbwaiters. The child in the photo was killed in a horrible accident on Christmas Eve, 1936. In Minneapolis. The article gave the address as the Heatherbrae's residence in Mendota Heights. Unfortunately, it gave way too many boring details about counterweights and guide rails. I kept asking Wallis to speed it up but that only made things worse."

"Wait a minute. Wait a minute. Cynthia Dickerson, the librarian from the state historical society, pulled up the news articles on that tragedy but it gave the family name of Williston. She and I assumed the accident took place at the Williston residence and not at the Heatherbrae's. The article she found didn't list the address. We made an assumption and it was wrong. But now, everything's starting to make sense."

I gulped my coffee so fast I started to choke.

"Slow down, kid. Don't need another accident."

"I'm fine, Max. I'm fine. Better than fine. We know who that kid in the picture was – Kent Williston. He was six years old according to Cynthia's news article. The Williston's must have been friends of the Heatherbrae's. Did Wallis' article give any more information?"

"In a technical sense, yes. Dumbwaiters today remain closed until the cart appears at the designated floor. Not so back then and that's what the article was contending. Long story short – the door opened, the kid jumped in, horsing around no doubt with Helena, and fell to his death."

"How gruesome. How absolutely gruesome. Poor Helena. That had to be the reason she switched the rooms around when her parents died. She couldn't bear to have that dumbwaiter in use. By switching the rooms and installing a new system, she didn't have to. She had the perfect excuse. Not to mention, she was installing a new state-of-the-art system. No one could argue with that."

"Pretty good deduction, I'd say. However, it doesn't bring us any closer to solving this case."

"Maybe. Maybe not. What if someone in the Williston Family was seeking revenge?"

"Why wait decades for that? And who? Who would be around? The parents were long gone, and if Kent had a sibling, he or she would be Helena's age. No, I don't think it's revenge for the kid's death."

"You know what the saddest part is? That hidden room of Helena's. She must've been haunted by that accident. And back then, no one would've gotten her any help. Not like today where we have counselors, psychologists, and all sorts of specialists who can help kids deal with those kinds of things."

"Yeah, a sad case all around. Maybe we'll get lucky with the next lead. That is if Phoebe can pull off that fingerprint stunt of hers. Then we can find out once and for all who Anna Gainson really is. By the way, I think I'll make a call and have another chat with Martin Vogel. Once he becomes aware that we've got the dirt, so to speak, on his son, he may want to let us in on any other information he's kept to himself. What do you say?"

"This is scary. We're beginning to think alike. I've got a few appointments today and one on Thursday but tomorrow looks good. What about your schedule?"

Max pulled open his desk drawer and pulled out a large paper calendar. "I've got a nine o'clock but that shouldn't take long."

"How come you're not using your computer calendar?"

"Takes forever. Technology's supposed to make things easier. There's nothing easier than writing things down on a paper calendar. It's worked for hundreds of civilizations."

"If you say so…Um, I know it's probably a colossal waste of time, but I'm going to check into the Williston's. See what I can dig up."

"Knock yourself out but don't put too much credence into it. I'm not much of a believer in that saying, 'Revenge is a dish best served cold.' The Williston kid died over eighty years ago. The only thing cold is his grave."

"His grave. Oh my gosh. His grave! That *had* to be the grave Helena kept visiting at that cemetery. What was it called? Oh yeah, Acacia Park. I need to make a call, Max. I—"

"Yeah, yeah. You're on to something. Don't let me hold you back."

I snatched my coffee mug from Max's desk and raced to my computer. Harry Sorenson's phone number was somewhere on my desk. All I needed to do was shove around the stacks of paper and find it. Or I could save myself some time. I doubled back to the front office.

"Angie! Can you get me Harry Sorenson's phone number? He was the chauffeur at the Mystery Castle before Helena died."

"No problem. I'll pull it right up with the other employee information from that place and place the call if you want."

"Yes. Yes. Go ahead."

I wanted to tell Max to forget technology and forget paper calendars. As long as he didn't forget to give Angie a raise each year. A minute or so later, I had Harry on the phone.

"Mr. Sorenson. Harry. This is Marcie Rayner. I'm still looking into Helena Heatherbrae's death and I need your help."

"I can only talk for a few minutes."

"I'll be quick. You told me you used to drive Helena to Acacia Park Cemetery. And I know you told me where you turned. Which road you took. But my memory's foggy. Do you think you can email me the exact directions to the area where that grave was? You still have my card, don't you?"

"Uh, sure. Yeah, I can do that."

"Great. I really appreciate it."

"Hey, mind telling me what that has to do with Helena's death?"

"I'm not one hundred percent sure, but I think there was a connection between Helena and the deceased. I need to see who else was buried in that area."

"No problem. I'll do if after work."

"That's fine. Thanks so much, Harry. Have a good day."

The next call I made was to Max because I was too lazy to get out of my chair again.

"Humor me, Max. After we meet with Martin tomorrow, we need to swing by the Acacia Park Cemetery. I need to check something out."

"You didn't have to call me. I already knew. The minute you said the word 'grave.' What do you think you'll find?"

"I'm not really sure but it's like having an itch that won't stop until I scratch it."

"All I can say is there better be some damn good eateries up that way."

Other than two cases involving tracking down birth parents, my work load was light. Of course, I knew that was apt to change given a busy appointment schedule on Thursday. I dove into the paperwork on those cases although my mind kept drifting back to Helena. Finally, at a little before eleven, I started my bona fide search on the Williston Family, reading every article I could find, including old advertisements from their stores.

They were a prominent Minneapolis family that started out with a mercantile business in St. Paul at the end of the Civil War. That business expanded to a number of department stores in Minneapolis/St. Paul as well as Rochester by the early 1930s. Somehow, they remained unscathed in the Depression but that changed at the beginning of World War II.

It seemed the CEO of the Williston department store chain committed suicide on Christmas Eve, 1941. I re-read the date. It was exactly five years after little Kent Williston's accident and the CEO was none other than his father. The article went on to say that Kent's mother suffered a major breakdown and was institutionalized until her death in 1953. There were three surviving children but other than their ages, listed at the time of their father's passing, no further family information was given.

The department stores were bought up by another chain and remained in business until the 1960s when they merged with yet another company.

It was as if I was reading a Kate Morton novel. I nibbled on the tip of my pencil before jotting down the ages of those children – eight months, two years and three years. I did the math. If they were alive, they'd be in their eighties. And maybe…just maybe, one of them visited their brother's grave and signed the cemetery guestbook. It was worth a shot. Even if Max thought otherwise.

At a little past noon, Angie rapped on my partially opened door and stepped inside my office.

"Max left a little while ago to meet with a client. He said to tell you he called Martin Vogel and you should be ready to leave at ten thirty tomorrow. Also said he'd buy you lunch if you drive. The Mystery Castle again, huh?"

"Yeah, you remember me telling you about Scott Byrd aka Scott Vogel? Maybe the dad knows more than he originally told Max and me."

"Like?"

"Like maybe he was the one responsible for Helena's demise. Maybe she confronted Martin about Scott's burglary and Martin had no choice but to...well, you know."

Angie took off her glasses and rubbed the bridge of her nose. "I suppose it's as good a conjecture as any. Considering there's no real evidence."

"I know. I know. Don't rub it in. My mind keeps flitting from one theory to the next. I keep going back to motive and that's where I get stuck. On the off chance it could be related to the death of one of Helena's childhood playmates, Max and I are also checking out another possibility – revenge."

She smiled and pulled a chair closer to my desk. "He mentioned something along those lines while you were fast at work behind closed doors. Said it wasn't on his A list but there was no harm in being thorough."

"That's Max, all right. More systematic than I'll ever be. If you ask me, he's got his money on Anna Gainson. Once we find out what she's hiding about her identity, we may have our answer."

"Her fingerprint. I know. I'm supposed to be on the lookout for anything from a Phoebe Leyton."

"If she comes through, it'll be a miracle. Along with not losing her job in the process. It's almost as if Phoebe is particularly anxious to rid herself of her boss."

"If Max's theory is right and Anna was the one responsible for Helena's death, then Phoebe will get her wish. By the way, it's after twelve. Want to order something from the deli?"

Food hadn't crossed my mind but the minute she mentioned it, I was suddenly famished. "Ham and cheese on rye with mayo and tomatoes. And a Coke."

I dug out a ten-dollar bill from my bag and gave it to Angie. "Thanks. I didn't feel like going anywhere and those fiber bars in my desk are worthless."

"Max threw out an entire box this morning when he

thought I wasn't looking. Tried to bury them under the throwaway cups."

"Next time cite him for covering up evidence."

CHAPTER TWENTY-SEVEN

M artin didn't want to meet at the Mystery Castle so Max and I found ourselves once again at the homey Fischerville Coffee House in Mendota Heights. It was lunchtime and the place was packed. We had left our office at twenty till eleven but traffic was surprisingly light and Max agreed to hold off on any fast food stops until we arrived.

"We're early," he said. "Might as well get a croissant or better yet, a sandwich and a pastry."

I settled for a large cranberry scone and coffee while Max took full advantage of their menu. We were almost done with our food when Martin walked in.

"Thanks for agreeing to meet with us," Max said. "Let me get you a cup of coffee or something."

"No need. I've been hankering for a strawberry tart all morning. Be right back."

"This is really uncomfortable," I whispered to Max. He shrugged and muttered, "What else is new?"

Martin came back to our table and took a seat, carefully placing his coffee and tart in front of him. I was relieved we were able to be seated next to one of the windows and away from the crowd. Martin spoke before Max could open his mouth.

"If you must know, I'm in as much shock as anyone. Blew the air right out of me. Cripes. Go figure. My own son, a thief. He called me once he obtained legal counsel. Some attorney out of St. Paul. Doesn't matter. I saw Anna Gainson yesterday and offered to resign. She said there was no need. It was odd, though. She seemed almost relieved when I told her."

Max gave me a kick under the table and winked. "Tell me, Mr. Vogel, how do you think your son was able to secure a master key?"

Martin clasped his hands in front of his face and bent his head down. After a few uncomfortable seconds he looked up. "It wouldn't have been hard for him seeing as he knew that place like the palm of his hand. Been keeping me company there since he was six. Mostly after school and on weekends. Followed me like a puppy. When he got into that tween stage, I guess that's what you call it when you're too young to work and too old to play, I found him odd jobs to do around there. You know, like changing switch plates or light bulbs in the wall sconces and table lamps."

"Scott's what? In his late twenties? That was a long time ago," I said.

Martin's hands were still clasped in front of him, only now he began to wring them.

"It wasn't all that unusual for Scott to drop by and visit me while I was working. Especially if he was meeting with clients up this way. We don't have the kind of relationship where we spend what they call 'quality time' together. No dinners. No ball games. Just a 'hello-how-are-you-doing' kind of thing."

Max took the last bite of his blueberry scone. "Uh-huh. So, about the keys...how was he able to get his hands on them?"

For a moment, there was nothing but silence. Finally, Martin answered the question.

"The keys were in an old key cabinet inside the long kitchen pantry door. Real easy for Scott to make himself a copy. Hell.

They were all labeled – front door, kitchen door, grotto… It wasn't as if I was watching him every single minute. And he knew I changed the locks when Helena insisted upon it a few months before she died."

I took a sip from my coffee and looked directly at Martin. "You said Scott knew his way around the castle. It's no secret that place was built with hidden passages. Are you saying he knew about those as well?"

Martin let out a nervous laugh. "What do you think kept his attention all those years? Heck, he was the unofficial tour guide for the tour guides so to speak. Once they found out how well he knew the castle, they'd be all over him to show them the secret staircases and stuff. Especially the girls. Heck, while most teenage boys were busy with cars, Scott was scouting out that labyrinth as if he was expecting to find hidden treasu—" He paused and rubbed his eyes. "I guess he did after all."

"Mr. Vogel," Max said, "I know this isn't easy but is there any possibility whatsoever your son could've had anything to do with Helena's death? Let's face it, he was in the most private of places – her sanctuary."

"I'd like to think I know my own kid. And Scott's no killer. He confessed everything to me. The gambling. The demanding fiancée. The pressure to have his company succeed. It all got to him, and before he knew it, he was in over his head."

Max scratched his forehead and spoke softly. "What if he knew who was really responsible for what happened to Helena? Would he be likely to share that confession with you as well?"

It took a second for it to register, but I knew what my boss was doing. Waiting to gauge Martin Vogel's reaction. Max once told me everyone has a "tell." Something that gives them away when they're lying. Like a sudden look of distress before their expression changes. Martin exhibited nothing of the kind. He shook his head and simply said "Beats the hell out of me."

Then Max asked one more question. "Why did your son change his name?"

At that point Martin stood up and pushed his chair back.

"When he didn't want to be associated with a blue-collar worker like his father. Ironic, though. He kept the same name only changed it to English and spelled it with a Y. Vogel. It's German for bird. Look, that's all I can tell you. I've got to get back to work."

Max stood up and reached out his hand. It was a quick handshake but a handshake nevertheless.

"If you want the name of Scott's attorney, I can get it for you," Martin said.

Max shook his head. "That's not necessary. Thank you for your time. For meeting with us."

"Not a problem."

I watched as Martin walked out the door. "I wonder if Scott ran his own 'castle' tour business. It would've been pretty lucrative once word got out. What do you think, Max?"

"Entrepreneurship. It's the American way. Wouldn't surprise me a bit. The dad seems to be one of those hardworking guys who plays by the rules. Too bad that didn't rub off on his son. Tell you what I'm hoping might rub off..."

"What?"

"Martin's conscience if he does have anything to hide. If it turns out he's protecting his son or thinks Scott knows who was responsible for Helena's death, Martin might choose to give us a call instead of waiting to be questioned by the police."

I started fidgeting in my seat and moved my empty coffee cup around.

"Oh brother," Max said. "You're worse than a ten year-old waiting to go to the circus."

"Not the circus. The cemetery. Acacia Park's just off the I-10. We can be there in less than a half hour."

"You're the driver. What are we waiting for?"

It was a quick jaunt to the seventy-five-acre park that was more a refuge for wildlife than a resting place for previous lives. I drove past the steel bell tower and small chapel at the entrance and followed the directions Harry emailed me. Max was humming and grunting as he looked around.

"I suppose this is as good a place as any if you expect family and friends to visit your grave. As far as I'm concerned, I'd rather they go out for a thick juicy steak and have a toast to me."

"Um, yeah…I think the Williston's had a different take on the whole burial thing, considering Kent was a child."

"Can't argue with you about that. So, where's his gravestone?"

"A few turns on the different small roads. We should be coming up on the general area, according to Harry's information. He didn't know the exact spot. And we need to locate the gravestone first before we can check out the guestbook Helena signed. I found out from the cemetery society that the graves in the guestbook are listed by numbers, not names."

Max let out a long torturous sigh. "At least it's warm and we're not freezing our butts off playing 'Find the Tombstone.'"

"If you want, you can wait in the car and I'll scurry around."

"Nah, that would ruin all the fun. We'll get to the spot in question and keep fanning out."

"Now you're making it sound like a search and rescue mission."

"Good. It'll go quicker."

"How about if we up the ante and first one to find the gravestone gets a bonus?"

"Ha-Ha. It doesn't have to be that quick."

I had to admit, I looked forward to Max's acerbic sense of humor whenever we were on a case.

"We're here," I said. "Race you to the first grave!"

Some of the bronze plaques dotted small knolls while others were shaded beneath linden, elm, and maple trees. We followed Max's plan and began at a grave marker for Agnes Wellington Scott, 1868 – 1925. It took us less than ten minutes to locate Kent Williston's final resting spot. It read, "Kent Royce Williston, 1930 – 1936, beloved son of Frederick and Emma Williston."

There was nothing unusual about the grave marker and nothing to indicate that anyone had been there recently. No flowers, nothing. A smaller bronze plaque discreetly placed below the grave indicated its number – 457.

A few feet away were the graves of his parents and another Williston. A younger sibling by three years. That meant the two remaining siblings might still be alive.

"Don't get your hopes up," Max said. "I know what you're thinking. Just because you don't see gravestones for Kent's younger brothers or sisters doesn't mean they're still alive. Most likely they've had families of their own, moved out and died somewhere else. And even if they were alive, I seriously doubt they waited an entire lifetime to enact their revenge on Helena Heatherbrae for Kent's death."

"Yeah, you're probably right. I suppose we should check out the guestbook and be on our way."

"Number 457. Want to write it down?"

"I think I can remember it for the three minutes it'll take us to drive to the chapel."

We got back in the car and I drove to the entrance where the small stone chapel was located. The stones, according to cemetery information, came from the old St. Paul Courthouse. Max opened the heavy wooden door and we stepped inside a small foyer with two tables on either side. Straight ahead was the chapel itself – cozy, warm and welcoming. A bouquet of fresh flowers was the only adornment on the ornate table that took the place of an altar.

The guest books were lined up on the foyer tables and according to Max, arranged by number.

"Would you look at that? Even numbers on the right, odd numbers on the left. I'll be darned. Not that I'm an expert on cemetery guest books, but this is wacky, huh? I wonder what they do if they run out of room for signatures."

I grabbed the numbered book and thumbed through it. "Helena wasn't visiting her parents' graves in this cemetery. She was visiting Kent's. See for yourself. The first visit was

January 1, 1942. New Year's Day. And look, she wrote a short note. It says, 'I'll be your visitor from now on.'"

Max reached out his hand. "Let me see that book, will you?"

He flipped back a page and held it under my eyes. "Look at the visit before January first. It's a page back. December 24, 1941."

"Max! That was the date Kent's father committed suicide. And look, up until that point he'd be visiting his son's grave. Helena must have known that. My gosh. She must have been carrying that guilt around with her since she was a little girl."

"Those articles called it an accident. It wasn't her fault."

I took my time and made sure I had read every entry. The only visitors were Helena and Kent's parents. With the father deceased and the mother suffering a breakdown, only Helena continued to visit, occasionally writing short notes in the guestbook.

"Max, look at this note. It says, 'Will you forgive me if I get to Heaven?' and here's another one, written a year later. It reads, 'Whenever something sweet touches my lips, I think of the red candies you liked so much.'"

"That must've been one hell of an incident that Christmas eve. Who knows what she saw."

"This is like one of those heart grabbing Gothic novels," I said. "But you were right. Right all along. No siblings ever visited the grave. Guess we can cross revenge off our list."

"I crossed it off a long time ago. You had to see for yourself. I can't help but wonder about the Mystery Castle's own mystery – Anna Gainson. Who the heck she really is. And what motive she might have had to expedite Helena's death."

"Do you think Phoebe managed to nab those fingerprints?"

"Oh yeah. She was plenty motivated. Probably can't stand working with that woman."

I thumbed through a few more pages in the guestbook and then let out a gasp. "My God, Max. Read this one."

He took the book from my hand and looked at the page in question. "Whoa. Maybe she's exaggerating."

"I don't think so. It wasn't as if she was trying to get anyone's attention or anything. More like a confession if you ask me."

"I'll say."

I read the notation twice before placing the book back on the table. It said, "I was teasing when I threw it. I never meant to kill you."

"Max, what do you suppose she threw?"

"I have no idea. No idea whatsoever. But keep in mind, she was a troubled woman whose memory might have been fading. That accident with the dumbwaiter was just that – an accident."

We didn't say anything to each other until we were back in the car. Then, it was as if we had to get back to normalcy.

"Want to stop for another bite to eat on the way home?" I asked.

"As long as it doesn't say vegan, non-GMO, organic or have the word 'health' anywhere in the title, I'm fine."

CHAPTER TWENTY-EIGHT

M ax and I returned to New Ulm, stomachs full but coming up empty as far as theories and evidence went. The next day wasn't much better. In-between my new client meetings and Max's ongoing investigations, I thought we were going to hit rock bottom as far as getting any closer to finding out why Helena's body looked staged. Minerva, Arletta and Greta concurred that she would never lie down without her wedge cushion or she'd risk a GERD attack. And yet, there she was, flat on her back, dead as can be.

I wasn't about to accept the official cause of death as "natural" so that meant I had to probe further. I had to go through every last note I had taken and scrutinize it. Like squeezing out the last bit of juice from a lemon. It was onerous and by the end of the day, the only thing I was left with was a headache.

Then, if that wasn't bad enough, my mother called.

"What's taking you so long with that case? I ran into Alice Davenport at an estate sale and she had just got done speaking with her cousin Minerva. Alice told me that she told Minerva the case would go a whole lot quicker if Minerva had insisted on weekly written reports."

"Oh God no! What did you tell her?"

"What could I tell her? I don't know anything about the case. But don't worry, Alice said it was Minerva's problem and she could deal with it."

"Whew."

"By the way, The Weather Channel replayed footage from that storm. At least it was rain and not snow. You know I absolutely dread the unpredictable weather I'll be facing at Thanksgiving. It could be sixty degrees or six! If it wasn't so darn expensive, I'd rather have all of you fly down here."

"That's a lot of people for a two-bedroom condo, Mom. Plus, it's a really busy time for Hogan's brewery."

"How serious are you with him?"

"I don't know. Serious enough."

"Fine. If you don't want me to know, just say so."

"Mom, I—"

"Never mind. I'll talk to you this weekend. And hurry up with that case. I don't want to run into Alice again until it's solved."

Then stay away from estate sales.

"Okay. Love you. Bye."

The second I hung up, I heard Angie's voice. "Hogan or some secret admirer? Sorry. Didn't mean to catch you off guard. Besides, your door was partially opened and all I heard was the 'love you' part of the conversation."

"If you must know, it was neither. Only my mother. I swear, that woman needs a hobby. Badly. Max leave yet?"

"Uh-huh. A few minutes ago. You were on the phone. He said to tell you not to push too hard on the case. It'll only drive you crazy. Said to sit back and give yourself a break."

"I suppose that's what he plans to do."

"For the time being. Until the morning mail gets here. He's expecting that fingerprint. What I don't understand is, how on earth was he was able to get the secretary to get the print."

"Don't tell him I said so, but I think his real detective skills come from reading *The Hardy Boys*. He got Phoebe to use transparent tape or something."

"I really need to re-read that series. So, what's your gut feeling about it?"

"Anna may very well be hiding something. She only exists on paper for about nineteen years and before that—"

"She didn't exist at all. I saw an episode that like on *Castle*. Boy, I really miss that show. Anyway, it turned out the woman with the secret identity was a Romanian spy."

I laughed and shook my head. "I seriously doubt Anna Gainson is any kind of spy. A thief maybe. Or even an embezzler, but I doubt espionage is in her skill set."

"Well, good luck. Are you planning on staying late?"

"No, I'm beat. I'm going to put the timeline information on a flash drive and have a look-see at home. After dinner."

Angie walked over to my desk and gave me a tap on the shoulder. "At least you got to the bottom of that Loreen Larsen mess. You saved her from a miserable marriage. That's worth at least one pat on the back. Come on. Wrap it up. Tomorrow's another day."

"Okay Scarlett. I'm out of here."

I stopped by Hy-Vee's market on the way home and bought enough salad fixings to last through the weekend. I also made sure I had enough snacks and finger food to keep Hogan and me from charging into the nearest fast food joint. The only one in my household who was set for the week was Byron. Last things I ever wanted to run out of were kibble or litter. Especially litter. Byron could always eat some people food in a crunch. But no litter? Ugh. He'd be scoping out the potted plants or dark closet corners. I tried not to think about it.

After a light chicken salad and a cool shower, I walked over to my desk, turned on the computer and inserted the flash drive. The file was under Helena Timeline and I needed to familiarize myself with it again. Too many disruptions and tangents had pulled me away and I needed to be sure of the actual events that led up to the discovery of the body.

I took a deep breath and began to read the notes.

Helena's body was found on a Monday evening. Around five, according to Minerva. She and Arletta were the only ones in the house. The Mystery Castle tours end at four. Same with the office hours. Greta, who usually works until five, had left early that day to meet her niece from Willmar. I figured that had to be Tilda. Martin, the handyman, and Ernie, the gardener, had arrived early that day, around eight, and were gone before four.

According to Arletta and Minerva, no one else was in the castle and the doors were all locked. That included Anna Gainson's office. The information was verified by the police when they were summoned to the place by Arletta's nine-one-one call.

I read my side notes again. The police officer who had spoken with Max told him there were no cars parked in front of the castle when they responded to the distress call. Yet Minerva and Arletta certainly didn't walk to work. They had to be parked around back near the Garden Grotto or perhaps the kitchen entrance. That meant it was quite possible for someone else to have parked out back as well. The police made no mention of it. *Because they never looked.*

There simply had to be someone else in that castle. And I was drawing a blank. Just then, Byron leapt from the chair behind me and landed on the keyboard. I automatically jolted from my seat before realizing what had happened.

"Bad kitty! Bad bad kitty boy!" This being said while I stroked his back and rubbed his ears. He arched his back, meowed, and jumped down.

A strange thought crossed my mind. Something Max had said about people dying of fright.

"You'll have to try harder than that, kitty," I shouted to Byron who was now halfway down the hall to the kitchen, "before you scare the daylights out of me."

I went back to my notes and plodded on. Suddenly, it felt as if I was on the verge of piecing together the edges of a jigsaw puzzle. Unlike my boss, who waited until he had every shred of evidence in front of him before offering up a substantial and viable theory, I was doing the worst thing an investigator could do – making the evidence fit the theory instead of the other way around. Still, I believed I was on to something.

Max was at a Kiwanis breakfast when I arrived to work the next morning. Angie was already at her desk sipping a cup of coffee.

"I got in early, Marcie. Heaven knows. Max didn't want to take a chance on having us miss the morning mail delivery."

"The mail usually doesn't get here much before ten."

"That's what I said, but Max reminded me of three instances in which it got delivered before eight thirty."

"Oh brother. Anna Gainson is Max's final corner piece of the jigsaw puzzle."

"Huh?" Angie adjusted her glasses and took another sip of coffee.

"It's like this. Any one of the staff at the Mystery Castle could've killed Helena and had it look like natural causes. No autopsy. A quick cremation and the evidence literally goes up in smoke."

"Ew."

"Max was able to conduct thorough background checks on everyone except Anna. That's his corner piece."

"That makes sense."

"Yeah, and speaking of the devil, I'm about to give her a call."

Angie put her cup down and gave me a puzzled look.

"Relax," I said. "I need some mundane architectural information from her. If I'm lucky, I'll be dealing with Phoebe."

"Let me know how it goes."

I poured myself a cup of coffee and walked to my office. "Shall do."

I dialed the Mystery Castle's office number before I even booted up my computer. Anna Gainson answered it on the third ring.

"Oh. Um, er, Good morning. This is Marcie Rayner. I didn't expect you to be answering the phones. I thought Phoebe would pick up."

"Phoebe's not in today. How may I help you, Miss Rayner?"

Oh, I don't know. Maybe coming clean about who you really are and what you're up to.

"As you know, we've taken a look at the blueprints for the castle but there was nothing on file for the renovations. Something that extensive would've required permits and all sorts of paperwork. Even sixty years ago. Miss Gainson, we need to know the name of the contractor who handled the project."

"I'm not sure what you expect to find or how that's going to help you with your investigation but I'll see if we have anything on file. Either way, I'll get back to you."

"Thanks Miss Gainson. Oh, and one more thing. It should only take you a minute or two to find."

"What's that?"

"Greta Hansen's timesheet for that Monday. The Monday when Helena's body was discovered."

"Hold on. I can pull that up on my computer."

No cutesy music. No robotic information. Only dead air space as I held my breath and waited.

"Miss Rayner? Are you still on the line?"

"Yes."

"Greta clocked in at nine and clocked out at four. Hmm, that's odd."

"What do you mean?"

"When I left at four that day, Greta's car was still parked out back. Then again, she was probably a few minutes behind me, that's all."

"Wow. I'm surprised you could remember something like that."

"Only because some miserable bird decided to leave a deposit on my windshield and I had to stop and deal with it. I remember thinking, and this is not so nice, I admit, but I remember thinking to myself 'why couldn't it have been Greta's old car instead of mine?'"

"Um, well, yeah. We all think those things sometimes. Anyway, would you please get back to me as soon as you can about the name of the contractor? I'd really appreciate it."

"I'll look into it. It was nice speaking with you. Do give my regards to your boss."

"I will. Have a nice day."

No wonder Max had those bad vibes about Anna. Wishing bird poop on someone else's car. Still, that didn't make her a killer.

Just then, I heard Angie's voice. "The mail's here. The mail's here. Max was right. It came early. The letter he was expecting is in this pile. Should I call him at that Kiwanis breakfast?"

I grabbed my cell phone and looked at the time. "It's only twenty after nine. He's probably still eating. If I remember correctly from my dad, those Kiwanians have all sorts of speakers before and after the meal. Give Max another fifteen minutes and then call."

"You got it."

I finally turned on my computer and headed for my own mail. The electronic kind. Nothing that demanded my immediate attention or action. I wondered how long it was going to take Anna to get me that name. Then, I had another idea – Wallis. I pulled up his number and placed the call. A lady answered and I figured it had to be Camila, Wallis's wife.

"Hello. This is Marcie Rayner from Blake Investigations and—"

"My God! Max had a heart attack and it was from over eating, wasn't it? Doris was right all along. Where is he? When did it happen?"

I was so flustered by her response, it took me a second to get the words out. "Max is fine. He's eating breakfast with the Kiwanis Club. I called to speak with Wallis. It's important."

Camila let out a series of short breaths and gasps. "That's a relief. Max's probably drowning his pancakes in maple syrup.

Hold on, I'll get Wallis for you."

Unlike my call to Anna, there was no dead air space. Only Camila yelling, "It's Max's office. That investigator of his scared the daylights out of me."

CHAPTER TWENTY-NINE

"Honestly Wallis," I said. "All I did was to identify myself."

"Don't worry about it. Camila always imagines the worst thing first. So, how can I help you?"

"Is there any way for you to find out who did the renovations on the Mystery Castle? You know, when Helena switched the day room with the dining room and had a new dumbwaiter installed."

"Can you give me a general date? Are we talking 1940s, 1950s, 1960s…?"

"It had to be after her parents died. Hold on. I can google that information right now. Her parents were wealthy industrialists. Their names are bound to pop up. Hang on a second. I'm typing as fast as I can. It's coming up. Wow. Quicker than I thought. Randolph Harvey Heatherbrae passed away in 1961 and his wife died a year later. I'll wager those renovations happened shortly after their deaths."

"Mind telling me what you're thinking? Why this has anything to do with Helena's death?"

"I think that dumbwaiter, the original one, held a secret

that plagued Helena and might have come back to claim her life."

"Are you sure you're conducting an investigation and not writing a horror novel?"

"Pretty sure. So, can you help me out?"

"Depends. How fast do you need the information?"

"Yesterday."

"I can see my brother-in-law's trained you well. Okay, I'll look into it. Shouldn't be that hard."

"Wallis, I really appreciate it."

"No problem."

I put aside the Helena Heatherbrae case for the next hour and instead, concentrated on the new client cases I had added to my schedule - a missing sibling and bigamy. The missing sibling was my client's twin. Both were adopted by separate sets of parents in the late 1980s. I figured that case would be pretty routine. Mostly tracking down records. The second case was far more complicated. The client, a man in his early sixties, was concerned the woman he was about to marry was still married to someone else.

As I poured over my notes, my thoughts immediately drifted to Hogan. What did I really know about him? He had lived his life in the Glencoe Hutchinson area, graduated from the University of Minnesota, Mankato, with a concentration in agricultural studies and went on to establish a burgeoning brewery business in Biscay. All of that substantiated by friends, neighbors and customers. Surely someone with loose lips would've told me if he had a questionable past.

He certainly had the opportunity to "confess all" when I told him about my short-lived marriage. All he said was that he had dated but nothing serious. I looked at the possible bigamy notes again and rubbed my eyes. Nothing Hogan said or did gave me the feeling he was hiding something. Unlike Chester Wellsworth, who wasn't so sure about his engagement and had hired me.

No, Hogan and I were on solid ground and I was aching to

see him tonight. The more time we spent together, the more time I wanted to spend with him. Of course, those cobalt blue eyes of his coupled with a damn good physique didn't hurt anything either. He planned to get to my place around seven and we'd go out for dinner somewhere. A nice quiet meal that didn't include snooping on poker games or sneaking into mystery castles.

Caught between day dreaming and work, I jerked when I heard Max's voice in the front office.

"Marcie! Phoebe got us the fingerprint. Get out here!"

My chair squeaked as I stood up and left my office. Angie gave me the two thumbs up sign and went back to her computer. Max was waving the envelope around like a high school senior who had just gotten an acceptance letter from college.

"I knew we'd get that print. I think in the back of Phoebe's mind she's hoping her boss is an escaped criminal or something."

"Is it viable? The print, I mean."

"Oh yeah. I already made arrangements with a buddy of mine at the police station. He agreed to run the print. I'm driving it right over there. See you in a bit."

The expression "turning on a dime" took a more literal meaning as Angie and I watched Max spin around and race out the door, the envelope with Anna's print clutched under his arm. I didn't get a chance to tell him I had called Wallis.

"Too bad this isn't like one of those TV shows where they pull up the print and five seconds later, they have a solid ID," I said.

Angie nodded. "I hope Max doesn't intend to plant himself at the police station waiting for the results."

"Nah. He knows it'll take a while. But he'll be chomping at the bit. That much I can tell you for sure."

"Oh, before I forget, Elizabeth Chesney's office called a little while ago. Not her. The secretary. Snooty sounding man. Anyway, he said Elizabeth wanted you and Max to know the letters were sent out regarding Helena's will. She mailed a cc to

Anna Gainson and one to our office."

"Yeesh. Anna Gainson's really going to be fried when she sees how much money Helena left to her staff. And I think you've got Elizabeth's secretary pegged. Young kid. Twenties maybe. Trying to make himself look older with a short beard and mustache. Meanwhile, she's trying to look younger by moving from gray to auburn."

"Figures. So, what do you think those prints of Anna's are going to reveal?"

At that second the phone rang and Angie picked it up. "It's for you, Marcie. Arletta Maycomber's on the line."

I reached across her desk and took the call.

"Miss Rayner? Is that you?"

"Yes. How can I help you, Arletta?"

"I've got something to confess. Are you alone?"

"Give me a moment and I'll pick up the call in my office. I'm in the front office now. Stay on the line."

I mouthed "Oh my God" to Angie and charged into my office to grab the phone. I was bracing for a full-blown confession regarding Helena's death and could barely catch my breath.

If I stay calm and composed, she'll admit to it.

In the back of my mind I could hear my mother spouting "Don't you blow it, Marcie, by spooking her."

"Um, Hi Arletta. I'm in my office. No one else can hear us. What was it you wanted to tell me?"

"I feel horrible about this. Simply horrible. I'm not that kind of person, you know. Never was. I don't know what got into me."

My God! It was Arletta!

I kept my voice soft and soothing. "Uh-huh. I'm listening."

"I got a letter today. From Helena's attorney. Oh my gosh, I feel so awful. Helena left me in her will. In her will! I never expected that. Not in a million years. Full salary for the rest of my life. With cost of living, too. And to think I went ahead and did something so regrettable. Of course, I didn't know at the time…"

"How exactly did this come about? The events leading up to it."

"Same as always, I suppose. I was in her bedroom tidying up and she was seated in a chair next to her bed reading something. Helena never saw me bend down to get it. She was too preoccupied with whatever she had in front of her. I was very discreet."

"So, after you bent down, then what?"

"Not much. I picked the lottery ticket off of the floor and put it in my pocket. Never in a million years did I think I had a winning ticket. And then, when the numbers came in, I could have confessed to Helena and made sure she got the money. But no. I didn't. I was greedy. Greedy and selfish. I went ahead and bought myself a Fendi bag. Five thousand dollars. That was the exact amount of the winnings from that ticket."

Words couldn't come out of my mouth. I kept trying to process what she was saying.

"Miss Rayner? Miss Rayner are you still there?"

"Um, er, yes. Sorry."

"I knew you were admiring that bag of mine when we first met. Remember? That day in the Garden Grotto. I was so afraid you'd know it was an original and not a knock-off. My palms were actually sweating. I never should have done that. Helena probably had someone buy her a lottery ticket and it must have fallen from her dresser or wherever she put it."

By now, I had consoled myself with the fact Arletta wasn't a killer, only an opportunist.

"Arletta, was it customary for Helena to play the lotto games?"

"Not that I knew of. In fact, whenever the news would come on about a giant Mega Millions or Powerball pay-off she hardly paid attention. Why? Are you saying the ticket wasn't hers?"

The ticket happened to belong to a conniving thief by the name of Scott Byrd but I'm in no position to let that mouse out of the trap.

"Um, no."

"What do you think I should do now? Should I reimburse the estate the five thousand dollars from my winning? Because it was really her winning. I feel so guilty. So awful. It's eating me up. I felt guilty when I first took the ticket and cashed it in, but when the letter from the attorney came, I felt really, really horrible."

"Arletta, I know this may sound strange, but right now, don't do anything. Don't say anything to anyone and don't do anything. If Helena was still alive and you took the ticket, it would be a different story, but considering the current situation, I think it's best if you keep mum for a while. Until our investigation is complete. Then, I'll be in touch and you can decide what to do."

"But my conscience—"

"You made a spur of the moment bad decision followed by an enthusiastic response to winning. It's not as if you set out to deliberately steal anything or harm anyone. I'm not saying what you did was right, but please don't torture yourself over it."

"Oh my."

Talk about a conundrum. Giving Scott his winning ticket money would be tantamount to rewarding him for essentially breaking, entering, and theft. And while Arletta's motives for taking the ticket were suspect, it was more a crime of opportunity than a carefully articulated scheme to rob an elderly lady of her prized possessions. And if she did confess, then what? No real proof as to who purchased the ticket.

I took a deep breath and bit my lower lip. "Aretta, if I were you, I'd consider the Fendi bag a final gift from Helena and leave it at that. Your secret is safe with me."

"Really?" Her voice started to crack.

"Yeah, really." *Because Karma's a bitch, Scott.*

The rest of the morning was uneventful. Paperwork, phone calls and routine calls. That changed a few minutes before noon when Max thundered back into the office. Angie and I were at the copy machine trying to fix a jam when his voice startled us.

"Record time I tell you! It was record time!"

"For what? For who?" Angie asked.

"For the Integrated Automated Fingerprint Identification System to find Anna Gainson. By the way, expect a bill. The police route it to the FBI and they, in turn, charge a fee for civil searches. Normally it would've taken days but like I said earlier, 'I have friends.'"

"Forget the friends, Max," I said. "What did you find out? Does she have a criminal record?"

"Not exactly."

"I don't understand. What kind of record did IAFIS pull up?"

"Yeah," Angie added. "What did it show?"

"Her prior employment as Annalise Graustein, business teacher in Brewer, Maine. Just outside of Bangor. I thought I detected a New England accent in her voice."

I stepped away from the copier and crossed my arms. "Last I knew, there was no crime in teaching business classes."

Max didn't laugh. "Something was fishy. People don't leave secure positions with pensions and change their names so I did a little checking while I was at the police station."

"And?"

"It seems she was let go. No criminal charges but she lost her job and her pension."

Angie finished clearing the jam in the machine and walked back to her desk. "What did she do?" Fail a board member's kid?"

"No," Max said. "She was let go for reasons of conduct unbecoming a teacher. No specifics were given and she didn't take the case further. The entire matter was closed. Almost nineteen years to the date when she started as Anna Gainson for a business in Mankato. I was able to match the Social Security records with her original name, however I couldn't find the county or state where that legal name change was made.

"What do you think she did?" I asked.

Max shrugged his shoulders and let out a breath. "It could've been anything from stealing money from a club or leaving the classroom unattended to having an affair with a student or showing up to work under the influence."

My eyes darted from Max to Angie. "I can't fathom Anna Gainson doing any of those things. She strikes me as one of those Puritan self-righteous folks. You know, judgmental to a fault."

"Don't look at me," Angie said. "I've never met the woman."

Max poured himself a cup of coffee and walked to his office. "Well I have and I intend to dig deeper before I let this fish off the line. If it's a no-go, then we'll widen the net."

I followed him to his office door and waited until he put the envelope and his coffee on the desk. Then I spoke.

"I called Anna today. And Wallis, too. I didn't think Anna would get me the information I needed so I decided to try your brother-in-law."

"What information is that?"

"The same theory that's been bouncing around in my mind. That somehow, that stupid dumbwaiter has something to do with Helena's sudden and unexpected death."

"Wallis said he'd help?"

"Yes."

"Terrific. Now I'll be forced to have another enjoyable dinner with him and Camila in the not so distant future."

"I'm sorry, Max. I should've run it by you first but—"

"It's all right. You didn't do anything wrong. You're thinking and acting like an investigator and that's a good thing. Let's sit back and see if that brother-in-law of mine can make good at his end."

Sit back we did. Well, I did. I imagined Max spent most of his weekend drudging up anything he could on Annalise Graustein. Meanwhile, Hogan and I ate out a lot and even checked out the Crooked Eye Brewery's competition - Schell's

Brewery. Delicious beers but not as complex as the stuff Hogan was churning out. Of course, there was no getting away from work so I played out my theory (Ad nauseam) to Hogan.

"If you're certain, Marcie, then what?" he asked. "You can't simply walk up to someone and accuse them of something."

"I know. I know. In all those movies and mystery novels, there's always the Big Reveal where the investigators gather all the suspects together, review the clues and finally point out the murderer or murderess."

"Please don't tell me you have something like that in mind."

"I don't know what I have in mind."

"Look, be careful. Whatever you do. Last weekend at that Mystery Castle could've turned out a whole lot different for both of us if Scott really was a killer."

"I'm not even sure at this point I can get the information I need, but if I do, I'll make sure Max is with me. How does that sound?"

"Better." Hogan smiled and gave me a hug. A hug followed by one of those storybook kisses that I didn't want to end. It was tough saying good-bye to him that Sunday night. Byron was no help, either. He kept bumping Hogan's legs and rubbing up against him.

"I don't know which one of you will miss me more," he laughed. "I hate to say it, but I think it's the cat. So, next weekend a go? I have to work Saturday but I'll be done by five. If you get to Biscay when we close, we can go out to eat in Hutchinson and then head back to my place."

"Sounds great," I said giving him another hug before closing the door.

Byron made a beeline for the kitchen and jumped on the counter where I keep the small bag of cat treats.

"You win," I said. "I've got sucker written all over me."

CHAPTER 30

Max barricaded himself in his office Monday in order to "get to the real reason behind the words 'conduct unbecoming a teacher.'"

"I think he's talked to everyone in Brewer, Maine, by now," Angie said. "And by 'talked,' I mean "plagued.'"

"Yeah, he won't make a move until he has the facts underneath the facts. If that makes any sense."

I walked over to the coffeemaker and poured myself the second cup of the morning. "He must really be at it. It's twelve thirty and he hasn't said a word about lunch. Think we should just call the deli and order him something?"

Angie laughed. "He might not have said a word but he has every pizza parlor in a two-mile radius on speed dial. Little Sicily emailed me. They're delivering a large pie to our office in the next fifteen minutes. I was about to tell you when you stepped out here for more coffee."

"Wow. Max must be getting close if he doesn't want to leave his office."

"What about you, Marcie? Are you—?"

In that instant the phone rang and Angie motioned for me

to stay where I was. "Probably a quick call. We can keep talking once I'm done."

I gave her nod and took a sip of my coffee.

"Hmm. It's for you. It's Wallis."

"On my gosh. Wallis! That's great! Maybe he found something. Tell him I'll be right there. Transfer the call!"

"And you thought Max was a bit extreme."

My coffee splashed everywhere as I ran to my desk. "Wallis. Good morning. I mean, good afternoon. Did you find out the name of the contractor? Are they still in business? Who is it? Is it someone in Minneapolis? Who?"

"Yes. Yes. Yes. Now will you please take a breath?"

My heart was pounding and I knew I was getting so close to proving my theory that I was about to bust. "All right. I'll slow down. What can you tell me?"

I reached for a pen and the nearest piece of scrap paper.

"Since the house was on the historical register," he said, "I checked with their files first. Turned out to be a smart move because it saved me some time. The renovations were done by Wenworth Builders out of Minneapolis. They're now River Went Builders as of 1984. Took me over an hour to finally speak with someone in their office. And when I literally begged the poor woman to look into their old files and call me, she did just that. Can you believe it? It so happens that the old files were old paper files in a filing cabinet. Real easy for her to look up. Not all of that computerized stuff."

"And? And? What did you learn?"

"Here's where it gets real interesting. First of all, I have the city permit number for you. Did you want to jot it down?"

"Not right this second. What did you find out?"

"The project manager was a Gareth Johnson. He died in 1978."

"Very sorry to hear that. What else?"

"Gareth Johnson wrote copious notes. Actually, interesting and insightful tidbits about the renovations. Were you aware the new dumbwaiter system was electrical? Of course, it can still be run manually but one push of a button and Voila!"

"Wallis, were there any notes about the old dumbwaiter? The one that's sealed off?"

"Yes, certainly. I was getting to that. First of all, it's sealed off because it's a hazard. According to Mr. Johnson's notes, they were going to remove the internal system but decided it would be too unwieldy. So, they left the old ropes and pulleys in place. The only thing they did to that dumbwaiter was to use some sort of vacuum system to pull up the stuff that had fallen to the bottom of the shaft."

My foot was tapping faster and faster and my breath quickened. Not only that, but my breathing got louder.

"Marcie, are you all right?"

"I'm fine. I'm fine. Keep going."

"If you're thinking they discovered some sort of treasure or valuables, you're going to be disappointed. All they found were old dried up lollipops and one red Tootsie roll pop. Oh, and gumballs and other virtually unrecognizable candies. They did, however, recognize mouse droppings. Apparently, the children in the house used that dumbwaiter as a disposal of sorts. I'm surprised the remodelers took the time to categorize the contents from the shaft. Not the sort of thing today's builders would do. Of course, things were different back in the 1960s I would imagine."

"You said a red Tootsie roll pop?"

"Yes, among other things. What amazes me is that no one bothered to monitor the behavior of those children. All that candy and sugar. The only reason the place wasn't crawling with ants was because they used baking soda and ground cinnamon to ward them off. They must have had some idea of what the children were doing. Remnants of those substances were found with the candies."

"Wallis, you might have solved this case. Oh my gosh. I've got to speak with Max."

"Say, don't you want that permit number?"

"I'll transfer you back to Angie. Give it to her. Wallis, I can't thank you enough."

"I don't understand. What do decades old candies have to do with Helena Heatherbrae's death? It's not like she choked on one."

"No, but she might as well have."

I thanked Wallis again and transferred the call to Angie. Then I tilted my head back, clenched my hands above my head and shouted, "Whoopi!"

"You don't have to get so excited about a pizza delivery," Max yelled out from the workroom that doubled as our eating area. "Hurry up and grab a slice. I've got good news to share."

Both of us spoke at once and the words tumbled over each other. "I think I might have solved the case."

"I'll just work on my pizza if you don't mind," Angie said walking into the workroom. "You two can duke it out as to who goes first."

I grabbed the nearest slice of pizza and a napkin. "You go first, Max. You've been at this non-stop."

Max was all but gloating as he wiped a bit of pizza sauce from his chin. "You'd be surprised how many teachers never leave their original schools. Especially in small towns. I spoke to no less than a dozen of them who remembered Annalise Graustein."

"So what heinous thing did she do?" I asked.

Angie sat down and propped her elbows on the table. "Yeah Max, what? It must've been pretty awful if she was dismissed and lost her pension."

"First of all, I should clarify. She didn't lose her pension as a result of being dismissed. Pensions come from the state and no actual charges were filed. She lost her pension because she wasn't fully vested. Teachers need a certain number of years before they qualify and she lost out because she was dismissed a year before that would have happened."

"Aargh. That must've been a bummer for her," I said.

"Not as bad as it could've been," Max replied. "She was lucky in a sense. The school district pretty much gave her a deal. So to speak. She would resign immediately and they wouldn't pursue the matter any further. Back then, lots of school districts rid themselves of questionable teachers by offering those backroom deals. From what I heard during my conversations this past weekend, the districts are now required by law to file charges with the state and even involve local law enforcement if any criminal laws were broken."

"I'm dying here, already!" Angie shouted. "What on earth did that woman do? Set fire to the place?"

Max let out a short huff and continued. "Nothing that dramatic. Annalise or should I say, Anna, was a business teacher. She was also the advisor for the FBLA. The Future Business Leaders of America."

He paused for another bit of pizza while Angie and I were practically jumping out of our seats.

"Hurry up, Max," I said. "This is worse than waiting for a commercial to end."

"Fine. Fine. Anna embezzled money from the club and got caught. By one of her own students no less. I don't know what's more embarrassing. Anyway, it was the student treasurer who discovered the discrepancies and took it to the school principal. As a result of that whistleblowing, the poor kid was a virtual pariah for the rest of the school term. Seems Anna was quite a popular teacher and her students were more upset with the treasurer than with her. Go figure."

I rolled my eyes. "That's unbelievable. But what does that have to do with Helena Heatherbrae's death?"

"I think Anna became worried Helena was going to find out about the past embezzlement and fire her. That's why Anna was so insistent the castle be transferred to the National Park Service."

"But why now? Why all of a sudden? Anna's been working here for years."

"I wondered the same thing myself. Naturally, I did a little more digging and guess what I came up with? Hold your horses, you two, I'm getting there. The student treasurer, who reported the matter, went to college here in Minnesota. That's where he met his wife, none other than Anna's very own secretary, Phoebe. Anna had no idea when Phoebe was hired. That's because Phoebe never changed her name or wore a wedding ring. We were fooled, too, thinking she was single. Anna must have just found out herself."

My jaw dropped and I sat there, stunned. Angie slapped her cheek and shook her head. "No wonder Phoebe was so helpful. Anna's actions made Phoebe's husband a victim."

"Ah-hah!" I blurted out. "Someone's trying to make sure a good dish of cold revenge is served up."

I grabbed a second slice of pizza and chomped on it. "But wait a sec. Wait a sec, Max. You still haven't told us how Anna was responsible for Helena's death. In fact, she wasn't even in the castle at that time. She had gone home."

"That's why we're about to pay another visit to Anna Gainson this week. We need to be blunt and relentless this time. Anna lost her pension and needed that job. Helena was poised to take all of that away from her. Even once the transfer to the park service had been made. Anna would only have peace of mind with Helena out of the picture."

Angie stood up, a half-eaten piece of pizza in her hand. "I can call there now and set up an appointment."

"Good," Max said. "Check our schedules first. Change around any appointments we may have once you get a date and time from Anna. Oh, and make it for early afternoon. I hate the rush hour traffic into Minneapolis."

"Got it."

Angie went straight to her desk while Max and I continued to eat.

"So," he said, "What's your revelation regarding the case?"

"I'm not letting go of my original theory. That it had something to do with the dumbwaiter and the reason Helena had the rooms switched."

"And what was that?"

"Guilt. The woman was virtually drowning in it."

CHAPTER THIRTY-ONE

The words barely got out of my mouth when we heard the phone ring. A second or two later Angie rushed into the workroom.

"You are *not* going to believe this. Not in a million years. Anna Gainson's on the line. She called us. Not the other way around. An emergency, I think."

Max moved away from the table and picked up the extension phone that was on the counter. All Angie and I could hear was "Uh-huh, when was this? All right, uh-huh, uh-huh. You said you tried to call her? What? No. I can't force the police to issue a missing persons alert if the person has only been gone for three hours. She's not a juvenile. A ghost, huh? I doubt that. Give me an hour and a half, more or less. I'm on my way. Uh-huh. Uh-huh. Fine."

I took a few steps forward until Max and I were face to face. "What was that all about? What happened?"

Angie's stood perfectly still and didn't make a sound as Max spoke.

"Greta was told to thoroughly clean out Helena's apartment. I repeat – thoroughly. She went in there this morning at around nine and at a little past ten she charged out of the place and down the main staircase as if she had seen a ghost. Anna Gainson happened to be in the foyer talking with two of the tour guides when this happened. Naturally she ran upstairs to see what was going on."

Angie and I nodded like two bubblehead dolls and Max went on.

"There was nothing unusual in Helena's apartment. The bed was moved out from the wall for vacuuming along with some other pieces of furniture. Presumably for deep cleaning or whatever they call it nowadays. Anna looked around and said there was nothing whatsoever that would've caused someone to react like that."

"I take it Greta didn't stop to mention where she was going?"

"No, kid, she didn't. Anna tried calling Greta's home phone and her cell phone but no answer. She even sent one of the tour guides to Greta's house to see if she was home. Nothing. Anna's convinced something scared the daylights out of Greta. Said Greta's face gave the word 'ashen' a whole new meaning. Anyway, I told Anna not to touch anything in Helena's apartment and that I'd drive over there."

Then he turned to Angie. "If I have any appointments this afternoon, re-schedule them."

"Yeah, me, too," I said.

Max was halfway to the front door. "We can get there in ninety minutes."

"Stop! Stop!" I shouted. "She's not in Minneapolis. I think I know where she is and it's not Minneapolis. We need to drive to Willmar."

"Willmar?"

"That's what I wanted to talk with you about. I think I can piece this together."

Max squeezed his shoulders back and stretched his arms over his head. "We can't be two places at once. Do what you need to do and we'll keep in touch by phone. Angie, I need you to stay in the office in case something—"

"No problem," she said. "I won't head home until I hear from both of you."

"Willmar, huh," Max said as we walked across the street to where we had parked our cars.

"I wish I had time to explain."

"Be careful. You've got your gun, right?"

"Always, but I don't think I'll need it."

"Call me as soon as you know something and I'll do the same."

I was in my car and headed north on Route 15 in minutes, pausing only once to get a street address from the GPS system.

I was pretty sure I knew what Greta had seen when she pulled the bed away from the wall. It was something she recognized. That's what sent her flying off to Willmar, to her niece Tilda's classroom. It was only after my conversation with Wallis on Friday that my theory about Helena's death moved from plausible to probable.

I can't even begin to count the number of times the backs to my earrings have come loose. Usually I hear a "ping" on the floor and immediately look down for the miniscule piece of metal. But if the earring lands on carpeting or if it rolls under a piece of furniture, I know I'm doomed. And worst of all is when I lose it during the day and don't notice it until late at night when I take off my jewelry. That's probably what happened to Tilda. It was most likely annoying but not earth shattering. That's because Tilda never knew where she had lost that small piece of jewelry. Otherwise, she would've been the one whose color had drained from her face. Instead, it was her aunt Greta.

Traffic was light on the 15 but picked up as soon as I headed west on the 212. It got heavier still when I took the 71 into Willmar. Not wanting to risk a slowdown due to road construction or an accident, I took the first exit from the highway and let the GPS guide me directly to Roosevelt Elementary School where Tilda taught. Greta had mentioned the school when she first told me about her niece. For once I was glad I remembered that tidbit of information.

It was three forty-one according to the clock on my dashboard and I found myself behind a steady stream of school buses. That was good news. It meant I could get into the building without an endless verification process. All I needed to do was to locate Tilda's classroom and take it from there. If I was lucky, there'd be a staff listing by the office. If not, it meant another delay and that was the last thing I needed. What I didn't stop to consider was the timing.

Greta had left the Mystery Castle hours before I set out for Willmar. That meant she had already confronted her niece. Suddenly I felt sick to my stomach. Thoughts of Greta removing Cooper from his classroom and driving him back to Minneapolis came at me a record speed. She babysat him. He was her great nephew. Naturally her name would be on the approved parental release form. I couldn't stop my mind from the course it had already taken.

I circled the parking lot three times before a space opened up. Unlike larger schools, this one didn't differentiate between a faculty and visitor parking lot. Not that it would have mattered. Cars were everywhere.

Slamming the car door behind me, I rushed to the main entrance and walked in. I was right about one thing – after dismissal the doors would be open. I scanned the walls looking for a faculty directory. With the exception of the concert schedule and paintings from Mrs. Lichenstein's fourth grade art class, there was nothing. I stood motionless for a second when a cheery voice broke in.

"They're quite talented, don't you think? Mrs. Lichenstein does a marvelous job, doesn't she?"

"Um, what? Oh yes. The paintings."

I was staring at a short, slender red-head who appeared to be in her thirties.

"The paintings caught my eye," I said, "I was on my way to Tilda—" And then I stopped. I had no idea what her last name was. Of all the stupid things!

"Tilda Erling? The second-grade teacher?"

"Yes. That's her."

"Wonderful teacher. She was my daughter's second grade teacher two years ago. Her classroom is right down this hallway. Second room from the end. On your left. Are you going to be student teaching with her next year?"

"Er, uh, no. I had to see her about something."

Wow! I passed for a college kid!

"She'll be in her room. She's a regular workaholic. Well, have a nice day!"

"Thank you. You, too!"

My footsteps thudded on the linoleum floor as I hurried to her classroom. Second room from the end. On my left. Only it was dark and the door was locked. I stood for what felt like hours when I heard a man's voice.

"You missed her by a few seconds. She and another teacher left the building. Went out the door straight ahead."

It was the custodian, a stocky gray-haired man who looked to be Max's age.

"The other teacher. Did you recognize her?" I asked. "Do you know what she looked like?"

The man shrugged. "I assumed it was another teacher but I could be wrong. She looked too old to be a parent. Grandparent maybe. Short gray hair. No make-up. A plain dress. Does that help?"

The description fit Greta perfectly. "Yes. It does. They went out that door, you said?"

"Yep. Turn left and it'll take you straight to the parking lot."

I thanked him and walked as fast as I could. The only sound was the click, click of my shoes.

Half the time it's impossible to find my own car in a large parking lot and I know what my car looks like. I was literally flying blind as I scanned the area for any signs of Tilda or Greta. No make, no model, and no time to think. I asked anyone and everyone I came across if they had seen a sixty-year-old woman with a well-built woman who had short dark hair. The answer was consistently the same – no.

Suddenly, a sedan went screaming out of the parking lot and I took my chances. It turned right as it exited the lot but I could see it was stuck behind the traffic waiting for the light to change. Running as fast as I could, I jumped into my car, which thankfully was only a few rows away, and I followed it. Three cars separated us but two of them turned in the opposite direction. That made it easier.

The sedan zigzagged around city streets before turning into the Willmar Education and Arts Center's parking lot. I was only a few yards away and mirrored its every move. It was Tilda, all right. I made a dash toward her, unaware that someone was following me.

"Tilda! Hold up a second! Wait! I need to speak with you!"

My voice must've rattled her because she took off running.

"You won't catch up to her," Greta shouted from a few feet behind me. "She's leaving me no choice. I'm calling the police."

I spun around and caught my breath. "Greta, I—"

"I've been trying to talk sense into her since I got here. Had to wait in the teachers' lounge until dismissal. My nerves are absolutely raw. This is a nightmare. I think Tilda was the one who killed Helena. I told her to confess but all she said was 'you don't understand.'"

"Well, maybe—"

"I understand all right. I found her earring under the bed when I went in the room to do the cleaning. It was an earring I had given her for her twenty-first birthday. A cameo gold post that had been in our family for years. Oh my. Why would she do something like that? Why?"

"Greta, if you'd calm down and give me a chance to explain, you'll realize what happened. You'll see that—"

"Tilda should be going to the nearest police station. Not to the district office. Resigning from her teaching job isn't the answer."

"Is that what she plans on doing?" I asked. "Quitting?"

"That's what she told me. Said it was no use. Said she was too depressed to teach anymore and was tired of putting on a smiley face and pretending."

"She didn't kill anyone, Greta. Stay put!"

Tilda was at the front entrance to the building and I had to hurry. It felt as if I was pushing my legs but they weren't going anywhere. I opted for the only choice I had – a loud scream. "Stop Tilda! Don't go inside. I need to talk to you."

She paused long enough for me to get within speaking distance. "I know what happened. None of this is your fault."

"Tell my aunt that. She thinks I'm a murderess. My God. I can't even sleep at night. You have no idea how hard it is to make like nothing happened. No one will believe me."

"I do. And I can prove it. Please, will you give me a chance?"

Tilda nodded and we walked a few yards to where her aunt was standing.

"This isn't exactly the best place to have a conversation," I said. "There are empty benches by the side of the building. What do you say the three of us take a seat and let Tilda explain. But before she says a word, I need to say something."

Greta and her niece looked at me and waited for me to speak.

"Helena Heatherbrae's own guilt killed her and Tilda was the innocent bystander."

"Dear Lord Above!" Greta gasped. "What on earth happened in that apartment?"

Tilda spoke softly, looking down and wringing her hands every few seconds when she wasn't looking directly at her aunt.

"It was the Monday afternoon we were meeting each other in Minneapolis. Early school dismissal that day. Cooper was so excited he'd be seeing his Auntie Getta. I got to the city early and figured you were still at work. Naturally I drove straight to the Mystery Castle. The tours had ended but Cooper and I were able to walk right inside the building. They hadn't locked up yet. No one was around. I figured you were upstairs in Helena's apartment and said something like that to Cooper."

Greta pressed her hands together and waited while her niece continued to explain.

"Before I knew it, Cooper had raced up the main staircase and was headed down the hall. He must've remembered where you worked from the last time we were there. Anyway, I told him to slow down and wait for me but he didn't listen. I was especially adamant because he was holding a Tootsie roll pop I had given him and I didn't want him to fall and get hurt."

Tilda paused for a second as two women walked by. When they were out of earshot, she went on.

"I moved as quickly as I could until I was only a few yards behind him. 'Don't you go in there!' I said but he didn't listen. The door to Helena's apartment was un-locked and he shoved it open. I could hear him yelling 'Auntie Getta! Auntie Getta!' By then, I had walked inside but there was no one in the living room. That didn't stop Cooper. He charged ahead into the bedroom where Helena was sitting next to her bed. She was in lounging clothes as if she planned to retire early. Then…Oh God! I don't even want to think about it."

"What?" Greta asked. "What happened?"

"Cooper stood near her and she lunged toward him. Both arms extended. She kept saying 'Kent. Kent.' She must've scared him because he dropped the Tootsie roll pop and ran behind me. Like he used to do when he was a toddler. Then Helena started shouting 'Kent! Don't leave me again.' She was sobbing and babbling, all the while trying to reach out for Cooper. Next thing I knew, she started to breathe heavily and then collapsed. She fell forward on the bed but she was still in her chair. I told Cooper to leave the room and wait for me in the living room. Thank God he listened this time."

"Lord in Heaven," Greta mumbled.

"I felt for a pulse but there was none. I know this sounds heartless but I didn't want to subject Cooper to the kind of inquisition that would've taken place had I called nine-one-one. The bed had the linens on it so I acted quickly. I lifted

Helena's legs and was able to maneuver her onto the bed. It wasn't easy. That's probably when my earring came off."

"Uh-huh," I said.

Tilda bit her lip. Her voice was steady but detached. "I made sure her head was on the pillow, all the while trying not to look at her eyes. They were wide open and motionless. Cloudy blue. As much as I wanted to close her eyelids, I knew enough not to do that. People die with their eyes open. It would've looked suspicious if hers were closed. There was a wedge cushion off to the side of the bed and I remember putting it at the bottom, by her feet. I left the bedroom and found Cooper sitting by her computer. He was fiddling around the mouse when I grabbed him by the hand and told him we had to hurry."

"He didn't cry or anything?" Greta asked.

"No, I don't think he knew what happened. I told him Auntie Getta had gone home and that we needed to go to her house. The last thing I thought about was the Tootsie roll pop that Cooper had dropped."

Tilda put her hand over her mouth and shook her head.

"Then what?" I ventured.

"No one heard or saw us go back down the stairs and out the door. It locked behind us. I know because I tried it once we were on the front steps. There was no one outside, either, although we did see a car pulling into the driveway as we left the place."

"That would've been Arletta," I said. "She was returning from an errand. Helena sent her out for a box of chocolate truffles. Talk about close timing."

Tilda lowered her head and covered her eyes with the palms of her hands. "Dear God. If only she hadn't gone on that errand or if Cooper and I had gone directly to my aunt's house, Helena Heatherbrae might still be alive. This really *is* my fault."

CHAPTER THIRTY-TWO

G reta wrapped her arms around her niece and I excused myself to give Max a call.

"I located Greta," I said. "In Willmar. Like I thought. It was her niece Tilda who staged Helena's body but she didn't kill her."

"Hold on a second. I need to get someplace where I can talk. I'll call you right back."

I looked around the Art Center/School District Building and decided to sit on the steps to the side of the place. Greta still had her arm around Tilda when Max's call came in.

"Sorry about that. I was with Anna Gainson in her office. What's going on?"

I went on to tell him about Tilda's confession and how Wallis's information substantiated my dumbwaiter theory. The minute Wallis mentioned all those candies at the bottom of the shaft, I knew Helena's death had something to do with Tilda's son Cooper. It all made sense in a macabre sort of way.

"I'm telling you, Max, Helena never got over a childhood tragedy that happened on Christmas Eve, 1936. She and her friend Kent were fooling around with the dumbwaiter. Tossing candies in there and fiddling with the pulley like they had done countless times before. On the night of the incident, Kent went to jump on the cart only Helena must've inadvertently raised it, leaving an empty shaft."

"Are you thinking she threw Kent's candy in there and he went to retrieve it?"

"Yes. Only she didn't get the cart down in time. He was either too fast for her or she couldn't work the ropes quickly. Either way, it was an accident. A tragic accident and one that haunted her for years. That's why she had the dumbwaiter replaced and the rooms switched around. She couldn't stand the memory of that night."

"How did you make the leap to Tilda and Cooper?"

"Observation. Like you taught me. When Hogan and I discovered those hidden photos of Helena and Kent, I was stunned. Greta's great nephew Cooper resembled that little boy. Especially when he walked into Helena's bedroom holding a Tootsie roll pop in his hand. She took one look at him, saw the candy pop and her mind went to another place. Given her vision problems, she was sure it was Kent. Back from the dead. It was the shock that killed her. Not Tilda."

"I know. It's all making sense now. Anna confessed to having a major argument with Helena earlier in the day. Helena was so upset she had Arletta cancel her regularly scheduled appointment at the beauty parlor."

"What? What are you saying?"

"The official cause of death was heart attack from natural causes. The heart muscle stopped. Probably from an onslaught of adrenaline and calcium that rushed into the cells. I don't know the specifics, but like we discussed once before, it's really not that uncommon. Tilda witnessed a sudden and massive heart attack. There was nothing she could have done. Especially since Anna inadvertently set the whole thing in motion by having that earlier blowout with Helena."

"What were they fighting about? And how did you get her to tell you?"

"Helena still had to sign a few papers for the National Park Service and was taking her 'dear sweet time' according to Anna. So, Anna went in to see her and they got into a huge row. Anna said Helena's face turned red and she gasped a few times but she was all right when Anna left the apartment. In fact, she even signed the papers."

"Yikes. Helena was probably still agitated later in the day. And when Cooper came running in, the shock was too much. But how'd you get Anna to tell you all of this? I mean, it's not something she'd want anyone to know about."

"When we went into Helena's residence to see what could've possibly upset Greta, Anna took one look at the place and welled-up. Certainly not what I expected. She said the last time she was in there was during that argument. Seemed she's felt badly about it ever since and has been trying to cover up her emotions."

"Wow. Helena's death was almost like a basketball game."

"Huh?"

"You know. One player sets up the shot and the other one takes it. Only this time it was purely circumstantial. Unfortunately, Helena wasn't the only victim. Tilda's beside herself and it sounds as if we've misjudged Anna. Both of them have been keeping this bottled up for a long time."

"Listen Marcie. Tell Tilda to get past it if she can. I'm about to have the same talk with Anna. No crime was really committed and as far as the police go, they've already chalked it up to natural causes. The only one who really needs an answer is Minerva. What she decides to do is up to her. Oh, and by the way, good job! Even if it means I'll be suffering through another meal with Wallis's wife."

"Speaking of eating, one of us better let Angie off the hook or she'll still be in the office."

"No worries. I'll give her call. See you tomorrow, kid."

I walked back to Greta and Tilda and told them everything Max had shared. It didn't change anything but it certainly helped to explain it. When I got back to my car, I made another phone call. This time to Hogan.

"How would you like some unexpected company for dinner?"

His voice was exuberant. "Will the unexpected company be spending the night?"

"Don't I wish! Only dinner, I'm afraid. I've got a full schedule tomorrow."

"Dinner's fine. How does pizza in Glencoe sound?"

"It'll be the perfect place to celebrate."

"Celebrate. Oh crap. What did I miss?"

"Relax. Max and I solved the case. And all of it was possible because you found that secret room. Oh, and that lottery ticket."

"Keep going and I'll want to be on the payroll."

I started to put my phone back in my bag when I remembered to make another call. Like Hogan's, the number was on speed-dial.

"Hi Mom! I've got wonderful news for you!"

"You're engaged? So soon? I haven't even met him. You couldn't wait for Thanksgiving?"

"What? No. Not that. Other fantastic news. You won't have to hide from Alice Davenport anymore. We've solved the case."

"I see. That soon."

"That soon? You've been plaguing me for the past two weeks."

"All right. All right. So, who did it? Was it her personal maid?"

"Actually, she wasn't murdered in the conventional sense."

"Huh? Get to the point."

"She died of fright. Saw something and—"

"Ah-hah! I've been right all along. All those years when you and your brother just had to watch those horror movies. Chain saw murders. Decapitation murders by clowns. All those years….and didn't I tell the both of you that you could die of a heart attack?"

"Mom…"

"Well, didn't I?"

"Yes. Yes. I suppose you did. But this was different."

"It doesn't matter. Maybe the next time I tell you something, you'll listen to me."

I promised my mother I'd call her over the weekend and headed for Biscay. Then I remembered something and I quickly re-dialed her.

"Mom! I forgot to ask. How many relatives does Alice Davenport have in this area?"

"Oh sweetie, the Davenports are all over the place. New Ulm, Mankato, Hutchinson…"

"She's a murder magnet you know. A murder magnet."

"I know. Why do you think I gave her your number?"

THE END

J.C. Eaton is the pen name of husband and wife writing team Ann I. Goldfarb and James E. Clapp. A former teacher and middle school principal from upstate New York, Ann always had a passion for writing. As a sideline to her career in education, Ann wrote for a number of trade journals before turning her attention to mysteries. She got her feet wet writing YA time travel novels and then joined forces with her husband, James Clapp.

With a background in construction, a degree in business and a successful tour of duty with the U.S. Navy, James never envisioned himself writing cozy mysteries along with his wife, Ann I. Goldfarb. In fact, the only writing he did was for informational brochures and workshop material for the winery industry where he worked as a tasting room manager in his home state of New York. When he and his wife left the Snow Belt for the Arizona desert, he was hit with the writing bug.

The couple resides with their four-legged friends in Sun City West, Arizona, where sunshine doesn't need to be shoveled.

Visit jceatonmysteries.com and timetravelmysteries.com for more information.

CPSIA information can be obtained
at www.ICGtesting.com
Printed in the USA
LVHW112026140821
695327LV00018B/1647